THE CURSE of the CARNAVAL
ADIE STURM MYSTERY

ANASTASIA AMOR

BRODT PUBLISHING

BRODT PUBLISHING
The Curse of the Carnaval: Adie Sturm Mystery
New uncut edition
AnastasiaAmor.com
Copyright © 2011 by Anna Brodt
All rights reserved.
ISBN: 9780992134303
Cover art by Anna Brodt
Author photo by Kristen Wells

ACKNOWLEDGEMENTS

My friends played a huge part in the writing of this novel. Jane encouraged me in my journey. Dave Maynard shared his knowledge of gunshot wounds and let me into Wolf's mind and body, Julie had useful weaponry advice and Peter, of the Toronto Police Department, gave me insight into the murders on which this book was based. Thank you to Kristen for her portrait photograph and to Bruce for his edits.

By *ANASTASIA AMOR*

ADIE STURM MYSTERIES

Corpse for Cozumel
Days of the Dead
The Curse of the Carnaval
Dead Delicious

PARANORMAL FANTASY SERIES

Havana Heat

EROTIC ROMANCE

Exploring Irresistible

1

Dark-red blood dripped on my toe.

It rolled under the double strap of my sandal and hid camouflaged by the scarlet leather strap. Like a bottle of rich cab-merlot carelessly spilled, the blood pooled at my feet. Crimson droplets speckled the oak grain of the table. But there was so much more…on the couch…on the white marble floor. Puddles of red rain.

A sickly-sweet smell permeated the room. Someone had draped the man's face and chest with a white fluffy towel the edges brushing the floor. A shroud no longer white. Blood-soaked terry cloth.

It wasn't a question of whether help should be called. Not anymore. No one could lose that much blood and live. Gulping down the bile rising in my throat, I brought my hand to my mouth and backed away to the entrance.

* * *

Hours ago…

I'd been standing with Janine on the powdery-white beach of the Primavera Hotel—the most exclusive hotel on the island of Cozumel.

"Not a problem," I said. "I'm going up to change anyway. I'll get the garter for you. Promise." I was wearing the requested silver-metallic bikini—not the usual bridesmaid attire by a long shot.

"Thanks, girlfriend." Janine grinned widely. "If you weren't right next door, I wouldn't have asked. Our rooms are in the other building. But take your time, no hurry. Dean said he'd take a nap before the real party begins."

I touched her arm. "I'm so sorry I arrived too late. There was an engine malfunction in Toronto. I was afraid I wouldn't get here until tomorrow. When I got in, I rushed over to the beach but the ceremony was already over. You forgive me?"

"No worries, Adie. Everything else went as scheduled. It was out of your control." Staring out at the Caribbean, she murmured under her breath, "Sometimes things are."

When I'd met Janine a few months ago, I'd been entranced by her vivacious personality. She was like a beautiful colorful bird, flitting about, chirping happily. Now I sensed an underlying sadness. This wasn't the Janine I knew.

I gave her shoulders a little squeeze. "Don't think about anything except your happiness today, Janine. After all, it is your wedding day and we're all here to celebrate it."

Her fist tightly clenched her gold cover-up. Looking down at her hand, she loosened her grip. "I'm so lucky you're here. Without you, I don't think it would have been quite the same."

"We haven't been friends long, but I feel a connection. Know what I mean?"

"Mm-mm, me too, Adie. Sam is a little jealous of you." Janine glanced at my silver string bikini. "She wanted the silver. I had to persuade her that the bronze was better with her coloring."

"You've known her a long time, haven't you?"

"We went to school together, took trips everywhere, and now," Janine frowned, "she works for Dean."

"Well, don't worry, we'll get along fine, I'm sure. You and Jim couldn't have picked a better time to get married."

"Yep, it should be a great party. I heard the Carnaval is just like the Mardi Gras."

I nodded. "Not quite as risqué but still a fantastic party. It's perfect planning for me to be here now, Janine. My latest research for the agency is the Carnaval. If I see enough interesting stuff, I'll be back next year with a tour group."

"Interesting it'll be."

When she clenched her jaw, I started to worry. For a newlywed, she lacked the sparkle I would have expected. But what did I know? My last fiancé had run away with my money and given it to his other fiancée. Hopefully, my instincts about men had improved.

Janine's clear gray eyes shot over to the reception hall where the sultry beat of a salsa drifted over. "Yep, the Carnaval will be a big bash. Should make the honeymoon fun. Tell Dean it's on the table near the door, Adie."

"Okay."

"Got to go. They probably need me in there. See you in a while?"

I nodded.

Janine sashayed away in her glittery gold bikini. That's what she'd worn for her wedding ceremony. In the end, Don, Janine's uncle, had persuaded her to drop the idea of an all nude ceremony on the beach. Even he, a laid-back sort of teddy bear from California, had drawn the line on that idea.

I dug out a translucent silver paraeo from my bag and tied it low on my hips. It was getting cooler with the sun near the horizon. The turquoise waters of the Caribbean lapped the shore, sparkling lavender in the rays of the setting sun. Shadows from the palm fronds danced on the empty beach. Or was it empty?

A tall athletic man stood silhouetted near the water's edge. As I drew near I saw him more clearly. My heart skipped a beat. A black, short-sleeved shirt covered his wide shoulders and hung open, displaying his strong chest and flat abs. Gold rays from the sun lent a glowing halo effect to his ruffled blond hair.

Wolf's lips turned up into a slow smile that spoke of secret pleasures. "Adie," he called out softly, "you made it."

My pulse raced wildly.

He strode confidently towards me, an untamed panther inspecting his jungle territory.

Electricity filled the air.

"Flight delay," I managed to whisper. I gazed up at a man who oozed sexuality with every breath.

His cool blue eyes met mine. "It's been too long." His voice was husky. With his finger he traced my lips. "We need to talk, but first…" He wrapped his arms around me and bent his head down to mine. His full lips pressed against my yielding mouth. Liquid fire surged from somewhere deep within me. I returned his burning message. My world ceased to exist. I lost myself in his kiss. Every part of me longed to remain in this state of borderless bliss— forever.

His tongue explored the tender inside of my lip, while mine

caressed his in a soulful, slow rhythm. I felt the warmth of his body through his silk shirt. Under the thin material of my bikini my nipples swelled to hard peaks.

My hands had a will of their own. Stroking his powerful arms, I let my hands slide down to his narrow waist. Under his shirt my hand lightly skimmed over his velvety skin. His familiar scent of soap and balmy ocean breeze assailed my nostrils. I pressed myself against him. His energy flowed through my body until it almost hurt for me to release him.

Brushing my hair away, he breathed lightly in my ear. His tongue discovered the contours, teasing me with each touch. Delightful quivers raced down my spine. I sighed softly.

Taking my hand, he kissed my wrist and journeyed over the palm of my hand to my ring finger. "Missed you." He pushed the tip of my finger into his mouth and sucked it.

Tingles ripped down my body. Wolf Du Lac was my sea god— unforgettable.

His sapphire eyes shot flames into my spirit. "I have a proposition for you."

"Um-mm." His words flustered me. It had been months since we'd been together. He was familiar yet strange. I tightened my arms around his waist again and felt the warmth of his body.

"Tonight," he whispered in my ear, "I want to be with you."

I closed my eyes, relaxing in his arms. "There's the reception."

"That'll be over soon enough." Wolf took hold of my face. "I want to give you pleasure, princess."

My pulse raced at his nearness, yet I resisted. I let my brain take over. Having graduated from the school of hard knocks, I hesitated. "Wolf, we should go in. I'm already feeling bad, having missed the wedding ceremony."

"Don't. You made it here and even if you hadn't, they still managed to get married without you." Wolf grinned. "Forget them. Think about us. You've been away too long, babe." He gazed seriously at me. "I'm making it my own personal challenge to see that you feel exceptionally good on this trip." Taking my hand, he steered me up the path to the hotel. "From this point on we'll have a good time."

I was having a good time—now that I was with him. Lustful thoughts danced in my head. I wondered how I could make it through the reception without imagining that buff bod against me.

Through the patio doors, I could see the party crowd, wearing a mishmash of outfits from bathing suits to T-shirts and jeans. With the doors open, mariachi music blasted out. From the loud buzz of conversation I could tell the pitchers of margaritas served were having an effect.

Wolf searched the crowd before he brought his eyes back to me. "Before we go in, we need to talk…" He draped his arm around my shoulders. "There's something I have to tell you."

Someone brushed against me. I knew it was a woman from the light floral perfume that wafted in the air. I turned my head.

A brunette in a bikini covered by a gauzy sarong sidled up to Wolf. The kiss she landed on him was quick and friendly. "Wolf! The toasts have started. Where have you been?" Her forehead furrowed. "Janine and Jim have said their speech and I told them we'd be doing ours next." Her brown eyes fixed on him. She sighed. "I hate this sort of thing, don't you?"

It was obvious she knew him—perhaps too well.

"Yeah." Wolf's eyes flicked to me. "Adie, this is Sam—my ex."

It was like a sudden blow to the head. Janine had told me her maid of honor was a school chum called Samantha but never in my wildest dreams would I have imagined she was *that* Samantha.

"Sam, I'd like you to meet my friend, Adie," Wolf said in way of introduction.

Samantha's smile didn't quite reach her eyes. "Nice to meet any friend of Wolf's." She gazed at his arm still draped on my shoulders. "So-oo," she said brightly, "you're dating again?"

"Adie and I go way back. Now that's she back in Coz, I plan on spending as much time with her as I can."

"Well, I hope you'll have some nights reserved for me, too, honey." She brought her hand to his windswept hair and pushed it back. "This is my first visit to Cozumel. Remember? I haven't seen any of the island. I would love to go dancing in the clubs."

"I'm sure you'll find any number of guides."

Sam's eyes shot to my silver bikini and matching paraeo. "Now I know who you are." Her lip curled. "You're Janine's friend—the bridesmaid that didn't show. Poor thing was so disappointed you missed the wedding. Where were you?"

I met her gaze steadily. "Flight delay."

Samantha swept her dark bangs away with her shapely, long fingers. "Jan and I go way back—high school. When did you meet her?" She snatched up a cigarette from her bronze lamé clutch. Holding it between her teeth, she held up a lighter to her cigarette. Before she could click it on, Wolf took it from her and flicked it.

As she inhaled deeply, he answered her question. "We all met a few months ago."

Samantha's eyes pierced me like a knife. "Months? And she chose you to be a bridesmaid?" Smoke blew out through her nostrils in a hazy stream.

I didn't feel much like it but I forced myself to play polite. "Janine and I hit it off at Don's party and when she heard I was coming back to do some research for my job, she asked me to be her bridesmaid."

"I was rounded up at the last minute too," Wolf said, noting Samantha's raised eyebrows. "Jim doesn't know anyone here. That's why I'm his best man."

"I see." She pursed her lips and took another drag, exhaling slowly. Her eyes took in Janine flirting with one of the waiters. "I was blown away when Jan decided to marry Jim." She rolled her eyes. "He's such a geek." Sam placed her hand on Wolf's arm. "When we were here together, she and JJ hooked up. Took off together for a few days—she stopped mid-sentence and shook her head as if in disbelief. "Jan's a free spirit—always has been that way." Sam turned to me. "You'll excuse us, won't you, er, I've forgotten your name." Not waiting for a reply, she urged Wolf. "Come on. We're wasting our time here. They want the maid of honor and the best man to start the toasts."

Wolf kissed my lips. "Later, okay, Adie?"

I stared at him. Was that what he had wanted to tell me? Why hadn't he e-mailed or phoned? I was cursed. I'd missed the wedding and even worse, the maid of honor turned out to be Wolf's ex. Nothing had been right on this trip so far except for that special feeling I'd had in Wolf's arms.

Watching them make their way to the center of the room, I wished I didn't feel the way I did. Abandoned and alone. After all, Wolf and I were..."

Lovers? My Logical Voice laughed dryly. Only lovers, right? No matter how much you want him, it doesn't matter, does it, if he's not committed to you?

And watching them together was a definite slap-in-the-face—an unpleasant rude-awakening smack. But I wasn't about to jump the gun on this. He'd just said he wanted to make love. They could be friends. People did manage that after a divorce.

At the front of the room, Samantha tapped her champagne glass. The crowd grew silent while she spoke imperiously about her very best friend, Janine. When she got to the part about being fellow cheerleaders, I zoned out. I had never been the popular type they chose for a cheerleader. It hadn't even occurred to me to audition—I couldn't manage a decent cartwheel. Besides, as far as I was concerned, high school was a cliquish hell-hole anyway.

"Have some champagne, Adelina," a husky voice said softly into my ear.

I swiveled about. "Diego!" I was taken aback by mesmerizing brandy eyes in an exceptionally handsome face.

"*Hola, mi amor!* You are radiant tonight! Silver is a beautiful color on you. But I'm not surprised. You would be resplendent in any color." Diego placed a fluted glass in my hand and motioned. Like magic, a waiter appeared with a glass of champagne for him.

Santiago Bolivar Alvarez flashed a show-stopping smile before he glanced at the speaker. "Samantha is an attractive woman," he noted softly, "but not nearly a lovely as you, Adelina. Still, a man would have a hard time forgetting her." He took up my hand and kissed it, his eyes sparkling with something indefinable. He added softly, "A divorced man like Wolf has baggage, *mi amor*. You don't need him."

I grimaced at the truth of his statement. I knew Wolf had been married for two years—two years I knew nothing about. I examined Sam's confident demeanor, her hand tucked into the crook of Wolf's arm. She was trying to prove a point to the women in the crowd. He was hers.

As he started his speech congratulating the happy couple, I couldn't take my eyes off of him. Wolf was a sea god. His unbuttoned shirt displayed a muscular chest and taut abs. And he wasn't top heavy either. Where his bathing trunks ended, his amazingly strong legs started. But it was his incredible face I was even more attracted to—irregular, rugged features combined in way that drew me in like a magnet.

7

"Perhaps they are too friendly, wouldn't you agree?" Diego ran his fingers down a strand of my hair, lazily studying my face. "I, on the other hand, am available. No ties and a heart that beats only for you." His hazel eyes sparkled hypnotically. "Are you staying at your condo tonight?"

His white silk shirt revealed a medallion that emphasized the shadows of his chest. Wavy dark hair fell on a high forehead. His face was perfect. In fact, the man was devastatingly handsome. I had to remind myself to breathe.

"Adelina?"

I shook my head, flustered by my body's response. "No, I can't. The bridal party is booked in here for tonight."

Diego glanced around dismissively at the elegant décor. "It's a reasonable hotel but surely you would be more comfortable at your condo?"

I did have a fabulous condo. Twice the size of my house back home and filled with expensive Italian furnishings, thanks to Diego.

You are so naive, My Logical Voice scoffed. Diego Alvarez is the richest man in Cozumel and you know what that condo means to him. He gave it to you conditionally. He wants to own you, along with his yacht, jet, and who knows what else. You've already got a man finer than chocolate and if you play your cards right he's yours for keeps.

My mind bounced back to a man that ignited a flame inside me.

Diego slid his hand along my arm. "It has been readied for your arrival, *mi amor.*"

My Hormone Voice couldn't help but take a jab at Logical. So what if she has Wolf? Any woman in her right mind would fall down on her knees and thank her lucky stars that a man like Diego wants her. This is Adie's chance to taste Diego's candy. Then she'll know for sure if Wolf is the man for her.

I checked out Diego's tight butt as he turned to say hello to a shapely Latina in a green sundress. She smiled demurely and eyed him from beneath her lashes before she moved on.

"Delores Montalvo, my assistant," he said, by way of explanation.

I nodded, wondering if he knew the woman had a thing for him. Across the room, Wolf raised his glass high for a toast. He called out, "To Janine and Jim. May they always be as happy as they are today."

Diego clicked his glass to mine and whispered, "And to us."

"Friends?"

Diego's eyes crinkled in amusement. "Very good friends."

There was a blast of music and a few guests hooted loudly as Janine and Jim took to the dance floor, grinding on each other in a wild merengue. Samantha pulled Wolf along with her to join them. The best man and maid of honor always danced next, didn't they? But seeing Sam snatch him so possessively caught me off guard. I sipped my champagne a bit too quickly and a bubble of pain shot straight up my nose.

Massaging my forehead to ease the sensation, I watched them critically but could find no fault in the way they moved. Both tall and slim, they imparted style and grace to the merengue. Too bad the dance was meant to be crazy and fun.

"They'll want you to join in. We shall dance together. Hopefully, they will be playing something else soon—something more romantic, but if not," Diego shrugged, "we'll dance and they'll," his eyes shot over to Wolf and Samantha, "take a back seat to us."

"Hey, Adie!" a deep voice boomed behind me. Brown wavy hair and a cherubic face. Don Carrera—a man who gave teddy bears a run for their money. He squeezed me tightly to him. "What kept you, darlin'? Let me guess." He chortled. "You met this buff dude on the plane and he wanted to start the Carnaval with a bang. So being a party girl yourself, you didn't want to leave him sulking on a bar stool by his lonesome." He nudged me. "Added him to your collection, did you?"

I rolled my eyes and was about to respond but Diego beat me to the punch.

"Adelina will set off sky rockets all right, my friend, but not until tomorrow. Picture it, Don." Diego gazed dreamily into space, gesturing with one hand. "Adelina in a translucent gold costume. The spotlight on her—the other girls merely a backdrop to her beauty. In the center of the float, she stands, an angel—blonde hair flowing, those pouty lips smiling as she waves to the admiring masses. No woman on any float will equal her. The belle of the Carnaval." Diego took my hand and kissed my wrist. "Will you honor me with your presence?"

I stared at him, puzzled. "You want me on your float? What do I have to do?"

"Help him drink his champagne and throw beads to the salivating men in the crowd." Don guffawed loudly. "Diego's got the best float in the parade. Royal Investments always does it up big time. He's the sheikh and I'll bet you're the lead harem girl!" He winked at Diego. "Am I right?"

Diego smiled apologetically. "Carmelita's designer prepared the costumes and she had him prepare one especially for you. You're not shy about showing your body, are you?" His eyes swept down my figure. "You shouldn't be."

"I'm not sure. I have to do some research for a tour group I'm bringing here for Carnaval."

"Well, even more reason to say yes then, isn't there?" Diego ran his fingers down a tendril of my hair and met my eyes. "Say you will, Adelinita. My sister will be so disappointed if you don't join us. I know it's last minute but Carmelita has gone to so much trouble..." He glanced over to Wolf and Samantha. "With this being your first Carnaval, what better place to view it than from on top of a float?"

I studied Samantha and Wolf's movements—like graceful hawks, swooping high in the sky.

"My driver will pick you up at four and bring you to the Merida Hotel. Carmelita has reserved rooms 101 and 102 and one of the dining rooms. We'll get dressed and have some dinner before the parade." He ran his hand lightly down my arm. "Believe me, *cariño*, it will be a fiesta to remember."

"I'll be there too, darlin', in my sheikh costume. If I'm lucky one of those harem girls might be interested in sharing my tent, if you know what I mean." Don winked. He turned to Diego. "Wolf comin'?"

Diego directed his gaze to the buffet table. Don was the first to spot my runaway lover. "My, my..." he remarked in amusement, "think he'll have any hair left after she gets through with him?"

I had always loved the feel of Wolf's blond hair—soft and silky. And now I wasn't the one touching him. The cobra was cutting into my action, smoothing back a fallen strand of Wolf's hair. Samantha wasn't looking at the food either, unless she considered him one of the choices. I gritted my teeth in annoyance.

Don squeezed my shoulder reassuringly. "Don't worry about her, Adie. She's as fickle as Janine. Wolf isn't rich enough for a gold digger like her."

I raised an eyebrow. "What do you mean?"

"When my lovely sister, Terry, set her sights on Dean, Sam decided he should be hers. Those two fought tooth and nail for Dean and his moollah."

"But Terry was the one who married him."

"Yeah, she won the war, but she wasn't enough for that bastard. He gave Sam a top-notch, executive job in his Woodbridge Branch as a consolation prize."

Diego smiled at me. "What's a man to do when he encounters two exciting women simultaneously?"

"Choose one?"

Diego rubbed my hand and smiled. "Sweet innocent Adelinita. Men would rather not commit unless they're forced to. Dean wisely took both of them."

"You're saying Sam is Dean's mistress?"

Don chortled. "You've got that right, darlin'. But she's a free agent with a mind of her own." He lowered his voice as he confided, saying, "Terry says the old dude's a pervert anyway. She's glad he's got Sam. My sister's way too civilized for his kinky scenes."

"Oh?" Diego's eyes traveled down the length of Sam's slender frame.

"Where is Terry?" I asked, scanning the room for a curvaceous redhead.

Diego thrust his chin in the direction of the entrance. "There. See her? Beside the security guard."

A lovely woman in a slinky red gown leaned against a bodybuilder in a black uniform in a way that suggested more than a casual acquaintance. Once again it surprised me how that dazzling Aphrodite and teddy bear Don came from the same gene pool.

"Excuse us, Don," Diego said, taking my hand and leading me away to the dance floor where the music playing had changed to a slow rumba. "They're playing this for us."

The Cubans call the rumba the music of love. It is. As he swayed with the beat, Diego's amber eyes glowed excitedly while

he led me into a turn with the flick of his wrist. I felt my cheeks
flush with his intense glances. From the corner of my eye, I noticed
Wolf leave the buffet table without Sam.

"Adelina, you'll come, won't you? Everyone loves the
Carnaval." Diego pulled my hand to one side and I stepped
smoothly alongside him.

He had a point. Why should I wait for Wolf to ask me out
tomorrow? The way that snake slithered around him, I'd be lucky
if I got to see him tonight. "Okay, Diego. I will."

"Where's that vivacious lady I know?" Diego swiveled around
and pulled me close. "Come now, Adelina, cheer up. I'm not
asking you to go to a funeral. You love a good party and you'll
never see a better one than the ones we have here. Forget about
that selfish bastard. He doesn't deserve you and you know it."

Diego led me into an open step and I followed his lead, shoulder
to shoulder, thinking all the while of Wolf. I wouldn't let a little
thing like an ex wife stop me—after all, I was a student of karate
and one thing that was drilled into us from day one is the motto
never give up. "You're right," I said, thinking of a plan. "I'll do
my research and have a good time."

I glanced over at Diego when he suddenly stopped in midstride. Wolf was cutting in and Diego was letting him. I didn't
think guys did that sort of thing anymore. But Diego smiled slyly,
like a cat with a canary, and said in an undertone, "Four o'clock in
the lobby, *mi amor*? I'll send the car around," before he backed off
into the crowd.

I stopped dancing.

"Princess?"

"I need to go to my room and change." Weaving my way off
through the crowd, I headed to the exit.

"Adie, wait!" Wolf's long stride caught up to me as I entered
the lobby. "Give me a chance to explain."

I pressed the elevator button and turned to him. "Yes, Wolf?
I'm listening."

Wolf grabbed my hand as the door opened. "Look, Adie. I
didn't know she was the maid of honor until a couple of days ago."
In the empty elevator, he swung around to me, his eyes sincere.
"Don't be angry with me. It was Janine's decision, not mine."

I knew he was right but something inside me rebelled. Why had he ever married that self-righteous slut? Given the opportunity, we might have connected years ago.

The elevator thudded to a stop and the doors opened. A security guard nodded politely and got on. He swiveled around and faced the metal doors, his sturdy back towards us. He pressed the button for the eighth floor.

We stood silently. I didn't want to talk in front of the man. This was way too personal.

On my last trip to Cozumel, I was sure Wolf had been ready to explore his feelings. As a parting gift, he had handed me the lease for a house on the cliffs. It was a beautiful place—wild crashing waves on a powdery shore. There on that dream weaver's carpet, we had lain in each others' arms, a magic moment after making love.

The elevator shuddered to a halt. The guarded stepped off on the eighth floor and we rode up to the ninth.

Wolf took the opportunity to plead his case. "Listen Adie, there's nothing between Sam and me. It's all in the past. We've both moved on."

When the elevator opened he followed me to my door. The wind blew my hair around wildly and I held it back as I turned away to dig around in my purse for my key. My emotions were jumping from anger to something else, indescribable. I didn't know what to say. I didn't want to fall for this guy and then be hurt.

From below us, I heard the sultry beat of Santana. The familiar rhythm of *Black Magic Woman*. Music that evoked a mysterious stirring inside of me.

"Adie?" his husky voice spoke into my ear.

Why was it so difficult to find the key? It was a large piece of plastic. I fumbled nervously in my bag before I felt myself propelled around, looking straight at Wolf. His startling blue eyes were intense with desire. Sparks flew between us. He brought me closer, wrapping his arms around me, his hard body against mine.

Wolf bent his head, brushing his lips on my neck. I shuddered with his caresses. Leaning my head back against the door, I invited more, my throat exposed to him. The tip of his tongue found that tiny hollow and slowly licked the spot. A bolt of electricity surged to my core.

He lowered himself slowly, his lips pausing to kiss the rise of my breasts and linger at the valley between. I breathed out with a sigh filled with longing. As if reading my mind, his hands lightly slid over my silver bikini top. Fingertips set my peaks on fire.

As he dropped to his knees, his hands lightly lit on my thighs before they slid to my calves. Startled, I felt my purse slide out of my hands and clatter to the tile floor. The wind rearranged the flimsy material of my paraeo, exposing my bare leg. I unfastened it. Wolf took over, tugged it off and tucked it into his waistband. And not wasting a precious moment, he journeyed back down my thigh with his fingertips, slowly stroking my leg. I shivered. His tongue tantalized the back of my knee. Desire awakened my core. I threaded through his wild ruffled hair, my eyes closed, caught up in this delicious sensation.

He took my foot in his hands, slipping off my sandal. His lips sucked the tips of my toes. A moan flew out of my lips and I forgot everything and everyone.

"Wolf…" My voice was breathless and confused. I didn't know what I wanted to say or how to say it and yet I had to tell him how his touch stirred my passion. My soul had waited for a man who could give me this incredible feeling. I was out of control, like butter melting on a hot stove. What was he doing to me?

His tongue flicked magically on the back of my calf as if in response to my question. I trembled as his tongue torched my thigh. His hot silken tongue sparked tremors down my body. Tiny teasing kisses.

Tinkling laughter trickled to us. Down the hall a door had opened. Wolf got up just as a couple came out from their room. He pulled me close, shielding me from them.

"Hey, man!" a burly man called out behind us as he waltzed by with a tiny brunette. I didn't know them.

Wolf turned his head slightly. "How you doin'?"

"Great, man!" the bulky guy said happily. "And now for some serious partying. See ya there, dude?"

"Yeah, sure," Wolf said into my hair, reluctant to let go of me.

From the glazed look in the stranger's eyes, I assumed the guy had already started his party hours ago. It wasn't easy for the little brunette to maneuver him into the elevator but she managed.

I watched the doors shut. My eyes shot to Wolf. His eyes held a silent question. But it was as if my brain had been wiped clean. I needed time.

Flustered, I pulled away, struggling to explain. "I have to get changed, Wolf. Janine wants me back there and I promised to get her the garter." I slipped on my sandal, watching Wolf scoop up my purse from the floor.

"I'll wait for you downstairs." Brushing my arm, he handed me my things before making his way to the elevator. The contact singed my skin and lingered long after the elevator doors closed.

I felt sadly alone standing there. Again I searched for my key. This time I found it.

2

Dean had been generous when he'd booked the rooms for the bridal party. I had five days in this luxurious suite. A matching loveseat and chair were situated around a coffee table near the balcony and a king-sized bed took up space at the entrance. Very comfortable. I smiled. By the passion of Wolf's apology, I'd guess that bed would be up for a test run—soon.

Wandering over to the glass doors, I undid the latch. It took quite a push to slide them apart with the force of the wind combating my efforts, but the view more than compensated for that. It was sensational. The bright lights of the restaurant sparkled lavender on the Caribbean waters. Shimmering waves rushed the shadowed beach. On the patio below people partied, their laughter carrying up with the breeze.

The wind was cool and a string bikini didn't give me much warmth. I crossed my arms over my goose bumps, but I didn't feel like going back in just yet. The Caribbean held me in its grip. I couldn't take my eyes off the waves rolling in. The surf was soothing. It made me forget all about the awkward situation I was in. The sea and shore were one of life's constants. Only a hurricane could change its beauty.

Leaving the balcony doors open, I strode over to my suitcase. Janine had this crazy idea—she wanted us to wear red, the color denoting passion, while the men were to wear a virginal white. I smiled, thinking the males were not likely innocent, but Janine must have thought one of them had to be. That wouldn't be Wolf and for Janine's sake I hoped it wasn't Jim.

I reached in for my dress but a strap caught on my umbrella hanging next to it. An impulsive purchase at the airport—a Burberry in magenta plaid. I'd been so pleased to find it in the duty free shop and with rain in the forecast, I thought I might be able to use it. Undoing it carefully, I lifted out my silky red gown and placed it on the bed while I searched for my bra and panties.

Some of my clothes were unpacked. I'd whipped out the important things before I'd changed into the silver bikini. In a way, it was a stroke of good fortune that I'd arrived late. Wearing a bikini for a wedding ceremony was really odd and not quite in my comfort zone. Jim must be a bit strange himself to go along with Janine's bizarre idea.

After fastening my bra, I pulled on some lacy panties and donned my dress. In my closet I found my red stilettos and slipped into them before retreating to the bathroom. Quickly I tugged a comb through my hair and wiped a mascara smudge before I picked up my evening purse and stepped into the hall.

A strong gust of wind blew under my skirt. I needed both hands to bring it down. The scent of rain was in the air. Across the road bordering the golf course, palm trees tossed their fronds wildly. Up in the hills, a few lights flickered from a solitary house. The moist humid air straightened my hair. I shoved my bangs away, wondering why I'd bothered to do anything with my hair.

Most of the people on this floor were wedding guests. It wasn't an enormous wedding, but considering Dean was footing the bill, a hundred guests in a five star hotel in Cozumel wasn't peanuts. In my case, he'd even included the air fare. I didn't know what kind of business Dean was in, but whatever it was, it paid off big-time.

Wolf must have gone to his room to change. Before I'd left Toronto, he'd e-mailed me about staying in the hotel tonight even though he lived here in San Miguel.

In this last year, Wolf had made inroads with his resort project. Cottages and a restaurant as well as a cantina. His idea was to combine the flavor of Mexico with the usual tourist amenities found in a hotel.

When I reached the elevator, I was about to press the button when it occurred to me I had forgotten the garter. I'd have to get it. Dean and Terry's room was two doors down from mine. The hallway ahead was empty. My gaze wandered back to the alcove where Wolf had given me a taste of bliss. The memory had been so powerful it even now sent a wave of heat down my body. I closed my eyes, imagining what could have happened had we not been unexpectedly interrupted.

Lost in my fantasy, I came to their room. The door was slightly ajar. I didn't know what to make of it. I knocked and waited. Hearing no one inside, I called out, "Terry?" but there was no answer. If Janine hadn't needed that garter, I would have left, but I knew time was short.

Hesitantly, I pushed the door open and looked around. A table stood near the door and sure enough, just as she had said, the garter was there. I picked it up and dropped it in my purse. As I turned to leave, the smell stopped me. Weed. The room had that clingy saccharine scent of marijuana. I knew the whole family indulged. But there was something else. A sickly sweet odor overpowered the other. I shot my eyes over to the couch. I saw the top of a man's head. Gray spiky hair. It had to be Dean.

My gut twisted uncomfortably. I stepped closer and called out, "Dean?" There was no answer. He could be asleep...or he might have passed out. My nose twitched from the smell in the room.

I glanced around. The suite was twice the size of mine. The bedroom would be behind the drawn oak doors. I was in the living area. Large still-life oil paintings hung on the forest-green walls behind the couch which was much like mine but larger—a green sectional with wedges of orange hibiscus flowers strewn over the fabric.

I shivered. The air conditioning had been set on high. Through the open balcony doors the wind blew in. The curtains swished erratically back and forth, rapping the glass in retreat as if in warning. By the steady rustling sound from outside, I knew it had started to rain.

I ventured towards the couch. The closer I came, the stronger the odor. I pinched my nostrils to block out the foul stench. Something wet dripped on my toe.

I froze. Blood was everywhere. On the cushions of the couch, no longer green and no longer floral. Red puddles pooled on the floor. A blood-splattered coffee table. The white beach towel covering the man's face and body was soaked red. I gulped down the vomit rising in my throat and backed out into the hallway.

* * *

The front desk was in the other building along with the manager's office. I should have gone directly there and asked for security. But I felt numb—like a sleep walker. What I saw hadn't registered yet. My mind had stopped functioning.

I don't know how I made it to the reception. Going down, I saw no one. In the banquet room, the guests were milling about eating and drinking as before. It was all a blur to me. It was as if I'd never left and somehow entered a time warp. The band was on a break but a hubbub of noise kept me from hearing the waiter. He handed me a glass of champagne. I took it from him, sipping it methodically. Had a nightmare entered my reality?

On the far side of the room, I spotted Terry and Jim, their heads close in conversation. Near the buffet table, Diego and Don were laughing, surrounded by an attentive slew of women. My eyes swept the room. He wasn't here. The strange trembling in my hands tipped my glass. The bubbles dripped on the floor. What I had seen was too horrible for words. My brain wouldn't accept it. But I had to do something. Accept responsibility. A man had been murdered—most likely Dean.

The newspapers back home told stories of corruption in Latin American countries. If I reported it, they would take me down to the station. Once they questioned me, they'd arrest me. Mexican law said a person was guilty unless proven innocent.

I looked down to my foot where the drop of Dean's blood had dried. I wasn't a coward but I was a realist and not a fool—foreigners had been arrested without cause, accused of crimes they hadn't committed. Tossed into jail, their families had to pay police for their freedom. Innocent people had been left to rot in jail. The consulate wouldn't be any help, either. They had no authority here.

If Dean had been murdered as part of a robbery by a local thug, the Mexican government would want to pin the murder on a foreigner. Tourists needed to feel safe in Cozumel.

From the beach entrance, Janine and Samantha, in identical red dresses, ambled in, giggling and jostling each other. They were wet and wasted.

Someone lightly stroked my arm.

"Princess?"

I spun around. "Wolf!"

He frowned. "You're not still angry?"

I shook my head in confusion.

"What is it? Are you feeling all right, baby?"

My knees wobbled like jelly. I gripped Wolf's arm tightly.

"Come on, Adie," he said, steering me over to the open patio doors. "You need some fresh air."

He led me over to a rattan love seat. I let myself sink down. My stomach was doing somersaults as my brain kept reliving the scene in the hotel suite. The bloody towel, Dean's spiky gray hair, the blood dripping down on my toe—all whirled in front of my eyes.

"Is it the champagne?" Wolf's blue eyes showed concern. "You didn't eat today, did you? Wait here, I'll get you something."

Before I could stop him he headed back in. I shivered not so much from the evening breeze but from my realization that I was in too deep. I had to let them know. It had to be reported to the police. And then there was the family. Terry and Janine had to be told. I rubbed my forehead in an effort to ease the built-up tension. From inside, the band lit into a soft rock hit. I didn't realize Wolf was back until I felt his hand on my shoulder.

"Adie, here." Wolf handed me a paper plate with miniature quesadillas. "Eat—you'll feel better."

I picked one up. My stomach tightened into a knot.

"Go ahead," Wolf urged.

I bit into one and chewed. It was a good thing they were basically cheese. I couldn't have swallowed meat. "Now talk to me. Did something happen? Is it Sam?"

"No, nothing like that." I set the plate on the table. I knew I could trust him but what could he do? "I had to go to Terry's room to get the garter and…"

Wolf drew me into his arms. "What is it, baby?"

The warmth of his body calmed me. "Something's happened, Wolf. Something horrible…" My eyes met his. "There's someone dead in that room—I'm sure it's Dean."

His arms loosened. Wolf stared. "Dead?"

"He's been murdered."

"How?"

"I don't know but there's blood everywhere." I glanced up at him. "I need to report it to the police."

Wolf frowned.

"You think I'm in trouble, don't you?"

"This is Mexico, Adie. Whether you had a motive or not, the police like a sure thing. And you," he stroked my cheek, "might be just the target they need. It would be better if you kept out of it."

Janine called out from the doorway. "Adie!" Her words slurred out. "Ya better come in. Ah'm throwin' the bouquet." She tripped but righted herself and stepped out. Janine was three sheets to the wind and her sail was blowing over. "I need the gartah, Adie. Give et to momma!"

From my bag, I pulled out the piece of frill and dropped it in her hand. Flipping off her shoe, Janine grabbed my arm for support. She tottered precariously in a high-heeled sandal. Her other leg wobbled unsteadily. Before she lost her balance and buckled down on the patio stones, Wolf seized her around the waist and propped her up.

"Wow! Thanks!" She smiled slyly up at Wolf and slid her hands down his biceps. "Mm-mm, nice guns. Just my luck I got myself hitched, today." Pushing her dress high, she pulled on the garter, giving us a full view of her red lacy thong. Janine giggled. "He'd better not get these two mixed up, eh? Wolf, tell him he needs to pull the blue one off. Although, you could tell him the red one is for later. Poor guy needs some advice from someone in the know." She gazed up at Wolf. "And that would be you."

"Hey you guys!" Don boomed from the doorway. "We're all in here waiting. Got the bouquet for you, darlin'."

"Take her arm, Adie," Wolf said quietly. "Let's get her in there."

As soon as Janine threw the bouquet I'd see the manager. In the meantime, I did as Wolf suggested and helped him pull Janine into the restaurant.

The guests had cleared the dance floor and the women stood on one side as Don announced the throwing of the bouquet. "Attention ladies...singles, divorcees, and widows. This is your ticket to marriage," he said, grinning from ear to ear. "Janine is about to throw the bouquet." He pointed to a curvaceous female in the crowd. "Darlin', come up here."

The brunette flashed her wedding ring and shook her head. Don looked a little disappointed but went back to his job of hustling the ladies in for the toss.

Janine looked out at the group of females gathered in front of her. "Where's Adelina Sturm? Adie!" she yelled. "Ya can't avoid this 'un. Ah wantya right beside Sam and all these otha girls."

Don trotted over, grabbed my arm, and propelled me over to the group. "Got her, Janine. You go ahead now, darlin'."

Janine staggered as she swung around, her back to the assembled women. She waved the bouquet and raised her arm.

I made up my mind. As soon as this was over, I'd speak to the manager and get him to contact the police. I couldn't let this go on any longer.

"Ready, ladies!" Don shouted. "Okay, Janine, throw!"

The bouquet of roses shot straight for my head. I was forced to catch it or let the thorns rip into my skin. If I hadn't caught it, Diego's enthusiastic assistant would have. As it was, I had to block her with my forearm or have her finger jammed into my eye. I scooped up the roses with my free hand.

"*Mierda*...shit." Diego's voluptuous assistant hissed the word.

It was hardly my fault they were flung into my face. If looks could kill, I would have been dead meat.

Don disrupted with a shout, "Bring your hands together for the lucky lady, Adelina Sturm."

I stood there, a hot flush rising to my cheeks. A few guests hooted appreciatively.

Marriage was the last thing on my mind. I had to get out of here now. I pushed through the women and started for the door.

Don made a stop gesture with his hand. "Before this party ends, we need the groom up here for the garter." He peered out into the crowd. "Jim?"

"He's not heah," Janine shouted. "But doan worry, Unca Don." Janine giggled. "Wolf kin pull ahf my gartah." She waved her hand. "Yoooo-hooo! Come up heah!"

Don waved to Wolf. "I guess you've been nominated, Wolf. I think..." In mid-sentence Jim appeared at the doorway. "Wait. Relax, big guy. Looks like the groom remembered his duties, after all. Come on, boy, we're waiting for you."

But Jim stood glued on the spot. His face was white, his freckles even more visible than usual. "Dean's dead. We need to call the police."

* * *

The guests filtered out quickly—no one wanted to be there when the police arrived and security under direction of the hotel management decided it was bad publicity to detain anyone. Janine and I supported a hysterical Terry. She rushed up as soon as Jim made his announcement. But with the arrival of the police, all the family members were ushered away into a room on the ground level for questioning, and I was left alone standing in front of the buffet table.

"Señorita Sturm, you remember me?" the slim policeman in a

tan uniform asked politely.

I nodded, recognizing Hernandez. He was one of the few fluent English-speaking detectives in Cozumel.

"Is Señor Du Lac part of the bridal group as well?" He glanced over to the doorway where Diego stood speaking with Wolf.

"Yes, Detective."

He frowned. "And Señor Alvarez?"

I shook my head. "No." I motioned to Sam speaking to JJ. "That woman is the other bridesmaid and Señor Du Lac is the best man."

Hernandez seemed relieved. "We will need the bridal party to wait in the other room." He called out, "Señor Du Lac! I need your presence in room 107 immediately. *Por favor, señoritas*, come with me."

I'd met Hernandez on my other trips to Cozumel, always under unfortunate circumstances. I could see from the dark look he shot me, he was thinking he was cursed. Wolf caught up to us and took my hand.

In the suite, a uniformed cop stood by the door. Wolf and I took the couch while Sam slid into the armchair. Hernadez grabbed a chair and pulled it over to face us.

From his pocket, Hernadez tugged out a pad and pen. "I'll need a statement from each of you."

Wolf said quickly, "Señorita Sturm and I were together."

"The entire evening?"

"Yeah," Wolf said, meeting my eyes a moment before he returned his steady gaze to Hernandez.

I nodded.

Hernandez glanced at Sam. "I need your name, Señorita."

"Samantha Stevens." She gave him a look. "This is an inconvenience, Detective. I'm tired and would like to go to bed. I don't know anything about Dean's murder, so instead of bothering me, you might find it useful to go after the killer."

"Murder, Señorita? An interesting choice of words. What makes you think it was murder?" Detective Hernandez eyed Sam suspiciously.

Sam's laughter sounded brittle to my ears. "I don't think we'd be sitting here if he died in his sleep. Would we?"

"Where were you tonight, Señorita?"

"Here, there, and everywhere. Not in his room, that's for sure."

Hernandez lifted one eyebrow, studying Sam intently. "Interesting you assumed Señor Firenze was murdered there."

Sam rolled her eyes. "Of course he was. Where else? Jim saw him dead in his hotel suite or did Dean get himself murdered in the honeymoon suite?" She threw Hernandez a disgusted look.

"Do you have any reason to suspect anyone?"

Sam snickered. "Maybe you should find out more about your victim, Detective. Dean Firenze was a wheeler dealer. Enemies? He had plenty."

"You seem to know a great deal about the man, Señorita Stevens."

"I am, or should I say was, one of his managers."

"I see." Hernandez scribbled a few words in his notebook. He turned to Wolf. "And you Señor Du Lac? What did you know of Señor Firenze?"

"He was here during the summer on business. I met him then. He was staying with Diego Alvarez."

"Señor Alvarez had dealings with him?"

"That's a question for Alvarez to answer."

Sam got up from the armchair. "I think it's clear none of us had anything to do with Dean's murder." She stared at Hernandez who had also risen to his feet. "How was Dean murdered, anyway?"

"That is classified information, Señorita Stevens." Hernandez stroked his chin thoughtfully. "You will be allowed to return to your rooms for the time being. However, I will require your passports."

Sam's face flushed. "This is outrageous." She turned to Wolf. "Surely you can do something, Wolf. You live here."

Wolf stretched out his long legs and leaned back in the couch. "'Fraid not, Sammy. I'm sure the *policia* will have this tied up in no time. Right, Detective Hernandez?"

Hernandez pursed his lips. "We shall see. I will send an officer to each of your rooms for your passport."

Wolf helped me up. "Mine's in my house. I could drive over and get it."

Hernandez clenched his jaw. "I would like you to stay. I need to speak to you further, Señor Du Lac. Señoritas, you may leave." He opened the door and called out to another police officer and spoke to him rapidly in Spanish.

At the elevator the young man caught up. "I'm Officer Sanchez. What floors are you on?" he said to us, but stared at Sam.

She thrust her chin up. "The second, 204. It's not necessary for you to come. I can leave my passport with the front desk tomorrow." She yawned delicately. "Go with her." In the elevator, she pressed the button for the second floor.

The doors closed and I pressed nine.

"Sorry, Señorita Stevens. I'm coming with you. Detective Hernadez would like those passports now. The *capitan* would jump to conclusions if you do not give it to me. You wouldn't want that, would you, Señorita Stevens?" The elevator thudded to a halt and the doors opened.

"You are being annoying." Sam glared at Sanchez. "This way," she tossed over her shoulder.

"I will see you shortly," Sanchez said to me. "What room?"

"901."

When the elevator thudded to a stop and opened on six, a darkly handsome security guard stepped in. He nodded and said, "*Buenos noches*," before he pressed the button for the ground floor.

"*Buenos noches*." It suddenly dawned on me where I'd seen him. He'd been on the elevator with Wolf and me earlier. While he stared at the panel, I studied him. Strong and solid—tall too. A long narrow face and hooked nose. Spanish heritage with maybe a touch of Mayan ancestry. He was the guard Terry had been friendly with. Good looking. Had that Bruce Willis look—a shaved head that gave him an edgy appearance. I was a hair woman. I liked hair long enough to be a sensational experience for my fingers. Wolf's silky waves always excited me. That and his clean soapy smell. The elevator shuddered, jolting me back to earth.

In the corridor, the wind tossed my hair into my eyes. Hotels in Mexico often have open air hallways. This one had the advantage of a spectacular view with the golf course stretched out past the Primavera gardens all the way to the Dorado Hotel.

I expected to see an officer outside the crime scene. What caught me by surprise was the maid who exited that room with a cart full of cleaning supplies and towels.

Dirty towels brought it all back. A bloody white towel. The pungent smell of weed mixed with the putrid odor of blood. Murder.

With trembling hands, I unlocked my door. Once inside I switched on the light. The entrance way lit up but the rest of my room was still dark. The patio doors were open the way I had left them, the moonlight flickering in as the curtains swayed with the wind. Where was the light switch? My eyes shifted to the wall but I couldn't see one. There was a lamp on the table next to the couch. I crept over to the table and felt around for the button and flicked it on. My couch was in the same position in the room as theirs but mine was a green floral, clean and unblemished by splattered blood.

I felt a chill. The air-conditioning had been set on low. The last thing I needed was a reminder of those blasting, cold Canadian winds. But it wasn't the room temperature that made me tremble. It was the memory of Dean. The tips of his gray hair pointing randomly in all directions gelled up for a party, unaware of what fate had in store for him. I shuddered at the memory.

A snappy ring tone went off in my purse. It was a text message: *Baby, we have a problem. Be there soon. Wolf*

What could that mean? Hernandez had dismissed me too easily. Had Hernandez cornered Wolf into admitting he'd lied? I knew now I shouldn't have dragged Wolf into it. There was no doubt in my mind we'd both be arrested. I sat down on my bed and brought my hands up to my temples, circling my fingertips. I should have admitted to entering Dean's suite while I had the chance. Hernandez was a fair man. He would have realized I had nothing to do with the murder.

I picked up the remote and flicked on the television. A cop movie in English with Spanish subtitles. Three quick raps on the door startled me. Could it be Wolf? I strode over to the door and peered into the peephole. Sanchez.

I let him in.

"*Hola,*" he said, quickly peering around as he stepped into my room. He wasn't the shy type, buzzing around touching things I'd left on the dresser.

"I'll get my passport." I watched him wander over to the bedside table.

He nodded and examined a book I'd started to read. "Are you staying here alone, Señorita Sturm?" He glanced up from the paperback.

"Yes. The bridal party is staying here at the hotel."

"So you must know most of the wedding guests?"

"Some," I said guardedly. Knowing the only way to get rid of this bloodhound was to hand over my passport, I dug in the side pocket of my purse and came up with the key to the safe.

Sanchez regarded me intently. "An attractive woman such as yourself is seldom alone."

I met his eyes. "As you can see, there is no one staying here with me."

He smirked. "For now. Perhaps you have plans?"

I stalked over to the closet. The small metal safe inside contained my jewelry and travel documents. Snatching up my passport, I brought it over to him. "I'm assuming this will be returned promptly?"

Sanchez's eyes flicked to my foot. "An injury?"

"What?" I said, puzzled.

"There's blood on your toe."

I felt heat rise to my cheeks. "Just a scratch. When do I get my passport back?" I opened the hallway door.

"We are thorough here in Cozumel. Don't make any plans to leave."

I opened the door for him and watched him head over to Dean's room where another officer stood on guard. Shutting the door, I realized my mistake. The blood had dried on my toe. I scooted over to the night table and snatched a Kleenex to wipe it off. How could I have forgotten that? What was Sanchez thinking now? I shook my head. The man was searching for anything to implicate me. I could see it in his eyes.

I dug out my cell from my purse and pressed Wolf's number. His voice mail clicked in. "Don't come tonight, Wolf," I said tensely. "There are police everywhere. Meet you for breakfast at nine." In the bathroom mirror I saw a pale, drawn face that didn't look like the Adie Sturm I knew. A flight delay, a murder, and now a suspicious cop. The situation was going from bad to worse and I had no idea what problem Wolf was dealing with. I reached into my makeup bag and opened a bottle. A sleeping pill was exactly what I needed. I had them for emergencies and tonight definitely qualified. Washing it down with water, I breathed easier.

My red dress slipped off my hips. Bra and panties were next. I looked at them regretfully. Wolf would have liked to have run his hands over the silk of my dress and I would have been the happy recipient of his journey. He would take the lingerie off...ever so slowly. I imagined how I would have unbuttoned his shirt, running my fingers over his powerful chest.

I breathed in and emptied my lungs slowly. Wolf would not be mine tonight. I might as well face the facts. A shower and sleep is what I needed.

In the bathroom, I turned the faucet on. As the water adjusted to warm, I removed my makeup. After testing the water with my toe, I stepped in. The warm flow relaxed my tired shoulders and my tensed up muscles. My chocolate shower gel filled the steamy air as I smoothed it on. I sighed. If only I had bought some truffles at the airport instead of the umbrella. They always made me feel better. Creamy milk chocolate coating my tongue with the delightful flavor of cacao—Mayan gold.

Rubbing the shampoo into my scalp, I closed my eyes. My thoughts returned to Wolf. He was a master when it came to massage. His hands would magically work in the shampoo and then knowing his creative mind, he'd have other ideas. My very core would ache for his light, sensuous touch. But I had messed all that up. Right now he was dealing with a problem that should have been mine. If anything went wrong in that interview room, I would speak to Hernandez and confess. There was no way I would let Wolf get in trouble because of me.

After I rinsed off, I dried myself and walked into the bathroom and slipped on a robe. My skin was flushed pink from the hot water and readily soaked up the body butter I spread over my legs and feet. The blood stain on my toe was gone.

Feeling somewhat relieved, I switched off the light, padded over to the bed, and climbed in. By the time I drew the covers over my shoulders, my body cried out for sleep and in no time, I drifted into a heavy slumber.

The thudding on the door woke me. I picked up a thin silk robe, pulled it on, and tied the belt. With the urgency of the knocks increasing, I assumed it must be the police or Wolf. Unlatching the door, I pulled it slightly open. I was thrust back as a husky gray-haired man pushed by. With the lights off in my room, I didn't recognize him at first.

Dean laughed. "Fooled ya, Adie Sturm." His eyes glittered in the dim light.

"Dean?"

"Surprised?"

Dean was dead. What was he doing here? I pulled my robe together where it gaped open.

"No need to cover up, honey. I'd like to see all of you."

"Get out!" I tried to push him back into the hallway.

Dean stood his ground and whipped the door shut with his hand. He grinned. "Don't do that...I have a treat for you." He gripped my chin and pushed it high, forcing me to meet his eyes. "I've been dying to have some of your sugar."

I jerked away from him and retreated backwards into the bedroom, holding up my arm to ward him off but he followed me in.

"Yea-hh! Now you're thinkin'." He chuckled. "Why waste time? Let the party begin, eh?" He reached over, swung me up, and abruptly dropped me down on the bed.

My robe loosened.

"I like the view, Adie."

I sat up and tightened the sash. None of this made sense. I had seen him dead a few hours ago and now he was here hitting on me. "Stay away, Dean," I warned him.

A laugh rumbled deep in his throat. "You don't mean that, honey."

A deep chill entered my body. Somehow I couldn't move. I knew how to defend myself but it was like Dean had put a spell on me. His dark piercing eyes riveted into me. Frozen, I sat there as he sidled up closer and tugged on my sash, undoing my robe. His eyes ate me up. "Nice boobs." With one finger he slid his finger over a mound. "So silky." He gazed at me. "I know you'd rather have me than Alvarez. Admit it."

I felt powerless, watching him. I wanted him to go but some force was stopping me from taking action.

Suddenly he stood up. "I'm so sorry, honey. I've been so selfish. Of course you want to see me." He grinned slyly before he tugged his T-shirt up and pulled it up over his head.

Blood gushed out of his neck, flowed down his chest and onto the bed. A crimson river spread on the duvet, covering my feet.

Wet sticky blood. Dean fell forward, his head landing in my hands, his gray spiky hair brushing my fingers.

I screamed—again and again, the cry echoing in my brain. Pearls of sweat coated my skin. I sat up searching the darkness but I was alone. Heavy banging brought my eyes over to the sliding doors of the balcony. Wind and rain rammed the curtains against the glass, rattling them erratically. I shuddered, remembering what I had just seen. I needed the comfort of human warmth but there was none to be had.

Groping for the switch on the night lamp, I flicked it on. The room was empty. The light reassured me a little but not enough. I dragged myself out of bed and padded over to the heavy doors, shoving them shut. My eyes shot down. I had nothing on. Had Dean been here? Was he really dead?

3

The mind can play tricks on us. We all know that. The heat and the bright tropical sun on the way to the open-air restaurant made the nightmarish image of Dean with his neck streaming blood seem ludicrous. It couldn't have happened. The whole thing was impossible.

The bartender was busy setting up for the tourists having an early morning start, typical of an all-inclusive in Mexico. I was late. My eyes searched the restaurant. It was twenty past nine. Would Wolf be angry? I saw him before he saw me. He was sitting at a round table staring out at the turquoise waters of the Caribbean.

A railing bordered the restaurant from the beach. His table was next to it. A few birds resembling blackbirds, flitted around, hoping for breakfast morsels. I figured the brown birds were the females when the black ones charged in, scaring away the others. They pecked at the crumbs from a plate left behind. Typical males always wanting to have theirs first. With a plastic covered menu, a waiter shooed away an overly assertive bird, while Wolf smiled in amusement at his efforts.

Seeing him happy like that was encouraging. Even though it was difficult to tiptoe in wedges, I approached him silently from behind before I popped out into view. I was good but he foiled my plan at the last second, swung himself around, and grinned a hello.

I dropped my beach bag into the empty chair and sat down across from him. "Sorry about being late but I forgot to set my cell alarm and couldn't seem to wake up this morning."

Wolf's blue eyes sparkled like the waters of a fast moving stream. "That wouldn't have been a problem, babe, if we'd been together last night." He smiled a slow smile. "I would've happily provided that wake up call."

Those irregular features and that smile made my temperature rise. In a black T-shirt that emphasized his wide shoulders and muscular chest, Wolf set my pulse pounding.

He leaned over and took my hand. "You look a little wiped, princess."

"I had a bad night." The nightmare was still fresh in my mind.

Wolf looked concerned. "That cop hassle you?"

My mind flashed back to the blood on my sandal. "Sanchez is suspicious with good reason."

Wolf frowned. "I don't like the sound of that." He stood up. "I'd like to hear everything but first, why don't we grab something to eat?"

We walked over to the buffet table. "By the way, I have a story for you, as well."

Now I was worried.

"Food will make you feel better." He stroked the furrow on my forehead. "No more negative thoughts. You need some food."

A chef was preparing omelets. They looked delicious. The smells made me aware of how hungry I was but I was also conscious of the lean man standing next to me. And, yes, he was as appetizing as anything displayed on the buffet table.

Wolf was tall and powerful. But unlike those workout junkies in the gym, he was no stranger to physical labor, having worked hard for his father's construction company. Formerly a manager at Blackberry, he was smart too.

I filled a bowl full of ham and onions and handed it to the man with a pin on his white uniform that read Jesus.

"If Jesus can't make those omelets right, I don't know who can," Wolf whispered in my ear.

That brought a smile to my lips. And he was right. Jesus-the-chef did a bang-up job of the omelets. I had to search for ketchup but in Mexico that was par for the course.

But I couldn't forget the fix I was in. I needed to know what happened with Hernandez after I'd left. If Wolf was in trouble, I was responsible and had to fix it.

While we sat down, a waiter appeared to pour us coffee. Reflectively, I spooned in some sugar. I was almost afraid to ask. "Tell me, Wolf, did Hernandez figure it out? Does he know I was there?"

Wolf's eyes crinkled at the corners as he sipped his orange juice. "You've forgotten how smooth I can be."

I laughed. Upfront, yes, mysterious true, but smooth? "You shouldn't have told him you were with me, you know. I appreciate it but I don't want you ending up in jail."

"Hernandez is the least of our problems, baby."

"Why? What are you talking about?"

"Well…" Wolf stretched out his long jean clad legs and sat back in his chair before he glanced over and said, "It's Sam. She told Sanchez she saw me alone at the bar. It must have been after I took you up to your room."

"How did you find this out?"

"Sanchez popped in to tell Hernandez. He'd just been with her. He didn't know that I understand a fair bit of Spanish."

"And did Hernandez ask about me?"

"I gathered he sent Sanchez to check out Sam's story first before he dug into ours."

"So she decided to put in her two cents worth."

Wolf shook his head. "It was most likely accidental."

With a woman like Samantha, I hardly believed she would just let something like that slip. But Wolf was a typical male—unaware of the devious nature of females. "So Hernandez wanted to know about me?"

"First it was all about Jim. What I knew about him. Hernandez was digging and wanted someone to bury."

"And you told him what exactly?"

Wolf buttered his toast and said, "Jim was Dean's CEO. The guy's nerdy but brilliant. Dean would have done anything to lure Jim into running his operation."

"How, exactly?"

"A six figure salary. Not too common for a guy his age."

"Do you think that's why he married Janine? To get in tighter with Dean?"

"He doesn't strike me as the calculating type, but I might be wrong. Dean's ventures certainly benefited from Jim's expertise. If Dean expanded his acquisitions to Mexico, Jim could hold the reins back in Canada."

"So that's why Dean contacted Diego."

"Right."

"I thought you didn't know if he actually had a business deal?"

"I'm putting two and two together, Adie. Alvarez had a lot of deals going and Royal Investments is a growing company."

"It doesn't mean it's bad or illegal."

Wolf raised an eyebrow.

"Okay," I conceded, "Diego's dealings have been in the gray area in the past but that's not unusual with billionaires, is it?"

"My point exactly and don't forget he's got the law on his side."

"You mean, his cousin the captain of the police?" I leaned in. "Do you think Sam really did see you?"

"It's possible but I didn't see her." Wolf stared out at the beach where the waves gently lapped onto the sandy beach. "Maybe she thought she was helping—establishing an alibi for me."

"Or one for her?"

"Possibly. She might be worried about her relationship with Dean and a motive. I suppose she could be making it up."

"She'd do that?" I frowned. Of course she would. She was one of those spitting cobras—the venomous kind.

My Logical Voice added: Giving Wolf an alibi helps her but not you, Adie. You're the loser here. And let's face it, she'd do anything to win. She'd make sure you get the Monopoly card—do not pass go, go directly to jail."

"Hey, Wolf!" Jim called out from the interior of the restaurant. He sprinted over to our table, his pale face flushed. "Er-rr, Adie, hi!"

The guys brought their fists together in a handshake.

"Pull up a chair," Wolf said. "How'd it go with the police?"

"Bad." Jim sat down. "They had all of us cloistered in that room for hours. Hardly slept. Just took a shower and headed down here to get a bite."

I bit into my toast. "Where's Janine?"

"Don't know. She was gone when I got up. She might have left with Terry for the airport."

"Why?"

"To meet Dean's brother. He was meant to come to the wedding but he was delayed." Jim shook his head. "I still can't get over all this. Gawd, you should have seen the blood in that room last night. Couldn't believe what the hotel did though…"

Wolf shot him a look. "What do you mean?"

"It's all cleaned up. Maids came in. Terry said there's no sign of the blood at all."

Shocked, I stared. "She's back in there?"

"No, she wanted a new room and they gave it to her."

Wolf stirred his coffee. "What about forensics?"

"No forensics. The room is corded off but the big boys from the mainland haven't arrived yet."

"Odd." Wolf shoved his plate away.

I set my cup down. "They must think it's bad for business to have a murder on the premises."

"Yeah, that's my take," Jim said. "Stuff like that goes on in this country. I read they brought in a street cleaner truck when a tourist was killed in a supposed hit-and-run."

"Here, in Cozumel?"

"No. It was this club in Acapulco."

"Drugs—Mexican mafia." Wolf bit on his toast. "The club owner didn't want any evidence left to implicate the local thugs."

"Nothing like that here," I said with conviction. "Hernandez is an honest cop."

Jim shot me a look. "Then why didn't they leave the crime scene intact? I'll tell you why. They're looking to blame it on one of us."

I was afraid he was right. Sanchez wanted to pin it on me. I pushed my plate away, my appetite suddenly gone.

Further down the beach, I saw a familiar slim redhead strolling by. Janine. It had to be her. I glanced over at Jim. I wouldn't tell him. Let him talk to Wolf. He'd let down his guard if I wasn't around. "Wolf, I'm going to find a chair over there," I said vaguely, gesturing to the beach.

Wolf caught my eye. "Okay, babe. I'll catch up with you in a while."

Good. We were on the same wave length. "See you," I said, waving to them, before I headed through the restaurant to the entrance. It had emptied out fast. Most of the hotel guests were outside sunning or swimming.

I hiked over an arched bridge that brought me to a beach bar and looked around. Already, a few balding men with spare tires were ordering *cervezas*. One of them whispered something to the other dude and he called out, "*Hola!*" as I passed by.

I smiled and said, "*Hola.*"

The other guy chuckled. "See, dude, she knows what that means. Am I right or am I right? " He banged his beer bottle on the bar. "That there is a smart blonde."

"By golly, Bobby Ray, ah've been fooled agin."

Men! I rolled my eyes. So now I was a blonde joke. It was hard not to take it personally. Could be that's why Sanchez thought I'd make the best murder suspect. A stupid blonde tourist. And if he found out anything about my history with Dean, I was toast.

I stopped at the edge of the steps to look around for Janine. It wasn't long before I spotted her. Topless. She was getting plenty of attention from the males deliberately passing by. What did they care if a woman was big or small—boobs and butt were all they were interested in.

I took off my wedges and carried them as I made my way through the beach crowd to Janine's chair. Beside her there was an empty one with a book balanced on it. "Hey, Janine. Is it okay if I take this chair?"

"Hey, Adie." Janine sat up, grabbed her bikini top and tied it on. "You can put the book on the table. I was saving it for Jim but he's probably not coming. With those freckles of his, he's not big on tanning."

I laughed. What was that—the pot calling the kettle black? "I'd think with your fair skin you should be careful yourself. I hope you've loaded up on sunscreen." I tugged off my tank top and shorts. Straightening the strings of my bikini, I stretched out on the lounge chair.

"Did that, but," Janine added, "it's not really about tanning, Adie, in case you didn't notice." She waved her cell. "Got a few phone numbers."

I pulled out my towel and placed it on the chair, straightening the wrinkles before I stretched out beside her. "Reality check, girlfriend. You're married."

"And I'll be single by the end of the week."

I shot her a look. "What?"

"It was a big mistake, Adie," Janine said, wiggling down further on her beach towel. "With all the money ol' Dean's left me, I'll be free as a bird. And now that Dale's here..."

"Dean's brother?"

"He arrived this morning. We're just waitin' for Dean's lawyer."

"The reading of the will?"

Janine nodded. "This afternoon."

"So what happened with the police?"

"They're busy rounding up the usual suspects." Janine smiled mysteriously. "Don't worry. I didn't tell them."

I tensed up. "Tell what?"

"About you and Dean."

"There was no Dean and me. Nothing happened, Janine," I said sharply. Memories of Dean flashed back in my mind. "If he told you otherwise, it was a lie."

"I believe you, girlfriend, but when he got stoned one night, he said the two of you hooked up."

"That's not true!" I felt my cheeks flush in indignation.

Janine smiled knowingly. "Nothing to be ashamed of. Sam said he was good in the sack."

"We never hooked up, Janine. I wasn't interested in him."

"He said it happened in Cancun—at the beach house."

"Nothing happened. You'd asked me to stay over that night, Janine. We had drinks. I was feeling strange so I went to my room and lay down. Dean came to the door, asking if I was all right." A sudden flashback brought back the dreamlike state I had found myself in. "I'd left the door unlocked. He came in..."

"I know what he was like," Janine said tightly.

I had a sudden vision of Dean lying on the bed beside me, stroking my leg. Had he done more? "The drink was potent and I was out of it, Janine, but I'm sure he didn't rape me."

Janine nodded. "I can see why you hated him."

"What do you mean?"

"He dropped a roofie in your drink. You didn't figure that out?" Janine frowned. "He was always doing stuff like that. And he'd brag about his easy conquests." Her eyes flicked to me. "Roofies are deadly. Makes you feel numb and spacey. You forget everything later. It's so easy for a man to do anything he wants to you." She pushed her sunglasses firmly back on the bridge of her nose. "So you don't think you had sex with him?"

"I didn't. I'd remember that."

"Not with a roofie you wouldn't, but he could have used GHB. It's almost the same but you'd remember more."

"I recall him coming in and touching me but somehow I worked up the strength and punched him."

Janine giggled. "You hit him?"

I glanced at my friend. "I don't know if you know this but I'm trained in karate."

"Really? So you got him in the nuts?"

"No. I went for his eye. It was closer and I was wasted. Dean was furious and left."

Janine pursed her lips as she considered my story. "So you didn't find him hot?"

"Damn right, I didn't!" I stared at her in disbelief. "He said I did?"

"Later that same week we were all together at Diego's nudist resort. He told us. When Terry and Sam started fighting over him, he said you were more woman than either one of them."

"And he said I liked him?"

"Yep. Dean said after your initial resistance you pleased him like no other woman. He said if he'd had another night with you, Diego would be history." Janine added, "He thought you were Diego's mistress." Janine waved a waiter over. "A margarita, *por favor*. Make it *dos*." She studied me. "Looks like you need one, Adie."

Once the waiter wandered off in the direction of the bar, I said, "But you knew I was seeing Wolf."

"Yeah, but I didn't bother clueing in the bastard. You were safe in Coz with Wolf, anyway." She said hastily, "Not that Diego was there, either." She grinned. "Too bad he wasn't though. I wouldn't have minded seeing him in the buff." Janine shrugged her shoulders. "So what if Dean thought he could have you. In fact, I was hoping that Wolf would get wind of Dean's plan and punch his lights out." She laughed. "Or Diego. Now that's a thought. He'd send one of his thugs over and cut his balls off."

"I guess someone's nose was out of joint—seriously. You know who that could be, Janine?"

"Plenty of people hated the creep, Adie."

"Is that how you felt, Janine?"

For a moment, I wondered if she'd heard me. She stared out at the ocean. "What's important is that he liked me, Adie. Me and Terry. We were afraid he'd leave it all to Sam."

I was about to speak when the waiter arrived with our margaritas. "Was he thinking in that direction?"

From a small bottle, Janine squeezed out sunscreen into the palm of her hand. "He threatened Terry. If she didn't do what he wanted, he'd leave everything to Sam." She smoothed on sunscreen and passed the bottle to me.

"But he didn't."

A hint of a smile curled Janine's lips. "No, and now it's too late."

Slowly, I stroked the lotion on my forearms. "So you'll be independently wealthy?"

Janine sucked up the margarita with her straw. "I'm not the only one, Adie. Dean left shares of his company to Dale and Sam, too."

"What about Jim? Why do you want to divorce him?"

Janine readjusted her bikini strap. "I like him and he likes me, Adie. He won't suffer. I'll let him work for the company."

"Generous of you."

"Do I detect a touch of sarcasm, Adie? Jim should be grateful for his highfalutin' job." She glanced at me. "I'll do your back, sweetie." Taking the lotion, Janine pressed a small amount into her hand. "Turn."

I did as she said and she spread it over my back and shoulders. "Where's that hottie of yours, anyway, or should I say those two hotties of yours?"

"One's with your soon-to-be ex and the other is probably making last minute arrangements for his float."

Janine put the lotion on the table.

"Thanks." I relaxed on the lounger, stretched out on my stomach.

"Royal Investments?"

"Um-mm. Don said Diego had a fabulous float last year."

"I don't know about his Carnaval floats but I've got the feeling the man has a habit of doing fabulous things." Janine glanced at me slyly. "How's he in bed, Adie?"

His bed—yes, I'd spent a brief time on his bed at his beach house. I thought of us together lying there on his king-size brass bed with a satiny cover and an erotic mural on the ceiling. But as far as his skills were concerned, we hadn't ever gone that far. "Can't tell you about that, Janine."

"Can't or won't?" She scrutinized my face. "You mean you have never…" She smirked. "But I bet you wouldn't mind finding out if a man can be both rich and satisfying."

"Wolf is great. I don't need to find out."

"Wolf is successful and cream-your-pants hot. No denying that but you and I know that Diego is drop dead sexy besides being filthy rich and powerful. He snaps his fingers around here and they kiss his toes," she snickered, "or higher." Janine pulled her hair back into a ponytail. "But that's not the problem is it? You aren't ready for a commitment, are you, girlfriend? That's your problem."

"Problem?"

Janine giggled. "Oo-oo-hh, I see. You are more devious than I'd thought." She pointed her finger at me. "You plan on having them both and then deciding, don't you?" She laughed. "Good plan. That's what I'd do."

"Hey, hot stuff. I'm here!" Jim called out from the bridge.

"Shit! He's back! Thought we'd have more time together. Just when you were about to reveal all to Auntie Janine." She patted my hand. "We'll need to continue our heart-to-heart later, sweetie." She sat up, pointing. "Hey babe, grab that chair over there and bring it here."

Jim followed orders to the letter. Dragging a lounge chair over the sand, he brought it next to Janine. He spread a towel over the chair. Unbuttoning his Hawaiian shirt, he whipped it off and sat down. "This is going to be one big happening day!"

I glanced over at Jim. His face was flushed with happiness. Janine had obviously not shared the divorce news with him.

"Yeah? You talk to the board of directors?" Janine asked.

Jim tugged off his shirt, revealing his strong shoulders and chest. "They know about the murder." He propped himself on the arm of Janine's chair. "I'm coming to the reading of the will. Targette, Dean's lawyer, said I should be there."

"When?" Janine asked.

Jim glanced at his watch. "We've got two hours."

In my mind, Jim looked a little too smug about it all. I didn't know him well but something told me he had a secret that he wasn't about to share.

"There's something you're not saying, isn't there, Jimmy?" Janine said, confirming my suspicions. I had the feeling he knew something important about Dean's will.

Rolling onto his stomach, Jim muttered into the towel. "Time will reveal all, Janine. Terry said we're to get together in her suite."

I pulled myself up on my elbows. "What happened to Wolf?"

Jim turned his head. "He had a phone call. Told me to tell you something's come up."

I'd been counting on Wolf to make me feel better, if not with good news, at least with his sexy smile. The sun beating down on my back and legs was uncomfortably hot. Any more of this and I'd be as red as an overly-ripe tomato. I stood up and gathered up my towel, folded it and pushed it into my bag.

"You're going, Adie?" Janine asked.

"Um-mm. I think I'll take a swim and have a shower. Diego invited me to be on his float tonight."

Janine stroked her lower lip with her finger. "Does that mean what I think it means? Why don't we meet for coffee tomorrow?"

"Sure."

"Lorita's?"

"Ten o'clock?"

Janine's eyes twinkled. "Can't wait!"

"See you!" I called out, heading up the stairs to the pool. I decided to place my things on an empty chair.

No one else was in the water. I stood on the ladder and pointed my toe into the water. The water was cool in contrast to the steamy air. From here I could see the beach—a few people snorkeling, but the rest of the guests were either in the restaurant or getting fried. This would be my workout. Sinking in bit by bit, I held onto the ladder. If I wanted to stay fit I'd have to suffer. There was nothing worse than an out-of-shape martial artist.

At the far end of the free-form pool my eyes lit on a shapely redhead stretched out on a chair. Terry. I was about to call out to her, when I noticed the handsome security guard from last night. He bent his head down and whispered something in her ear. Whatever he said had quite a reaction. She jerked up and grabbed her wrap. Quickly she tugged it on before she slipped her feet into flip-flops and took off in the direction of the elevator. He watched her a moment before he headed in the opposite direction.

Sliding into the water, I did a sidestroke, under the bridge towards the unoccupied chairs near the far end where Terry had been sitting. I had to swim hard or let the cold numb my extremities. This was twice now I'd seen her with the guard. Of course, the hotel management might have sent him. Her husband had been murdered and possibly they'd want to question her. I touched the end and swiveled around to swim back, slowing down a bit now that my body had acclimatized itself. I sank into a back stroke, relaxing in the water. What I wouldn't give to go back to my room and have Wolf waiting for me in my king-sized bed. What was that goal of his—to make me feel better? Give me pleasure? I smiled, thinking of his sensuous lips on my body, making me melt faster than butter in the tropical sun. Soon. It had to happen soon.

I grabbed the ladder and climbed up. Grabbing my things, I started towards the elevator where Terry had disappeared. Too bad I couldn't be a fly on the wall this afternoon when they read the will. I had the feeling there'd be some surprises for everyone. Hopefully, Don could tell me the details later. He'd said he'd be on the float—one of the sheikhs. It was hard to believe Diego would allow other males up there. I could imagine Diego standing proudly on that float, knowing he was born to be the king of the Carnaval.

Sexy brandy eyes. I could hardly trust myself not to throw him down and kiss those succulent lips while I explored his svelte body with my fingers. Could I really believe he wanted me or was I just an ornament for his arm while he sat on his throne before the admiring masses? I'd have to be a fool to think this meant anything to him. Billionaire Santiago Francisco Bolivar Alvarez with tour group leader, Adie Sturm.

* * *

The bed was big, comfortable and sadly empty. That sexy man of mine was busy doing who knows what. I resigned myself to my second choice. Sleep. There was still time for a nap before getting ready to meet Diego's driver in front of the hotel. I set my clock alarm and lay down. Sweet sleep—dreamless sleep. That's what I needed. If only my bad luck would end. Through my open balcony doors, birds squawked noisily. Those were the last sounds I heard before I sank into a deep slumber. The drone of the alarm jarred me awake.

I pressed the button and sank back into my bed. I wasn't feeling up to this whole Carnaval thing or those men. Ooops! Did I say men?

Yes, you did, My Hormone Voice whispered. You're finally

wisening up. Wolf is avoiding you, so take this as a sign. Diego will offer himself to you tonight and he doesn't have a cobra hanging around—a definite advantage for you.

No it's not! My Logical Voice chimed in. She's always screwing up as far as men are concerned and let's face it, Hormone, she's getting closer to the big Three-Oh. Adie Sturm is no teenager. She has to consider a permanent relationship before all the good ones are gone.

Hormone chortled. Did you ever miss the boat! Diego is "The One"! Rich and hot doesn't come along every day!

Right, Logical said dryly, she should go for a player! He'll use and abuse her in no time. Besides, money isn't the most important thing—love is.

"Shut up, already!" I said aloud in the room. I grimaced. I was seriously losing it. I needed food. Snacks. Diego had mentioned eating before the Carnaval parade. I glanced at my watch. "Hold on, stomach," I said consolingly, "soon, twenty minutes max."

From my dresser, I dug out a rose camisole and my denim skirt and slipped them on. High heeled, metallic sandals and the jade pendant that Wolf had given me, but nothing else. No need for jewelry since Diego would have me out of my clothes in no time. No, that wasn't what I meant. I did have some common sense. What I meant to say is, his sister, Carmelita, a model with her own designer line, would have a costume for me and jewelry.

Romantic music. I headed over to the sliding doors. Enrique Iglesias crooning a song about his woman coming closer and hearing her breathe. Aa-ah, I sighed. To have Wolf breathe in my ear tonight and his body next to mine would be all I would need.

I glanced out to the area surrounding the pool below. It was quite a distance down from where I stood. So beautiful—the palms swaying, the Latin music and the warmth of the sun.

At the pool I spotted a lean, lanky blond guy sitting next to a brunette. Wow, I thought. He was hot—like Wolf. Such a lean yet athletic body. I leaned over the railing. If I had been holding a glass I would have dropped it. Luckily, for those people below, I was empty-handed. That man below so like the sea god was Wolf. And he was speaking to the viper perched on his chair.

4

Outside, sitting in the driver's seat of a white limo, I saw a familiar face. Ernesto popped out to greet me. "*Buenos tardes, Señorita Sturm.*" He hurried over to open the door and assisted me into the soft leather seat in the back. I glanced around. Wide seats facing each other and a partition separating the chauffeur from the passengers. Right now, the partition was down and the chauffeur seemed eager to renew our acquaintanceship.

"*Hola.* How are you, Ernesto?"

"*Muy bien*, thank you, Señorita Sturm." He grinned widely. "It is good you are here this week. You will like the Carnaval."

"It sounds like fun."

"Very much dancing, music, and you will enjoy the floats. They are something to behold."

"I was told Señor Alvarez has a wonderful float."

"*Si!* And the costumes and the prizes are fantastic."

"Have you seen the costumes?"

"No, not yet. Although I have heard Señora Bolivar Alvarez has some of them in her winter fashion line."

He was talking about Carmelita. I'd forgotten that married women kept their mother and father's name. She had her own fashion house now. Knowing what fabulous designs she had, I was sure my costume would be spectacular. The woman was a creative genius in the fashion world and a hot dog in the real world. I missed her—she was a friend I could count on.

On the crowded main drag there was a flavor of anticipation in the air. The white pillars along the sidewalk were decked in gold and purple, the Carnaval colors. In the distance out in the harbor, I spotted cruise ships anchored at the dock.

As we approached the town center, Ernesto explained, "We'll need to turn here, Señorita Sturm. The street is closed off for the Carnaval."

We took a roundabout route through the residential section. The houses were brightly colored with red tile roofs, mostly bungalows. In front of the supermarket the locals crossed the street, oblivious of the limo or the other cars. On a motor scooter, two ladies in tight pants pulled up beside us and honked at Ernesto. He looked pleased at the attention and waved.

Making a right, we drove back up to Raphael Melgar, past the ritzy shopping plaza of Punta Langosta, and finally parked in front of the Merida Hotel. Whether it was legal or not was of no concern to Ernesto who took his time helping me out of the limo and escorting me to the rotating doors.

A doorman rushed out. "Señorita Sturm?"

I nodded. He looked relieved as he held the door for me to enter. "I will bring you to Señor Alvarez. He is waiting." He called out something in Spanish to the bellhop who scurried over to stand by the entrance, while he lead the way to a double door with elaborate brass handles. Swinging the door open, he gestured for me to enter.

My eyes widened as I stepped in. The place was elegant— chandeliers, oil paintings, and a long buffet table stacked with food that made my mouth water.

Diego, in a white silk shirt and jeans, strode towards me. "How lovely you look, *mi amor.*" He paused a moment to peruse me, his eyes lingering on my cleavage. "I'm so glad you decided to come tonight." Taking my hand in his, he kissed my wrist. A whiff of citron met my nostrils. His brandy eyes sparkled green in the dim light. "Come sit down. I had them prepare your favorite." He placed his hand at the small of my back and led me to a candlelit table laid out with a silver tureen and white china dishes.

That set my stomach gurgling happily. "How thoughtful of you, Diego."

"I want to fulfill all your desires, *mi amor.*" Diego flashed me a celebrity smile. "Food or otherwise." He pulled out the chair for me.

I sat down, curious as to what the tureen contained, but had to wait while the server poured Diego a portion of red wine to sample. After Diego swirled the wine in the goblet, he examined the glass before he sipped. When he nodded, the waiter poured me a glass and disappeared to the bar with the bottle.

"To us." Diego clicked his glass to mine.

"*Salud!*" I met his eyes. He was particularly dashing tonight, the white shirt setting off his broad shoulders and the buttons open at the neck displaying an enticing chest. How lucky I was that I had someone who adored me. Wolf was another story. He obviously had other fish to fry.

Just as I set my glass down, my cell tinkled a ringtone. "Excuse me," I said to Diego, recovering my cell from my purse. A text message.

Tonight is ours, spicy woman.

Hastily I clicked it shut and thrust it back in my bag.

"By your expression, I surmise it's not good news?"

"Nothing has been good for me lately, Diego."

"Ah-h, yes. Dean's death was inopportune, was it not?" Diego studied me over his glass. "Hopefully, you weren't bothered unduly by the police?"

"The family was detained for hours but the bridal party got off with less. Unfortunately, they took my passport and..." I hesitated, recalling Sanchez and his suspicions.

Diego took my hand. "What is it, *mi amor?* You look distressed."

I sipped the wine contemplatively. "I hardly slept last night. A bad dream. No, that's not true. It was a horrible nightmare."

"Tell me about it. Perhaps it will help."

"I dreamt about Dean."

Diego raised an inquiring eyebrow.

"He knocked on my door and when I opened it, he pushed by me."

"And?"

"He wanted to have sex with me, Diego."

Diego smiled slightly. "Yes, I can see having sex with a dead man would be upsetting." Diego signaled for the waiter who trotted over with the wine bottle. At Diego's nod he refilled our glasses before he scurried back to the bar.

"That's not all..." The image of Dean with the blood pouring out of his throat jumped out at me. I shuddered.

Diego took my hand. "What else, Adelina? You look so upset."

"I..."

"You can trust me, *cariño*. It might help to tell me."

"It was an awful dream." I didn't want Diego to know I had entered Dean's room and had actually seen the blood. "What you don't know, Diego is, he really did come on to me and it wasn't at all agreeable."

Diego patted my hand. "Of course not, Adelina. The man had no finesse."

"He put a roofie in my drink that night I stayed at their villa."

"The swine!" Diego hissed out the words. "He forced himself on you?"

"He was drunk and...let me explain."

Diego's eyes narrowed.

"Do you remember when I came here on business for the travel agency?"

"You were checking out the condos on Cozumel. I believe I was in Mexico City. Unfortunately, we couldn't get together. With my father in the hospital, I had to manage his business."

"I stayed at Dean's house at Janine's invitation. We all had drinks. Later he let himself into my room." I paused and frowned. "I was feeling dizzy and disoriented. I thought it was the daiquiri, but Janine told me Dean slipped a roofie or GHB into my drink."

Diego's hand tightened on mine. "You said he didn't rape you, but are you saying he assaulted you?"

"He tried. When he started to touch me, I hit him and told him to leave."

Diego laughed. "You struck the bastard? Excellent. In the *cojones*...the testicles, I hope."

I studied his face, wondering if he was telling me everything. "You didn't know about this before, did you?"

"No. I didn't know you punched the bastard. But I do remember how you hit with a powerful blow. When we were in Tulum together, I was fortunate not to have been kicked lower. I recall a painful strike to the chest."

"You deserved that one."

"I would take any punishment to be with an enchantress like you." Diego kissed the inside of my wrist. "But I am worried about your state of mind. Dean's murder is bringing back unpleasant memories."

"I suppose so. I didn't like him."

"Not many did, Adelina. Perhaps, it would help to speak of something pleasant. I am so blessed with the pleasure of your presence tonight." He stared at my glass of wine. "How is your wine?"

"Interesting. I like it…soft berry flavors."

"And?"

"A hint of oak."

Diego grinned. "I am envious of your palate, *mi amor*, but you are missing something."

"Ah-hh." It was in the finish. The flavor was distinctive and unforgettable. A taste that set my endorphins hopping. Diego had found an exceptional shiraz, once again. "There's chocolate in the finish, isn't there?"

Diego nodded. "It's Australian—Lily's Garden. New but impressive." He motioned to the server who sprinted up to the table. "We're ready for the soup."

And I was. My stomach reminded me with a rumble. But my brain told me not to forget my reconnaissance mission. As we ate sopa de lima I considered how to approach the man referred to as the godfather of Cozumel.

"You like it, Adelina?"

"Um-mm, it's excellent, but Diego," not wanting to be sidetracked, I touched his sleeve, "tell me about your deal with Dean. What was it all about?"

Diego paused, his spoon airborne, and regarded me intently. "Deal? Who told you I had a business with Firenze?"

"Janine said he was interested in your condo resort on the Mayan Riviera."

Diego shrugged. "We were in the process of negotiation." He stroked my hand. "But it would be better if you forgot about the bastard and his dealings. Focus on this dinner and on us, Adelina. A beautiful woman, such as you, should not be concerned with boring business details." He signaled the waiter who rushed out with a tray.

That caught my interest—soup can only go so far in satisfying a hungry woman's appetite. When he set my plate down, I nearly swooned at the sight of lobster tail, out of the shell with a dish of melted butter. "Diego—" I breathed out his name.

He smiled indulgently. "For my lovely, Adelinita."

"How did you guess?"

"You told me of your liking for lobster before and you know how I want to please you. Try it," he said, his voice husky.

He moved his chair next to mine so that our knees touched. The heat of his leg radiated out to me. His brandy eyes set me on fire and those well-formed lips begged to be kissed. I gave him a flirtatious look but my stomach rumbled. Diego was placed on the back burner as I forked up some lobster and dipped it into the golden liquid. He watched as I brought it to my lips and let it slide in, savoring the heavenly morsel—my eyes shut, I swallowed, my senses steeped. Diego watched me lay down my fork.

"Good?"

"Oh, yes, delicious. Nothing can taste better."

"Really?" Diego brought his hand to the back of my head.

Soft lips met mine, pressing gently, sliding over the coating of butter until my mouth parted for his tongue to enter. I dropped my fork. Slowly he teased my tongue and inner lips and then withdrew his tantalizing weapon.

"I have more for you, beautiful Adelina!"

Confused, I opened my eyes to see another forkful of lobster ready for me, this time on Diego's fork. I let him feed me until it was almost gone. "Stop, Diego, you need to eat."

Diego picked up his wine glass and tilted it to his lips. "I'm not hungry." He smiled. "That is to say, not for food."

Oh! My Hormone Voice exclaimed. He wants you badly. Tell him you want to be with him too.

"Did I tell you about my soiree following the parade? You will allow me to escort you tonight, won't you?"

See! Hormone screamed in my brain. Say yes before he chooses someone else.

I thought about Wolf's message. What did it mean exactly? Was he investigating the snake, finding out what she was up to? Or was I being naïve? I twisted my hands nervously. Where was he anyway?

Diego ran his fingers through a strand of my hair, gazing into my eyes. "It will be a costume party at my beach house."

"And I will wear the costume Carmelita has for me?"

"Yes, and believe me, it was made for you. You will look beautiful." Diego set his glass down. "Speaking of which, are you ready to go?" Diego pulled out my chair as I stood up. "Carmelita said she'd meet us there. Come," he said, leading me to the double doors and swinging one open.

We headed down the hallway to a room next to the dining room.

Inside, it was a hubbub of activity with dressing tables and women in various states of undress. Carmelita, a pretty, willowy brunette came charging out at Diego. "You are not allowed in here. Go!"

Diego laughed, shrinking back from his sister as she shoved him into the hallway and pulled me in. She flipped the door shut with her foot and gave me kisses on both cheeks. "Amiga! How are you?"

"Great and you?"

"Couldn't be better, Adelina. How wonderful of you to agree to this. This is such a good opportunity for me. My designer has out done himself." Her eyes shot up and down, surveying me. "I have the most fabulous costume for you."

"I hear it is rather revealing; I hope not too much so."

She grabbed my hand and brought me over to a curtained change room, eying me with amusement. "Don't look like that, Adelina. You'll have all the males of Cozumel panting for you. What more could you want? I'll help you." She pushed the curtain aside and we entered a large change room. On the wall, a gold costume was draped over a hanger. "Get undressed, amiga."

"Do I keep my underwear?"

"No, but don't worry. I have these." She held up a gold thong in one hand and picked up a sheer demi bra. "Aren't they something?" She watched as I undressed. "You will certainly do justice to the costume."

When I stripped down to my underwear, Carmelita handed me the bra. I felt a little self conscious with her studying my breasts before I pulled the gold fabric over them and fastened it.

"Very nice," she said obliquely. I wasn't sure if she was referring to my breasts or the bra. "A perfect fit." Her glance swung down to my panties. "Those are pretty, Adelina. High-cut, lacey and black. Hm-mm."

"What?"

She shook her head. "I feel bad giving you a thong." She smirked. "Some man, perhaps even my brother, would be more thrilled to see those lacey undies. Ultra feminine." She pulled out a cloth beach bag. "I'll put your clothes in here. You'll probably want to take them along when we leave. I doubt if you'll be coming back here tonight!" She laughed. "Who knows where you'll be later?"

I rolled my eyes. "Carmelita, you need to tell me something." I tugged down my panties. "Did Diego invite Wolf?"

Carmelita handed me the thong. "You shaved. Excellent." She giggled. "We don't want to give them too much of a show."

I pulled on the thong and looked at her significantly. "Well?"

Carmelita shrugged her shoulders. "Anyone, who's someone, appears at my brother's parties." Her eyes twinkled. "And I'd say Wolf is someone—*un hombre muy guapo!*"

"Hot he is, but he and Diego are not friends."

"Personal conflicts, Adelina. Nothing to do with business. Seems to me your mysterious Wolf is involved in a condo deal that my brother is putting together." She handed me the harem pants, sheer gold with purple edging.

"What? Not the one Dean Firenze was involved in?"

"Firenze..." Carmelita curled her lovely lips. "He needed his hands chopped off—that pathetic particle of pond scum."

I pulled on the pants. "I gather you didn't like him?" I took the glittery top from her. Fastening it, I noticed it did little to cover the bra. It was so sheer.

"Thought he could touch the goods, but he was mistaken."

"He came on to you?"

"Only once. Churo paid a little visit to the slimeball and he lived to regret it." She smiled maliciously. "But I'm not the only one who hated the *cabrón*. Someone obviously agreed with me and went to the trouble of slitting his throat."

I thought of what she said. Churo was massive and one of Diego's trusted security guards. He would have caused Dean some pain but from what I knew of him, Eduardo was the meanest of Diego's security guards. It would have gone a lot worse for Dean if Eduardo had been sent.

Carmelita adjusted my top to reveal more cleavage. "There, that's better." She gazed at me. "I detect a touch of hostility, amiga. You didn't like him much either, did you? Did he try something with you?"

"Yes, but he didn't get too far."

"Oh?" Carmelita lifted an eyebrow.

My jaw tightened. "I hit him—hard."

Carmelita's laughter tinkled. "I would have liked to have seen that! I hope you really hurt him." She glanced down at her Cartier watch. "Come, amiga, it's time." She tugged on my hand and brought me out of the dressing room. Here she looked around before calling out, "Alejandro, please! We need you now!"

A very stylish man in tight jeans and a print shirt emerged from behind a curtain. His flashing black eyes surveyed me. "Ah-hh, yes, Señorita Sturm. How nice to see you again. I am looking forward to the challenge." He ran his fingers through my hair. "My, my…you have been taking care of it. Staying out of the salty water, have we?" He glanced at Carmelita. "I worked wonders with Señorita Sturm's hair before but today it will be much easier. It will be exceptional once I add the extensions. You shall see, Señora Alvarez."

Carmelita grinned. "You are the guru of the hair world! I have no doubt of that, *cariño!*"

Alejandro inclined his head at the compliment and snapped his fingers. A rotund Latina appeared with a case. "Bring the extensions over to that dressing table." Alejandro motioned arrogantly. "We are ready to start." He glanced over at a fair brunette sitting at the next table. "Isabel is all set to do the makeup, I see. Her skill will certainly bring out the best in Señorita Sturm."

"My brother will be pleased."

Alejandro smiled. "And grateful, I am sure." He turned to me. "Come with me, Señorita and we will begin."

"We will make Adelina the belle of the Carnaval, Alejandro. No man will have the power to resist her charms."

5

I was perched high on a float. That in itself made me nervous, especially with the copious amounts of champagne Diego kept pouring into my glass. He, on the other hand, looked well suited as the sheikh and totally comfortable with both the champagne and the lustful glances from his harem girls.

What girl in her right mind wouldn't want a guy like that? He had decided not to wear a shirt. A purple sash, a pair of white loose pants, sandals, and the sheikh headdress were the extent of his costume. The makeup lady had given him a touch of eye shadow, a smoky gray, eyeliner and mascara, to increase the sheikh mystique. When I glanced at his wide shoulders and well-defined chest tapering to a narrow waist, I was tempted to savor his candy.

His smoldering bedroom eyes met mine. "I have..."

With the noisy crowd surrounding the float shouting for beads the harem girls threw, his voice drifted away.

"A present," he said in my ear.

I like gifts and one from Diego was bound to be exciting.

From out of his pocket he drew out a velvet drawstring bag and gave it to me. Undoing the strings, I tugged out a wide silver bracelet. The design was unusual. In the center I saw the voluptuous figure of a woman in profile, a snake coiled on her head.

"Here, *mi amor*, let me assist you." Diego opened it and clasped the bracelet around my forearm before I could protest.

"Ixchel?" I tilted my head, admiring the intricate workmanship. "Lovely, thank you, Diego, but I really can't accept it. You know you shouldn't buy me gifts."

"But I want to. Wear it at least for a while."

I smiled. "All right but..."

Diego kissed me quickly on the lips. "Hush—look closely, Adelina. She's the young Ixchel, the fertility goddess."

I laughed. "As opposed to the crone Ixchel?"

"I forget sometimes how knowledgeable you are. Beautiful and intelligent—a rare combination."

"Ever since I started bringing tour groups here, I had to do my research on Mexican celebrations. Four days of Carnaval before Ash Wednesday, isn't it?"

"Yes, *cariño*. And I'd like you to be here on this float, for all the parades if you can. Fat Tuesday will be the biggest procession. They end the Carnaval on that day. It's not until the Wednesday they award the prizes for best floats." He grinned. "My goal is to capture first prize."

I glanced down at Carmelita's models in their skimpy purple harem costumes and nodded. "The girls are beautiful and the crowd likes the beads and candies they're throwing out." I suddenly felt guilty. "I should be helping, shouldn't I?"

Diego brought his hand to the back of my head, stroking my hair. "No," he said, "yours is a much more important job." He glanced down at my cleavage and then back to my lips. When he pressed his lips on mine, the crowd reacted, cheering and waving their arms back and forth. Diego looked out at them as they shouted something loudly in Spanish. "I think we should follow their wishes, Adelina."

I was puzzled. What was it they wanted?

"Come, we'll go to the next level," Diego said, holding my hand, helping me down. He snapped his fingers and the music changed to a Moorish rhythm, nouveau flamenco. Diego put his hands up and started swaying to the music. I didn't have a choice, I had to join in. "That's it, Adelina, show them your hip motion. See how they love it." He swiveled to the crowd behind him and brought me over to face them. "Let's make them envious of our skills." He slid his hand fleetingly down my arm. Shivers of delight coursed down my body. With his hand on my bare waist, I was very much aware of how revealing my costume was. My breasts were barely covered by the flimsy gold material and the shimmering fabric did little to conceal the metallic hues of my thong.

As I spun around, I met the eyes of a blond man in the crowd. It was only a fleeting glimpse and for a second I thought it was Wolf. My heart raced. Could it be him? He would be angry if he'd seen me on this float with Diego. My eyes searched him out again but he was too far away.

I was drawn into Diego as the music ended. His warm strong

arms wrapped around me, and he leaned down, his lips greeting mine with a slow dance of their own. My inhibitions diminished after the champagne, I parted my mouth. The crowd went wild with our kiss and realizing then what I was doing, I hastily pulled away but not before I noticed Diego's wicked grin.

Behind our float, a troop of merengue dancers in satin blue wove down the street in three lines. The float had come to a standstill as the harem girls and our token eunuch, Don, threw out T-shirts and beads. He was not the Don I knew. Here was a dynamic man, with dramatic makeup and a beard and moustache. Who said eunuchs don't have fun? The girls were clinging to him, especially Diego's assistant, Delores. Between flirting with Don, she shot lustful glances at Diego. And, no, I did not feel sorry for the besotted Latina. Anyone who scrambled that hard to catch a bouquet was one tough cookie. She deserved to suffer after nearly taking my eye out.

I sidled up to Don and waited to get his attention, while Delores took that opportunity to drag Diego off. "Don," I said, coming up to him from behind.

Don jerked around. "Hey, darlin'." His eyes settled on my body. "You are one sweet babe tonight! Diego has this contest in the bag with you on his float." He slid his arm around my waist. "Give me a kiss, Adie. That should make the girls jealous."

I gave him a quick peck. "What happened at the reading of the will?"

Don looked serious. "Big blow to our girl, Janine. If she wants the moollah she needs to stay married to the chump. I could tell she didn't expect that little twist."

"And Jim?"

"The boy keeps his CEO job with company shares as long as he doesn't leave her."

"That must have made his day."

"The kid was pleased as punch." Don frowned. "Don't trust him, though. He looks innocent enough but..."

Letting go of me, he grabbed a handful of beads. "Give these to Diego. They'll be your excuse. From the looks of him, he's seething with jealousy."

I glanced over to where Diego was talking to Delores yet all the while watching me. Deciding Don was on the mark, I made my way over. "Don gave me some of the silver beads. Do you want to throw them now?"

"Let's wait. Come." Taking my hand, Diego led me up to the throne and waited for me to sit down first.

"Listen, Diego, I am uncomfortable about your gift."

Diego's eyes met mine. "Why, *cariño?*"

"The bracelet is very beautiful and it's extremely generous of you, but I can't accept it."

He let his hand drift to a tendril of my hair. "Why not, Adelina?" Diego said with concern.

"We are not in a relationship, Diego. I don't want you to believe that we are more involved than we are."

"Please accept it. I especially selected it for you. It's merely a token of my admiration for my beautiful Adelina—a gift for my special friend." He gazed beseechingly at me with those brandy eyes. "I know how you are fascinated by the goddess."

"I appreciate it. I really do," I laughed, "but Ixchel is the fertility goddess and I'm not ready for that."

Diego grinned. "As much as I would love to see you pregnant with my child, that is not my intention in giving you the bracelet. I think you should know Ixchel does more than that. She protects women from danger."

I stroked the jade figure hanging on a silver chain around my neck. A few months ago Wolf had given me this jade Ixchel for protection. Unfortunately, I hadn't worn it the day I discovered Dean's bloody body. And now there was this bracelet from Diego. It was exceptional and I really liked it. I had to wonder if a powerful goddess like Ixchel could help confused women who couldn't decide on which man.

"I don't mean to sound ungrateful, Diego. The bracelet is lovely, but remember I am dating Wolf."

"Keep it, *mi amor*. Remember all things come to an end. It's only a matter of time before you see him for what he is."

"Which is?"

"A man who has tight ties with his lovely ex."

I frowned. I visualized Sam sitting on his chair, cozying up to him. They had looked friendly—way too friendly for my liking.

Diego put his arm around me. The champagne and his warmth made me relax against him. He would love me completely with no distractions. If I forgot about Wolf, I could let Diego into my life.

My Hormone Voice added: And into your bed...

Yes, that had some possibility. Diego's lips on my neck made me tingle. Sweet kisses that sparked my inner flame. My eyes flicked up. He was devastatingly handsome and I could so easily be caught in his web.

The night breeze felt cool after the moist heat of the day. I shivered—ghosts walking across graves. Thoughts of Dean occupied too much of my time. I had to forget what I saw.

The float rounded the bend and we headed down the other side of the boulevard. Here the crowds were thick with both locals and tourists. What stood out were the numbers of children still up with their parents. Cozumel was a happy place for children. No wonder it was the home of Ixchel, the fertility goddess.

"Wave, Adelina. They like that sort of thing." Diego pulled me up and we waved in unison. Seeing the happy faces out there made me more enthusiastic. But it wasn't really me to be up on a float; I would have preferred to have been down in the crowd with that special man of mine, his arm around my waist. But he apparently didn't care about me the way I did about him.

Diego deserved more from me. "Let's throw some beads." I handed him the strands Don had given me. "Come on, Diego, if you want to win, you need to participate."

"You might have something there, Adelina. We're slowing down again." Diego grinned. "Why don't we throw some of the gold beads, too? They're especially prized."

A huge bucket of gold beads had been placed near the edge of the float by one of the girls. "If they dance for you, throw some, okay?"

"To the good-looking women, right?"

Diego smirked in reply.

Spotting some kids, I leaned over and tossed them beads. They must play baseball, I thought, seeing them spring up and land the beads. A heavy set middle aged woman, wrapped in an aqua shawl, stood stoically beside the kids. When I tossed her the beads she gave me an unexpected smile.

"Honeh, heah!" a bouncy blonde in a cowboy hat shouted up at me from the float's edge.

I had to give the beads a spin to get them to her outstretched arms. Luckily she was a tall woman, a head above the crowd of locals. Up the street, we stopped again. A bulky gray bearded man with a military crew cut gyrated wildly in front off me, his bulging middle swinging with his jerky movements. "Hubba, hubba, sweetheart! You got some of those for me?"

I had to give him an A for effort. I threw him some beads but someone behind him caught them. "Sweetheart!" the bearded guy begged loudly. "Over here!"

I bent down, picked up another strand, and threw them just as the float started off. He caught them. Smiling triumphantly, he gave me a thumbs-up. I waved but when I saw the man beside him, my hand dropped. He was wearing the beads I had just thrown to the bearded guy. Dean grinned and waved.

6

Lanterns glowed brightly orange on an immense kidney-shaped pool, the warm hues shimmering in the evening light, lending it a romantic air for Diego's party. Interlocking stone surrounded the pool area and beyond that, there were gardens heavily planted with palms, hibiscus and bougainvillea and something else that was wonderfully spicy and sweet. From the corner of the bar, a guitarist strummed a soft melody to those sitting nearby.

Carmelita, decked out as Cleopatra, was in the midst of a boisterous crowd. Well-supplied with pitchers of daiquiris, margaritas and beer, the revelers gathered on the deck.

Diego and I headed over to a table but before he could sit down, his flustered assistant, Delores, arrived to inform him of a problem. "It's business." Diego kissed my cheek. "My apologies. I'll be back as soon as I can, sweet one." He looked about. "Don't let someone steal you away. Wait! There's Don." He waved.

Don nodded and started towards us. One of Carmelita's models was not about to let him leave without her. Blonde, lithe and exotic, Lourdes was exceptionally beautiful. Don knew a good thing when he saw it. With Lourdes on his arm, he sauntered up. He smiled winningly at the blonde model before reluctantly turning his attention to Diego. "What's up?"

"I have a meeting at the house, my friend, and am loathe to leave Adelina with all these sharks."

Don appraised me with a grin. "I can see why, Diego." His eyes shot over to a group of partying Musketeers having a few beers at the bar. "They've probably spotted her already and are deciding who should come over as soon as you leave. Hah, you're lucky the big man isn't here. He'd give you a run for your money."

"Stop it, you two! I'm not a prize. I do have a brain and can speak for myself."

Diego grinned. "Certainly, but you're unaware of how enticing you are tonight. Men are lining up for a chance to meet up with the belle of the Carnaval." He stage whispered, "So much hotter than the Queen of the Carnaval."

Lourdes giggled. "Don't say that too loud. She's here tonight, Diego. I hear she likes to win and don't forget she's not too fond of you."

Diego's eyes twinkled merrily. "I'll keep that in mind, Lourdes, but you watch out for this scoundrel. Don is not as innocent as he seems." He flashed us a sparkling smile in leaving.

"He should watch out for the Carrazone girl—evil temper and hates to lose." Don scratched his chin. "Her carriage was awesome. and did you see the costumes? The thing rivaled Diego's float. The Carrazone Family is almost as rich as the Bolavars but she hardly qualifies to sell popcorn at the square, let alone be the Carnaval queen." He grinned. "Well that's Mexico for you. Money buys anything."

Lourdes snickered. "She'd kill Diego if that would guarantee her first prize."

I'd stopped listening. That man in the crowd was a dopplegänger for Dean yet he couldn't be Dean. I had to remind myself the man was dead. What was happening to me? First the dream and now visions. Was I going insane? I just wanted to head back to my hotel room and curl up in bed.

Lourdes tapped my arm. "Hey, amiga. I didn't mean to worry you. The queen won't kill you. It's Diego she hates. Besides the float business, she doesn't think much of him." She snickered. "They grew up together and he never dated her. She tells everyone he's a user." Lourdes grinned. "But when it comes to Diego Alvarez, what women wouldn't mind a little abuse from a man like that? Would I ever love to scrape my fingernails down his bare back."

"You women are aggressive little creatures. But so much fun. I'd think you," he ran his finger under Lourdes' chin, "as one of Carmelita's models, would be a peaceful type—a woman of zen. Isn't that Carmelita's thing—organic food, yoga, and zen?"

Lourdes pinched his cheek. "Oh-hh, Don. You are so funny. I think you mean pilates. Those keep the abs trim." She became suddenly serious. "No, *cariño*, I think you don't understand our Carmelita. She's a Bolivar Alvarez, after all. For all her new world philosophy, she has a dark side. I wouldn't recommend crossing her."

Don nodded. "Guess the queen found that out."

Lourdes tipped back her drink. "The hard way."

I was really puzzled. "Are you saying Carmelita did something to her?"

"You're surprised, amiga? I admit she's charming and she's the best friend a woman can have—kind, generous and loving, as long as you don't stab her in the back. That was the queen's mistake."

"Oh? What did she do?"

Lourdes smirked. "Flirted with Fede."

I was puzzled. "But she doesn't like him."

"That probably saved the queen but Fede is her husband, Adelina, and as such is her possession."

Don grinned. "Putting the rat in her room was priceless."

"Rat?"

Lourdes nodded. "In the bed. The queen and the Carnaval group were staying here a few months ago." Her eyes twinkled. "The queen must have slipped her hand where it didn't belong. You have to admit it was a bit extreme."

I frowned. "True, but Lourdes, Carmelita has always been wonderful to me."

"That's because she wants you for her brother." Lourdes pointed her finger in the air. "She'd do anything to make that happen."

I shot Lourdes a look. "I find it hard to believe that Carmelita would be so harsh. We've been friends for awhile and I think I know her."

"And I'm her friend too, Adelina—make no mistake. But you weren't here when she had that falling out with Dean."

"Dean? What do you mean? They were involved?"

"I think it was a fling. They'd been together a few times for fun and games."

"Are you sure about that? Carmelita said she didn't like him."

Lourdes smiled slyly. "I don't think she'd admit she was attracted to him. And don't forget, Fede is always with some woman."

"So it was revenge on her part?"

Lourdes shrugged her lovely shoulders.

"But Carmelita is married, Lourdes. How did she manage to..."

Lourdes grinned. "With difficulty, amiga. But remember Fede has been away in Mexico City for a while. He's been learning the import-export business with her dad."

"When Francisco Bolivar calls—Fede runs." Don stopped a waiter and grabbed a seafood appetizer. "I think Carmelita's dad wanted to keep an eye on him. Diego must have told him about Fede's affairs."

"I think her affair was just a challenge." Lourdes laughed, revealing perfect tiny teeth.

Don gazed tenderly at Lourdes as he inserted a scallop between her full lips. "And she wanted to make Terry suffer."

"Why?"

Turning to me, Don grimaced. "Terry treated her like crap." He glanced over to the crowd gathered at the bar. "Speak of the devil! Ladies, excuse me a moment. Carmelita summons." Quickly, Don hugged Lourdes before he headed over to Diego's sister in the midst of a crowd of admirers.

"She's always been nice to me."

Lourdes' eyes swept over at Carmelita holding court. "That's because you didn't cross her. Dean was ignoring Terry and paying attention to Carmelita. Bought her some valuable art. That made his wife furious. I mean, she already had to contend with Samantha. She deliberately spilled wine on Carmelita, justifiably so, but remember one thing—Carmelita is a Bolivar. She's Cozumel's royalty. Nobody treats a Bolivar like that. She got off lightly when Carmelita decided to take Dean from her."

I bit my lip. Terry was pretending to like me. She had to be angry, thinking I'd slept with Dean. Had she wanted revenge? It would have been easy for her to set me up for his murder. And what about JJ? Had he helped, knowing he'd get a piece of the pie?

Suddenly, Lourdes grabbed my hand and squeezed it, her eyes riveted on someone behind me. "Oh-hhh! Adie. He's so-ooo hot! But don't look now," she said hastily, digging the tips of her nails into my arm. "He's coming over!"

I didn't think I needed any more guys in my life but this was a party and having fun was a party rule, wasn't it?

Lourdes' eyes glazed over. At the same time I felt soft kisses on my shoulder that awakened every fiber in my body.

"Excuse me, Adelina, I can see you have things to discuss with your friend," Lourdes said in a hushed tone, before she retreated to the bar.

I spun around. A lean, muscular pirate wearing a black hat and open white shirt stood before me. And those eyes—dark blue like a deep, fast moving stream, lined with black—à la Johnny Depp. The word sexy wouldn't begin to describe this god of the sea— Neptune in pirate's garb!

He stroked my cheek. "Elusive woman. I finally caught up with you."

I stared up at him, my emotions caught between anger and desire. "Are you alone, Wolf?"

He glanced around, grinning, his tight black pants showing off his enticing glutes to perfection. "Well considering we're in the middle of party—yes."

I took a deep breath and another fleeting glance. Wolf's eyes gleamed in the dim light. I returned my gaze to his face. I couldn't stop thinking about how well he filled those breeches. "There's a lot to talk about," I said lamely, trying not to glance down.

"There sure is."

I pulled myself together. "Serious stuff."

"Okay, let's start with Alvarez."

That got my blood flowing to my cheeks. I hissed out each word. "Are you sure we don't want to start with Sam?"

"Why don't we forget about both of them," he said, with a lopsided grin. Gripping my shoulders, he pulled me close.

My anger was replaced by a new type of heat. A red-hot flame ignited inside me and momentarily I forgot everything except his mouth and the sweet taste of his lips. The warmth of his body against mine shot tingles through my core—tantalizing tremors that surprised me with their intensity. When his tongue tenderly brushed my lips, my mouth parted involuntarily. He entered with a slow rhythm that stoked my inner fire. Our tongues and lips played with each other until we remembered where we were. As he pulled away, his eyes swept down my body. "You've outdone yourself, spicy lady."

"You were in the parade, weren't you?"

"Yes, babe. On the Black Pearl." Wolf grabbed a daiquiri from a waiter's tray and handed it to me. "I was conscripted this afternoon. My renovation buddy decided he needed a few more people on his ship." He glanced down at his costume. "I didn't mind the outfit so much," he grinned, "but when his wife brushed on that mascara…"

"Looks good, Wolf," I said causally, taking a sip of the slushy mix. I was annoyed but at the same time I couldn't take my eyes off of him. He spewed sexuality tonight. His rugged features suited the pirate role and with those blue eyes sparkling wickedly, enhanced with liner, he was sinfully delicious. But I wasn't about to say so. From the ladies' glances at the party, he had to be aware of the sensation he was causing. I caught a glimpse of Delores Montalvo. She would have trouble getting her mouth shut again unless I took him away pronto.

Wolf ran a finger down my cheek. "Guess I'll need your help taking it off, eh?"

I felt the heat surge to my cheeks and rush down my body.

Help? My Hormone Voice repeated in a daze. Yes, you do that, girl. Forget about the makeup…slide that shirt off and run your fingers over that strong hard body.

I felt my nipples perk under the thin fabric.

Wolf's glance dropped and I became conscious of my partially exposed mounds.

"You are every man's fantasy tonight, princess. I had hoped we'd be together on a float. I looked for you." Wolf searched my face. "Janine told me you'd run off with Alvarez." He motioned the waiter and said, "Dos Equis." He gazed at me expectantly.

"Diego asked me last night. I didn't get a chance to tell you with Jim there. After Janine and I talked, I went up to my room and took a shower. Jim said you weren't joining us. I figured you were involved in some business matter." Would he mention Sam or was he waiting for me to say something?

"I had to straighten out a problem."

I couldn't hold back any longer. "You mean that little tidbit your ex said to incriminate me?" I said sharply.

"She was lying out by the pool and I thought I'd find out exactly what she told the cop."

"And did you?"

"Yeah," Wolf said slowly. "And I told her she was wrong. I said you'd been with me until the time you'd gone to the washroom."

"And she believed you?"

"It's not her we'll need to convince."

I bit my lip. He was right. "Wolf, I didn't tell you but," I swivelled my head to see if we could be overheard and seeing no one close, I continued, "Sanchez pointed out that I had blood on my toe."

Wolf stared at me.

I whispered, "It's true. It was Dean's."

"Shit!" Wolf swore softly.

The waiter came over holding a tray. I waited while Wolf picked up a beer. We watched the server move on.

"There's something else."

Wolf raised an eyebrow.

"People think I had a thing with Dean."

"Who?"

"Everyone. He spread this rumor…"

"Hell, I knew the guy was a bastard."

"Well, something did happen. There was some truth to the rumor."

"What, baby?" Wolf gazed at me. "Tell me."

"Let's go over to the beach," I said nervously, afraid that one of the partiers would overhear.

Wolf nodded and took my hand. We made our way through the crowd.

"Hey, Wolf—Adie!" Batman called out.

Tall and dramatic in a black cape, Batman punched Wolf's fist. "Cool duds, Wolf."

I recognized Jim's voice.

"Is Janine here?" I asked.

He jerked his chin to the bar. "See the hot babe in the bunny outfit? She thought a pink mask would hide her identity." He chortled. "She's got the sexiest little ass. With those stilettos and tail, Hefner would recruit her in a flash."

Wolf appraised Janine in the silky low-cut white playgirl suit. Fishnet stockings on her shapely legs and her tight butt partially exposed by the high-cut bunny suit would set any man on fire. "How's married life goin', buddy?"

"Super," Jim said quickly. "Whatcha drinkin'?"

"Dos Equis."

"And Terry," I said, "is she here, too?"

"Yup." He shot his chin in the direction of the bar. "See the nurse chick with the doctor?"

I checked them out. Terry had on a short, tight white uniform. "Who's the doctor?"

Batman grinned, his eyes gleaming wickedly from tiny slits. "Terry's got a boyfriend—Juan Jose, Primavera security guard."

Wolf shot him a look. "Didn't take her long to forget Dean."

Jim grinned. "Mr. Popularity he wasn't."

We watched Juan Jose put his arm around Terry's shoulders.

Jim stopped a waiter and lifted a margarita from his tray. "He's a man of mystery, that dude."

"What do you mean?" I had never noticed Jim's eyes before. With the mask he looked positively evil.

Jim grunted in disgust. "Ask Janine." He punched Wolf's fist. "Catchya later, dude." He wandered off to the bar.

"Come on, Wolf," I said, pulling him into the garden with me. "Quick, before someone else comes along. We need to talk privately. There's the path," I pointed to a gap between the bushes, "I know a spot where we can sit overlooking the ocean."

Through tall Emperor Palms I led the way into the darkness. Flickering lights in the trees lit the path, but the shadows of the fronds waving erratically with the breeze lent an eerie atmosphere to our trek. I was anxious to discuss the murder with Wolf and I had the feeling that time was of the essence.

The surf became louder as we approached a bench just off the path.

"Let's sit here, Wolf. It should be private and we'll be able to see anyone coming."

Taking a seat on the bench, he put his arm around my shoulders. "Okay, baby." Wolf's jaw clenched. "Tell me what happened with Dean."

It took an effort to get it all out. I was nervous, thinking he might believe I brought it all on myself. Maybe he'd find me disgusting.

I inhaled deeply and began. "Janine had asked me to stay at their beach house. I didn't say anything at the time because I thought it was all my fault. I'd had daiquiris," I glanced at the half-empty plastic cup in my hand, "too many, but Janine said that wasn't it. She told me he must have put a roofie in my drink. By the time I went to my room I felt dizzy. When Dean came in, I was on the bed feeling disoriented. At first he only spoke to me. But I wasn't wearing much—only a thin robe. He pushed it away and touched me."

"Bastard." He turned my chin towards him. "Something more happened, didn't it?" Wolf's lips tightened. "You can tell me, Adie."

I placed my hand on Wolf's arm. "I somehow managed to punch him before he..."

He took my hands in his. "And then what?"

"He was angry but he had this inner calm that scared me…" I paused, as I remembered the smoldering depths of his brown eyes. "He stood up to leave but not before..."

"What?"

"He said he had an offer I couldn't refuse." I gazed over at the sparkling silver waters of the Caribbean. It was beautiful and it should have been romantic, sitting with a magnetic man like Wolf, but life casts shades of pain on everyone and tonight I could feel only that.

"Which was?"

"One month with him. He said he'd give me a house on the beach, anything I needed, necessities, car, clothes and stocks, but I was to be his exclusively for a month. I could keep it all afterwards, or renew my contract. That's what he said, Wolf. Renew my contract. I hated him then and now," I paused, on the point of tears, "I'm afraid. They'll want to blame someone. They'll blame me."

"Adie, you went into his room. Did you touch anything?"

"You mean fingerprints?"

"Yeah."

I thought back. Images jumbled in my head. "The door was open, but only a bit." I thought back to when I came there. "I pushed it." My eyes shot up to Wolf. "They'll be matching my fingerprints to those on the door, won't they?"

"That won't be so bad. There could lots of them—Dean, Terry, Janine, Jim. All of them would have been in and out. I wouldn't worry about that. Did you see the knife?"

"No," I looked down at my trembling hands, "only the blood on the towel. I didn't stick around to find it. It was so horrible, Wolf. You saw how Jim looked. I felt exactly like that."

Wolf put his arm around my shoulders and hugged me to him.

"You couldn't be one of their prime suspects, baby. You didn't get anything from the will, did you?"

"No." I pulled away and glanced up at him. "Did Sam tell you what Dean left her?"

Wolf frowned. "No, she didn't mention anything. You sure he left her something?"

"Janine told me the estate would be split up between Terry, Dean's brother, and Sam. Although, I wonder if Janine might get something."

"And you'd only gain if he had lived."

"And if I'd gone along with him."

Wolf's face was shadowed and I couldn't see his eyes. What was he thinking? Surely, he knew me well enough to know I wouldn't have done anything like that.

Ha! My Logical Voice spoke up. He knows you are interested in Diego and he's rich. How often has he enticed you with his wealth? No wonder he doubts you.

"I'm sure you have nothing to worry about, Adie."

I had a bad feeling about the whole thing but I didn't dwell on it. "Maybe, we'd better go back." I touched his arm. "And if you can, find out what Sam gets."

"Don't worry, baby. I'll talk to her."

A rustling noise in the bushes startled me. I tightened my grip on his arm.

A raccoon-like animal, maybe a coati, flashed through the trees. I sighed in relief.

"Let's go, baby. We'll put in an appearance," he glanced at me, "and head back to your room. I'd say go back to my cottage but there's some renovation going on there."

I was just as anxious to go as he was. The coati at the cottage had rattled my nerves. They were cute, until they curled back their lips and snarled, showing long, sharp fangs. I think this time I was glad it was to my hotel room.

The moon had disappeared behind dark patches of cloud and we stepped carefully down the shady path back to the party. The music was loud. A mariachi band played near the pool where the partiers danced. The costumes glittered under the lights while their colorful makeup sparkled brightly. My face was just as dazzling, but the makeup was beginning to feel uncomfortably dry. I felt like picking off the purple sequins and the gold dust around my heavily lined eyes and washing my face clean.

"Adelina, *mi amor*," Diego called out from behind me. "People have been asking about you."

"Who?"

"Don't look so serious, *cariño*. Your fans are everywhere." His eyes flicked to a group of men by the pool. "They're part of the Carnaval committee and," he slid his fingers down a tendril of my hair, "they were wondering where you had gone." He glared at Wolf, standing beside me. "So, Du Lac, you're the one who abducted Adelina. I should have had Churo watch her." He smiled but his eyes narrowed dangerously.

Wolf grabbed a beer from a passing waiter and glanced at Diego. "She's her own woman, Alvarez, and she doesn't like being held on a leash."

Diego motioned to a waiter who appeared with a tray of margaritas. He picked up one without salt and handed it to me. "Your favorite."

I was about to refuse, thinking I'd had enough alcohol to last me a month until I saw the slut pirate wench. Samantha, a shirt unbuttoned to her waist and breeches tightly glued to her legs, slithering towards us.

But if she conjured up sexy images for the male guests, they'd have to turn on her defrost button before she'd have anything to do with them. Sam had eyes for only one pirate. "Hey, babe!" she called to Wolf. "Where'd you take off to? The pirate crew has been looking for their captain and I said I'd bring you back."

I shot Wolf a look.

He explained hastily. "Sam was with me when my buddy started recruiting a few extra pirates. When he saw her, he decided he needed a female."

I grimaced, watching her pink tongue flick over her scarlet lips. She was a female all right—a female viper.

"And what a dazzling beauty, she is," Diego said enthusiastically, his glance wandering to her breasts that moved freely under the open silk shirt. "I would have asked you to join us, Samantha, but we were in dire need of a blonde. They are rather a rare commodity in Cozumel. Carmelita had already chosen a number of brunette models. I'm afraid I wasn't allowed to ask any others. Please forgive me, Samantha."

"Blondes, eh?" Samantha repeated with a frown.

"Nothing personal, *cariño*. Some believed the most famous goddess was a beautiful blonde."

"Ixchel?" I asked, glancing at the silver bracelet on my arm. The robed goddess sat in profile, her hair down, a coiled snake balanced on the crown of her head.

"How lovely," Sam said, studying the intricate design. "Your gift from Diego? What is she goddess of?"

Diego flashed her a wide smile and handed her a margarita from the table. "She is the fertility goddess. Ancient Mayan women paddled across from the mainland to sacrifice to her, wishing for fertility. They have shrines for her all over the island.

Samantha peered down at my naked abdomen as if to detect the presence of a bump. "And did she help your cause, Adele?"

"My name is Adie and my cause is *not* to be pregnant."

"Of course you must be considering it. Surely," she argued, "when a man wants your child as much as Diego does, you should give him what he needs, an heir to the Bolivar Alvarez empire."

Diego grinned in amusement.

I glared at her. "Diego and I are friends, nothing more."

Wolf glanced at the pendant nestled at my cleavage. "A few months ago, I gave Adie that jade pendant. She swore it protected her from danger." His fingers took up the pendant as he examined it. "And it did, didn't it, babe?"

Diego drawled, "Adelina won't need it now that she has this piece designed by one of the most famous artisans of Cozumel."

Wolf let the pendant drop back into the valley between my breasts. He glanced at the bracelet. "Um, yes, I remember this one. When I was in his shop, he suggested jade was the better buy." He stared at Diego. "Said jade was for the Mayan nobility. That convinced me it would perfect for Adie."

Seeing Diego's glare, I said, "I like the bracelet, Diego, but I also love the pendant. They're both beautiful. I think they go well together."

Samantha snickered. "Like and love? Are you sure you're not speaking about these two gorgeous men? Now which one is likeable and which one is loveable?" She glanced at me. "I'm sure you wouldn't mind if I take Wolf for a few minutes, Adele? It will give them time to cool off." She placed her hand on Wolf's arm, attempting to steer him away.

"Hey, everyone," Terry cooed from behind us. "What a lovely party, Diego." She grabbed Wolf's arm away from Samantha. "Such a surprise to see you on that pirate float, handsome!" She massaged his bicep. "My, what nice guns!"

Wolf looked at the redhead in amusement. "Owed my buddy a favor." His glance flicked down her outfit. The low cut nurse's uniform showed off an abundant cleavage—her creamy pale skin splattered with freckles.

"We could have used a lovely nurse with a good bedside manner," Wolf said with a smile.

Terry purred, "Had I only known—I would have made an emergency visit."

Sam scowled. "I'm sure your doctor had other plans that didn't involve Wolf." Her eyes narrowed. "Where is JJ? Haven't seen him tonight. Your boy toy run off?"

I took that in. JJ, of course, Juan Jose. Terry's doctor, the hotel security guard, had to be the guy Janine had a fling with. Both mother and daughter slept with the same man?

"Diego," she said, her voice smooth as silk, "you must have turned on the heat to have persuaded our lovely Adie to be your harem girl. Your float was magnificent, by the way."

Diego held up her hand and kissed her wrist, pausing a second to look into her eyes. "I had no idea you would want to party so soon after Dean's demise."

Terry giggled. "That's one way to put it, darlin'. Someone thought it was his time, all right. Fortunate timing. I was afraid he'd give it all to his 'ho'." She curled her lip. "Someone didn't think you should have it all, Sam."

Diego snapped his fingers at a passing waiter with a tray full of margaritas. He took one off the tray and handed it to Terry. "Let's think positively, *cariño*, you have a sizeable fortune now and a share in my resort."

Terry slurped the frozen green mixture contemplatively. "True, but so does she."

Diego smiled. "But you are all family. You, Janine, and her husband. Together you have the lion's share."

Terry scrutinized the goblet in her hand. "None of us will give you problems either, will we? We're an easygoing bunch."

Diego nodded. "That is wise of you, Terry. Leave the management and plans to me. No need to worry that pretty head of yours." His eyes swept to Sam. "And you, Samantha? What are your feelings about the resort?"

Sam's face tightened. "I'll be going home. I'm happy with the dividends. I wouldn't oppose your plans, Diego. You are the CEO of that project."

"So that leaves, you, Du Lac. Have you considered it any further?"

Wolf regarded Diego. "With Firenze out, I am giving it some thought."

"Feel free to visit," Diego said, digging in his pocket for his wallet. He opened it and pulled out a card. "Here, just give this to the manager and he'll show you around. No clothes necessary." Diego turned back to me. "I haven't shown you the resort yet, *mi amor*. You might be interested for your tour groups. There's a beautiful cenote right on the property. Crystal clear water, stalagmites—fabulous snorkeling."

"Sounds lovely." I set my glass down on the table. "I'm so sorry, Diego, but I think I should go back to the hotel."

Diego looked worried. "Not feeling well?"

I rubbed my forehead. "A headache."

"Sorry to hear that. I'd bring you back but," he glanced around, "there are a few people I need to speak with tonight but Churo could drive."

"Not a problem," Wolf said, smiling slightly. "I'll take Adie."

Sam frowned and Terry looked amused.

I met his deep blue eyes and at that instant I knew how much he wanted to be with me.

Undaunted by Wolf's words, Diego drew me close and kissed my cheek. "Would you do me the honor of accompanying me on the float tomorrow?"

"I don't want to make any promises," I said hesitatingly.

Diego ran his fingers through my hair, searching my face as he said, "Don't promise anything, then, *mi amor*. Let fate decide."

He was an exotic man—exciting because he was so foreign to my world. Yet as I turned back to Wolf, I was reminded how his tongue tore into my fiber with every hot kiss. Although the purpose of my trip was to research the Carnaval, I temporarily forgot that small fact. Wolf, on the other hand, was unforgettable. And he was so much like the animal of the same name. What choice did I have? I focused on his full lips.

His voice was husky when he spoke to me. "Come on, baby," he said, taking my hand.

I caught a glimpse of Samantha's grimace as we headed out.

* * *

Dramatic black liner rimmed slanty turquoise eyes. With sparkling gold eye shadow and glitter on her cheeks, the woman in the mirror had the unreal appearance of a wingless fantasy fairy. The unfamiliar image frowned at me. My skin ached for moisture. Opening a jar of chocolate body butter, I rubbed the creamy lotion into my hands, thinking of the slut pirate wench, Sam. I smiled, pleased I'd wrenched Wolf away from the viper. She'd lost this one and I would get the spoils of the victory.

I glanced back up. The makeup was beautiful. No doubt about it, but it had to go. There was no use delaying it. That woman in the mirror wasn't really me, anyway. "I have to wash this makeup off," I called back over my shoulder to Wolf. Picking at a sequin on my cheek, I knocked it off. It flashed purple as it dropped to the floor. Taking a cleansing cloth from a package, I started wiping off the glitter around my eyes. Running some warm water, I filled the sink and rinsed my face, ridding myself of the remaining glue and grime. With closed eyes, I reached over and grabbed a towel to dry off. After dabbing my face, I looked up to check my cleanup job. Most of the makeup was gone but some sooty black liner remained.

I reached over for another cleansing cloth. I felt rather than heard his presence behind me. I glanced in the mirror to see Wolf's ruggedly handsome face. From the mirror lights his bare broad shoulders and strong chest had a moist sheen. He wore black pirate breeches but that was all.

Standing behind me, he wrapped his arms around my waist and leaned down to kiss my ear. I bent my head away to allow him access to the curve of my neck, all the time watching him from half-closed eyes. His lips pressed softly, lingering with each kiss. His image oozed sexuality.

Seeing him in the mirror did strange things to me. It was as if he were a fantasy man and I was in a dream. When he pushed my hair aside for his mouth to nuzzle the hollow of my throat, fire blazed my body. His tongue and lips caressed me so sensuously I held my breath and let out a sigh that edged into a moan.

Slowly his hands left my naked waist and drifted up my sides. The journey of his fingers mesmerized me. I watched in wonder, my excitement mounting as they neared their destination. When the swell of my breasts received his light touch, my nipples stood to attention, waiting. His fingertips circled sensitively and with every movement I lost myself and entered his world.

Moving behind me, Wolf undid the tiny buttons of my gauzy top. His heavy-lidded eyes met mine. Quickfire surged down the length of my body. In the mirror I hardly recognized the woman whose eyes burned feverishly.

I shrugged off my gold top, letting it drop down to the tile floor. I stared back at his image as he pulled down the straps of my bra. My view was blocked for a moment as he moved forward, tenderly kissing my shoulder, while his hands lightly stroked my breasts through the silky fabric.

Behind me, he bent his head down. I could see his ruffled blond hair falling over his forehead. I felt him unfasten the hooks of my bra. Lifting my arms up to reach him, I ran my fingers through his tousled hair—smooth and silky-soft. I let my arms drop and my bra fell to the floor.

Delicious chocolate wafted in the air—the scent of the body butter lured me. Scooping out the thick balm, I brought my hands to my breasts and thickly coated them. He watched my fingers circle, slowly spreading the creamy lotion, stroking my palms over my nipples. Wolf pushed himself forward against my body, his eyes mesmerized by my hands gliding over my peaks.

Turning around, I gripped his pants to undo them but he took over and unbuttoned his breeches and pushed them down.

The aroma of chocolate lotion assailed my nostrils and again, I turned about and scooped out some out. Still facing the mirror, I reached behind me to spread the thick cream over the velvety texture of his skin, staring at his face.

In the mirror, his blue eyes glimmered, like the waters of a fresh-water stream, so intense was his gaze. I was riveted to the pirate's darkly lined eyes as he was to the reflection of the woman stroking him.

His eyes locked with mine but his hands reached around to the ribbons tying my harem pants, and unfastened them. The sheer fabric slid off my body. His hands smoothed over my hips, caressing my cheeks until the throbbing in my core was all I could think about. I pressed against my pirate lover but didn't have the strength to ask for what I wanted, so overwhelmed was I by the sensations flooding through me. I was in a river of molten lava and there was no getting out nor did I want to.

Strong hands lifted me onto the counter. Wolf's tongue and lips torched my throat. Tenderly, he cupped a mound and brought his mouth down to lick my hardening nipple. I sighed with each flick of his scorching tongue. Wolf glanced up at me and smiled, a mischievous glint in his eyes. Suddenly, he stepped back.

"Why are you stopping?" In alarm, I straightened up.

Wolf smiled slowly and scooped me up in his arms. "Worried, princess? Don't be. You're gettin' everything you ever wanted." Carrying me into the bedroom, he laid me on the bed.

I wasn't alone for long. Wolf rolled in beside me, pulling me into him. His eyes voiced his need. Sensuous lips against mine invited my mouth to linger. He teased me unmercifully until I returned his caresses with a fiery rhythm of my own. As I pressed into him, my hands slid down to his narrow waist while my lips sought out his heat. Our tongues played a secret game that lit a flame deep inside and spread like wild fire. Passion possessed me.

I pushed him down onto the bed and climbed on top of him. A moist film coated his hard body. At his neck, I took in his scent of soap and balmy ocean breeze. I licked. A slight salty flavor. I heard him catch his breath, but I journeyed on to his powerful chest, catching his nipple in my mouth. My lips pressed tightly. Control aroused me.

"No," he groaned, "stop—you know what that does to me." Wolf twisted away and shoved me down, reversing our positions. "I want to taste you."

Starting at my throat, he kissed his way down to my shoulder while his hands tortured my skin with his light strokes. I gasped when his tongue tantalized the valley between my breasts and lingered over the swells—everywhere except my taut nub. At last, he flicked lightly over my mound to the peak and hungrily captured my erect nipple. I heard a moan. It was mine.

"I've missed you," Wolf said softly, stroking my other breast.

My hand wandered through his silky thick hair, stirring my juices. I had this strong urge to touch every last bit of him. "It's been too long, pirate."

"Stealing treasure doesn't compare to capturing a harem girl...so much hotter." Wolf's kisses descended lower—down my abs to invade the recess of my navel with his electricity.

My mind had clouded into a dreamy haze. "Ah-hh, Wolf…" My mind had left and my body had entered a state of euphoria.

The pounding on the door startled us. A voice shouted loudly. *"Policia!"*

Wolf sprang into action. Grabbing his pirate breeches from the couch, he pulled them on. "I'll get it, Adie."

From the chair, I took up my robe and slipped it on.

Persistent pounding started up again.

Wolf called back from the hallway. "It's Sanchez."

"What's he doing here?"

"Bastard." Wolf looked over to me. "I'd better let him in."

I sprung up, tied on my sash, and stepped into a pair of high-heeled wedges.

"Señorita Sturm," Sanchez shouted, "Open the door! Cozumel Policia."

"Okay," I said tightly, "let him in."

Sanchez strode into the bedroom, his eyes taking in the state of the bed and our attire. He smirked. "I see you're not alone, after all, Señorita Sturm." He eyed Wolf. "You are Señor Du Lac. We've met. I am Officer Sanchez. *Perdoname*, but Detective Hernandez sent me."

"Why?" Wolf glared at him. "Isn't it a bit late to come calling?"

Sanchez's eyes gleamed in satisfaction. "Señorita Sturm has something in her possession I need."

I moved beside Wolf. "What?"

Sanchez surveyed the room. I could see he was itching to take a look at the articles I had laid out on my dresser but he turned to me and said, "I'm here for your shoes, Señorita Sturm."

"Shoes?"

"The red high-heeled sandals you wore for the wedding. Find them for me, *por favor*."

There was no getting out of this. Brushing past him, I went to the closet and slid the door open. They were all lined up like soldiers for inspection—tan wedges with tiny flicks of purple, gold woven sandals, quirky flip flops, black and white high-heeled sandals and finally, my favorite open-toed red patent leather slingbacks. "Both?" I asked hesitantly.

Sanchez held out a plastic bag. "Drop them in there, Señorita."

I had this sick feeling in the pit of stomach when I placed them in the bag. "When will I get them back?"

Sanchez looked positively slimy when he smiled. "It's not for me to say. I'm sure Detective Hernandez will be contacting you."

"Is he there at the police station right now?" Wolf asked.

Sanchez shook his head. "He's on day shift." He turned to me. "But don't worry, Señorita Sturm, you will hear soon."

With another smarmy smile, he swung open the door and stepped out into the hall. The door slammed shut behind him.

"Shit!" Wolf muttered.

"They think I did it." I plopped myself down on the bed. "How could they possibly think I could cut Dean's throat?"

"They must think you have enough motive."

"I don't get anything from the will."

"True, but he came on to you. Maybe…"

"Everyone thinks I slept with him. The police must think I hated him enough to kill him."

Wolf sat down on the bed beside me. He ran his fingers through his tousled hair. "A petite woman like you would have had a hard time killing him."

"They think I had help?" I shot him a look. "You? It wouldn't be easy for anyone to cut Dean's throat unless he was drugged up."

"Sanchez is implying that you had help and since I'm with you, we pulled it off together."

I shook my head. "Cutting someone's throat can't be easy and Dean was a big guy. But he was also a boozer and into drugs." I plopped back down on the bed. "Someone did it when he'd passed out. I'm sure of that now."

Wolf sat down beside me and draped his arm around my shoulders. "We'll figure this out."

"We have to…Wolf, tell me what you know about Dean."

Lying down on the bed, his arms behind his head, Wolf's eyes flicked to the ceiling and then back to me. "I didn't like the guy. I only met him once with Alvarez at a meeting with potential investors for the nudist resort. He bought a sizeable number of shares, as I recall."

"Which now go to his estate."

Wolf pulled me close. "To be shared amongst his heirs. Blood or money, isn't that what they say?"

I snuggled up to him. "Money—Terry, Janine, Dean's brother, and Sam." His arm around me made me feel safe. "But there's the other motive."

"Blood?"

"Mmm. Generally speaking, blood could be a relative or friend that hates or loves the victim." I rested my hand on his chest and glanced up.

"And Firenze did something that drove him or her over the edge." Wolf met my eyes. "A woman?"

"There's Carmelita. She had Churo rough up Dean after he…"

"What? He came on to her, too?"

"I don't know what to believe. That's what Carmelita said, but Lourdes had a different spin on it. She said Carmelita and Dean had a fling."

"So Churo beat up Firenze when Carmelita was through with him?"

"Or he upset her in a major way and she sent Churo to teach him a lesson."

Wolf frowned. "There's always Alvarez."

"You would think he had something to do with it." I didn't think Diego was the monster Wolf made him out to be.

"Alvarez wasn't too happy about Firenze," Wolf said slowly. "Something to do with the nudist resort."

"Diego was pleased that Terry wanted him to take over the resort management."

Wolf stared at me. "And, don't forget, if his sister was involved with the bastard, he might have sent Churo to finish him off."

"Diego wouldn't kill Firenze."

Wolf argued, "You sure about that?"

I thought back to Diego's bodyguards. Churo and Luis were massive men fiercely loyal to the Bolivar Alvarez family. And then there was Eduardo. Outwardly, he was attractive—tall, muscular and handsome, apart from the long jagged scar that ran down his cheek. But they say the eyes are the mirrors of the soul and when I looked into his I entered a cold, dark place that reeked of evil.

"We've got to find some answers, Wolf. Are you free tomorrow?"

"After twelve. What did you have in mind?"

"The resort. I think we could find out lots there. Meet me at the ferry dock? We'll take the one o'clock express."

Wolf nodded. "I'll be there."

7

Lorita's was situated smack in the center of the square. The owner was Portuguese but the menu was pure Yucatan. I had decided to have a pollo de mole with fried beans. Janine had chicken wrapped in tortilla. With the bright rays of the sun warming us and the band playing in the park, neither of us wanted to eat Canadian.

"Omigod! This is so good!" Janine licked her lip where a smidgen of salsa clung.

I forked up some of my chicken in chocolate sauce. "Mm-mm, I can't get enough of this stuff." Yes, I know, I'm weird that way. Who else would eat chocolate for breakfast? But Mayan food was known for its mole—chocolate sauce with chilies. It hits the tongue and tantalizes the taste buds. With this quirky addition chicken reaches a new high. Because of my chocolate obsession, I had this thing about trying it in every restaurant in Cozumel.

When a catchy ringtone went off in my purse, I hurriedly searched for my phone. "Excuse me, Janine. Got to get that." I clicked it on.

"Hey..." I was more breathless from identifying the caller than from my rush to find the phone.

"Remind me never to do that again."

"Do what?"

"Leave you without a proper goodbye kiss."

I vaguely remembered a soft kiss on my lips as I lay dozing. "I think you did kiss me."

"Key word, baby—proper," Wolf said in his husky voice, "or let's say…not so proper."

I must have blushed because Janine started to giggle.

"You were so beautiful sleeping, I had a problem getting my pants back on."

I must have looked like I put my head in an oven, I felt so hot and flustered. After Sanchez had left, I hadn't been in the mood and Wolf, sensing that, suggested we cuddle and sleep. It wasn't the scenario I had hoped for but neither was being indicted for murder—a situation that required some immediate detecting, or jail would become a reality.

"See you at the ferry dock at one?"

"Um-mm." I grinned, thinking how wonderful it would be to see him again.

"Jim wanted to come."

"Oh?"

"He said he'd like to check out Janine's property. It'll give us a chance to see what he knows."

There was something in that. All the heirs needed to be checked. One of them could be the murderer. "Good idea. See you soon!"

"Bye, princess."

Clicking the phone shut, I saw Janine's eyes on me.

"You're up to something, babe," she said with a smile.

I felt a little guilty but what was I supposed to do? Let them arrest me and throw away the key? "Just going to the nudist resort with Wolf. Diego invited him."

"Really…" She licked her lips. "Wolf nude—mm-mm."

"Jim's coming with us."

Janine raised an eyebrow.

"Apparently he wants to check on your investment."

Her mouth twisted. "That's something I should be doing." Janine's tone had an edge. "We were left most of the resort shares."

"The rest going to Dale?"

"And Sam." Janine sipped her coffee.

I looked up from my chicken. "How do you feel about that?"

Janine shrugged her shoulders. "I think it'll work out—she doesn't care much."

"Diego is the CEO. I think you're safe with him running the show."

Janine patted my arm. "Let's talk about that delicious man. You were awfully chummy on that float."

"The dancing?"

"And that kiss." Janine sighed. "Is he good?"

"Mm-mm."

"Okay—I sense excellent is closer." She stared at me. "Which raises the question, how does he rate with the man of the hour, Mr.

Sexuality himself?"

"Wolf?"

Janine rolled her eyes. "Who else!" She giggled. "Unless there's another guy breaking out in a sweat for you." She sat up in her chair and leaned forward. "Adie, tell!"

"There's nothing to tell." I twirled a strand of my hair reflectively. "Things have gotten in the way of us being together."

"Sam?"

I nodded. "And the police."

"Police?"

"They think I had something to do with Dean's murder."

Janine's fork dropped with a clang. "What! Why would they think such a thing?" She stared at me. "They must know about you and Dean?" She placed her hand on my arm. "I hope you don't think they got it from me?"

"No, I trust you, Janine. I think it was Sam." I shot her a look. "Did Terry think we were having an affair?"

"Mom was used to Dean's two-timing but I never heard her say a thing about you and Dean. After a while, I think she was relieved he was finding other playmates. Believe me, she's glad Dean's dead." She glanced at the pedestrian area in front of us. A troupe of dancers in satin blue costumes started setting up for a performance, along with their equipment and loudspeakers. "Hey, Adie, isn't this cool? They're goin' to dance for us."

"Um-mm." I pulled out my camera and leaned over the railing as the dancers took up their positions. When they saw what I was doing, two of the ladies grabbed the male's hand to pose for me. "*Muchos gracias!*" I called out to them before I sat back down.

"They're so sweet, aren't they Adie. It's amazing how they seem to be all ages." She gestured. "Look at that little granny in the middle—sixty if she's a day. Grandmas and mothers. Family is so special here."

"Janine, I was wondering…"

"What?" she said distractedly, watching them snake into a merengue line. "And look. That one must be her grandkid!"

"Why are you still married to Jim? I thought you didn't want any part of marriage. Second thoughts?"

"Yeah, well, Dean nixed it."

"What do you mean?"

Janine rolled up her last tortilla and brought it to her lips. "Dean made sure I couldn't get my hands on my share unless Jim came along for the ride. Otherwise, it stays in trust 'til I'm thirty."

"Wow, that's unbelievable! What about Terry and Sam? Any restrictions for them?"

"Yup, Sam has to stay on as manager at the Woodbridge office for a minimum of two years and Mom's shares revert to me if she marries within the next five years."

"Why did Dean want you to stay married to Jim?"

"Jim's brilliant with the computer end and Dean thought the corporation would go down the tubes without him," she shrugged, "and I guess he thought he'd be a stable family guy I'd have kids with."

"What kind of business did he have?"

Janine shrugged. "Dean had lots of fish in the pan." She bit into her rolled up tortilla and chewed thoughtfully. "You know, I wouldn't mind going with you to the resort."

"You have to be at the ferry dock by one."

"No problem." She glanced at her watch and signaled the waiter. "Don't worry about the bill." She winked. "With two guys hooked, you've got more important things to worry about."

* * *

Turquoise waves lapped the sandy beach. With the sun filtering through fluffy clouds, Playa del Carmen looked inviting with its palapa rooftops and white stucco buildings. It was a half hour trip with the express ferry from Cozumel and we were lucky the day was beautiful and the trip was smooth. Jim and Janine stood side by side at the stern, while we lounged in some chairs with some other passengers.

"They look happy enough, don't they?" I tilted my head up to Wolf. "Who would have thought she wanted a divorce?"

"Already?"

I nodded. "But she'll have to stay married to Jim to keep her inheritance."

"You mean that screwed up bastard put stipulations in the will?"

"For Terry too. She loses her share if she marries."

Wolf rubbed his chin. "I wonder if Dale had to do something to keep his portion?"

"Dean's brother?"

"Yup. Heard they had a falling out years ago."

I glanced up at Wolf. "Interesting he was invited to the wedding." I looked out at a cruise ship crossing our path. "Mexico is a good place to do away with someone."

"Yeah, enough low-lifes for hire."

"He was late for the wedding, or so he said."

Wolf shot me a look. "You think he came early, did away with brother dearest, and pretended to arrive the next day?"

"I doubt if anyone checked his story."

"Hey, guys, we're dockin'." Jim gestured for us to come forward.

The crowd on the deck had the same idea. Grabbing their bags, they shuffled down the stairs to the lower deck. Although we were packed tight as sardines, the Mexicans were politely indicating that Wolf and I should go ahead.

"Gracias," Wolf said, as a man moved back for us to go first. His hand against my lower back, he guided me out onto the wharf leading to Playa del Carmen. Just ahead of us, Jim and Janine were walking hand-in-hand, blissfully in love, or so it would seem to any passerby. But I knew differently. Janine enjoyed money, so much she'd put up with a nerdy guy like Jim.

Playa del Carmen bustled with activity—vendors sold anything from jewelry to baskets. The place itself was picturesque with cobblestone streets and colorful buildings. I could have passed the day here, browsing the stands and watching the people but we had a nudist camp to see.

At a side street we stopped and piled into the jeep Wolf had rented and set out down the highway south to Tulum. The road wasn't particularly interesting but seated beside a hot man like Wolf I couldn't help but be excited. Sexy lips and tousled blond hair blowing about with the breeze reminded me of what a wild man he was. I began to fantasize about a natural location for some spontaneous lovemaking. Jim's voice startled me out of my vision of a white powdery beach and a long lanky man, his body entwined with mine.

"Hey, we might see some of the others today," Jim shouted over the wind.

I swiveled around to look at him. "What others?"

"Diego told the manager to expect investors. He's invited the family, besides Wolf, here." He grinned a Colgate smile. "It's cool you'll be there too." He made a fist and punched Wolf's arm.

Wolf looked amused. "You need some moral support, Jim? Too many women?"

"Nah," his cheeks turned bright red, "not with babes like Janine and Sam around. Even Terry is hot. Hey, dude, what more could a man want?"

I turned to Janine. "I thought Sam said she was going back home."

"She took an extended leave from her manager position." Janine tossed back her curls and giggled. "Guess she's not needed for her other job. You know, the girlfriend gig—boyfriend being six feet under."

I didn't find that as funny as she did. Dean was dead and Sam was still here. The sooner she returned to Canada, the better, as far as I was concerned. I'd bet my bottom dollar she was the one that told Sanchez about my supposed affair with Dean. Sam was trouble.

"How's Dean's brother handling his death?" Wolf asked over his shoulder.

Jim frowned. "Kind of an insensitive dude. Couldn't say anything nice about his bro. If that's what brothers are like, glad I was the only child."

We whizzed by another resort with an elegant gate and long driveway. I couldn't see anything of it from the road except the sign, which read *Paraiso*. "This area has lots of cenotes," I told Janine.

"What are those?" Jim asked.

"Limestone caves. The ancient Mayans got their water there and made sacrifices to the rain god."

"Young nubile men?" Janine asked with a grin.

The wind whipped my hair into my eyes. I brushed it away only to have it fly back. "And children mostly."

"What about the virgins," Jim quipped, "couldn't they find any?"

"It wasn't about virginity." I zipped up my window at the bottom but it was so hot I decided to leave the top open to flip freely in the breeze. "The rain god wanted a worthy sacrifice, possibly warriors captured in battle. Those would be the nubile young men, Janine. Strong athletic types that had the misfortune to lose the battle."

Jim sat back and stared at Wolf. "I'd bet they'd have wanted someone like Wolf, eh, Janine?"

The tip of Janine's tongue ran over her lip as she gazed at Wolf. "Definitely."

Wolf glanced over at me. "I'd sacrifice my pleasure for yours."

Janine giggled. "Now there's an offer you can't refuse, Adie."

Your pleasure, My Hormone voice said. You hear that? Get him to stay at the resort tonight. You'd be safe from everything...no police, no nightmares of Dean. He'd give you everything you'd ever want!

"She must be giving serious consideration to that proposition," Janine said slyly. "See how her cheeks are getting so flushed."

I gazed at Wolf's rugged profile. "Does that mean you want to stay overnight?"

His lips curled upwards. "Why not?"

"We should stay too, babe!" Jim said excitedly to Janine. "Think of it! Nature and us! This will be like a honeymoon within a honeymoon!"

I didn't catch what Janine said, but when I turned around she was looking smug. Strange. Maybe she had second thoughts about being with Jim. I glanced back at him. He wasn't bad looking— trim and well proportioned. Then why did I get this feeling deep in my gut that something was out of sync here?

According to the signs we were now in Tulum. It wasn't a big place. I guessed there were restaurants and homes back further back from the main street. "Is it far?" I asked Wolf.

"Almost there. Look for a sign that says Tulum del Mar."

"Ooooh!" Janine squealed. "It's on the right." She pointed at a grouping of palms with a signpost on a white pillar. "There it is...stop!"

Wolf swerved into the driveway in the nick of time. It wasn't paved and the gravel rolled under the tires, making a crunching noise as the jeep steadied itself. I gripped the handle at the door to keep myself upright.

"Hey, man! That's some drivin'!" Jim's mouth hung open.

I rolled my eyes. Jim would polish Wolf's Nikes if he had a

chance.

Wolf grinned at me but Jim was getting on my nerves. I'd be glad if Jim conveniently disappeared, too...maybe not dead, but gone. I didn't have a gripe with Janine. She was okay in my books, even if she was a little wacko.

When Wolf slowed to a stop, a grinning Mexican trotted over, and yes, he did have clothes on. "*Hola,* Señor! Are you planning to spend the day? We have a day rate." He opened the door for me to get out and took my hand to help me down.

Wolf explained to the man, then said, "We may want to stay longer. Señor Alvarez invited us."

The little guy visibly tightened at the mention of Diego's name. "Of course, Señor, I will be happy to take you to our front desk."

We followed him down a gravel path to an open clearing where a thin man stood behind a desk under a palapa roof. Palms and bushes bordered the reception area where the sweet scent of fuchsia bougainvillea flowers prevailed. It had a wild charm that made me think that if ever there was a paradise, it would be here. Approaching the desk, I wondered if Wolf had similar thoughts as he took my hand in his.

A serious man behind the counter looked up. "Señor Du Lac? I'm David."

"Call me Wolf." Wolf reached across the desk to shake hands.

"Señor Zamora is expecting you and your group."

"Good, *gracias,* but first, I'd like to book a room. One with a sea view." Wolf took out his wallet.

"For one night, Señor?"

"*Si,* with a king-sized bed."

"Adie," Janine interrupted, "we'll see you there. I need a drink. My throat is so dry. Come on, Jim. Let's go."

"Sure, Janine, but didn't you want to stay overnight?"

"Don't know for sure. We'll see. If we decide to go back today, no worries. We can grab a taxi."

"The other investors are over at the bar, Señor Du Lac. Alberto," David said to the stocky fellow fussing with some papers, "I'll return shortly."

Both David and the other front desk man were barechested. I half expected him to be nude but he had on baggy long shorts. Seeing my expression, he said in a superior manner, "The staff are allowed to wear clothing. Most of us do. For guests, clothing is optional. After a day or so, the guests tend to go without. You'll see the logic of it."

Trees flanked the gravel path that led to the bar. David left as an immense Mexican in a T-shirt and shorts approached us. "*Bienvenidos!*" His arms unfolded in welcome. He beamed at us.

"I am Jorge Zomara, the general manager. Come, Señoros, we have welcome drinks for you. Water or lemonade—whatever your pleasure. I'm sorry but we do not serve alcohol at this resort."

"Wolf Du Lac." Wolf shook hands. "This is my friend, Adie Sturm."

"A pleasure to meet such a lovely lady." Jorge bowed slightly. "This is an informal meeting. *Señor* Alvarez invited all investors to come to visit and stay if they liked. Now, if you'll follow me? I believe you know the others."

Wolf nodded. At the bar, I saw Terry, Janine, and Jim. Behind him a gray-haired man I didn't know stood with his back to me. He seemed to be in deep conversation with JJ, Terry's handsome security guard.

Wolf pulled me to him and whispered, "I have to be here at this meeting but if you want to look around, we could meet at our room."

"Do you know where it is?"

"No, but ask one of the front desk guys."

I nodded. "I have to check some things out."

Wolf let his finger trail down my cheek. "Be careful. Someone murdered Dean and he's still out there."

I nodded.

Turning on his heel, Wolf made his way over to Jorge. I reached for a glass of lemonade and had a sip. A perfect tart taste.

"Good, isn't it?" Janine said from behind me. "They make it from those lime trees. Take a look, Adie. It's really cool. And that tree next to it is a papaya."

Setting my drink down, I wandered over to have a look. One thing about Mexico is the wide assortment of unusual plants you'd notice. On a tree, high up, I saw small pale green fruit camouflaged in the leaves, and then scanning further over, I caught sight of melon-like clusters attached to the trunk. I glanced over at Janine suspiciously. Since when was she so interested in vegetation? The only kind of plants she liked were the smokable kind. My eyes shot over.

Terry had joined her and they seemed to be having a laugh about something. Janine shrieked uncontrollably, bouncing around on her bar stool until I thought any second she'd topple off. But whatever joke they shared must have been a private one because as soon as I neared them, their laughter broke off. I had that uncomfortable feeling that you get when someone's been gossiping about you.

"Hi, Terry," I said casually. "When did you get here?"

The pretty redhead pulled on a pair of sunglasses. "'Round eleven. Diego phoned and told me you guys would be here this afternoon. Jorge said he'd start the spiel when everyone arrived." She gazed at me. "You and Wolf seem tight. What happened to Diego? He lose the battle?"

Janine giggled. "More like a war."

I wasn't in the mood for their teasing. The afternoon heat was hitting me badly. "Excuse me." I squeezed my hand in between them and picked up my glass.

"Funny not to have alcohol, isn't it?" Terry tipped her drink back.

I thought she was staring but with those dark glasses covering her eyes, I couldn't be sure. My trust in her was rapidly diminishing. And Janine. What was she up to?

"Nature lovers find their own uppers," Janine said and eyed the opening to the beach. A hint of turquoise water glimmered through the trees. "I think I need to test out that water in my birthday suit. How about you, Mom?"

"I'll have to stick to the shade. It's way too hot right now to expose those tender areas. But, later, for sure."

"Sam didn't come?" I looked around but saw no sign of my nemesis.

Terry frowned. "She's here somewhere. But you know snakes, they hide in the grass waiting to strike when you least expect it."

I believed her. Sam had an agenda when it came to Wolf.

Janine leaned her elbow on the bar and rested her chin in her hand. "Sam didn't get that much with the will. Did she, Mom?"

"Getting anything is way too much for that cow. And let's not forget she still has her job as manager."

"How important is she to the company?" I asked curiously.

"Head office is in Woodbridge and she's runnin' the show." Terry twirled her swivel stick. "And even though I inherited the major portion of the estate, the bitch has a fortune." She turned to Janine, shaking her head. "Why did you ever invite her to be your maid of honor? That woman has no sense of the word."

Janine patted her mom's hand. "Don't let her get to you. We all have a slice of the pie now, Mom, and don't forget once she sees Wolf belongs to Adie, she'll hit the road. We can stay here in Mexico and she can go back to the land of ice and snow."

That would be fitting, I thought. Ice matched her personality perfectly. I downed more of my drink and nearly dropped my glass when I glanced across the bar. The gray-haired man talking to Jim was Dean! "Who the..." I said uncertainly, steadying myself on the back of Janine's bar stool.

Following my gaze, Terry laughed. "Whoa, Adie! Take it easy. It's not Dean." She shifted to stare at Dean's look-alike. "Amazing resemblance though, isn't there? Gives me the willies." She patted my hand. "That's Dale, his older brother. Came here to check on his fortune."

Spiky gray hair and those same dark eyes. Although the day was uncomfortably warm, I felt a chill. JJ stepped in front of Dale, blocking my view, and I breathed easier.

"Ladies and gentlemen..." Jorge cleared his throat. "I'd like to tell you about the resort and the fundamentals of our plans for the future. I realize you know very little about it but if you'd keep your questions until the end, I will answer everything at that point."

I took this for my cue to leave and discretely snoop around. The front desk would be as good a place as any to start.

As I headed out, the sun beat powerfully on my skin. A thin sheen of sweat coated my forehead. I wiped it off with my hand and took the path to the place we had come in.

A woman was with the desk clerk. I ran my fingers through my hair. Should I try flirting? I wasn't too sure—could be gay. I had to play it by ear. "*Hola!*" I smiled at David. Could I have the key to Señor Du Lac's room? I'm with him."

David's eyes appraised me critically. "You're his wife?"

I attempted to look head-over-heels in love. "His *novia*." Spanish people love romance.

"Ah!" the older lady, beside him exclaimed clasping her hands together. She said something in rapid Spanish to her companion.

David frowned.

"I'll need someone to show me to the room."

The lady with the name plate *Marta* smiled. "Give me the key, David. I will go with the lady."

Reluctantly David handed her the key. "Wait," he said, flipping a page in his book. "Your name is…"

"Sturm, Adie Sturm."

Studying the book, David nodded.

"This way, Señorita." Marta gave me a shy smile as we headed down a winding path. As soon as we were out of earshot, she said softly, "David is so suspicious. Too much so. He is…how you say, paranoid? Only with Señor Alvarez or our manager is he open. But perhaps he is right. Some of our guests can be trouble."

"That's too bad." I stepped carefully, avoiding a large stone. "I know my friend's stepfather stayed here a while ago. He seemed to like it."

"How nice, Señorita. What was his name?"

"Dean Firenze."

She stopped in her tracks and clutched my arm. "You know this man?"

"Knew," I replied, meeting her gaze. "He was killed."

Marta crossed herself. "I do not want to speak ill of the dead but he was a bad one."

"How so, Marta?"

"It's good that Señor Alavarez stopped him." She brought her hand to her mouth and looked at me in alarm. "You don't think Señor Alvarez had something to do with his death?"

"What made you think that?"

"I heard them argue. Señor Alvarez was opposed to Señor Firenze's ideas." She pursed her lips. "No, Señor Alvarez would not do such a thing. He is a good man Señor Alvarez. He is a man of God."

"What were Señor Firenze's plans?"

"You don't know, Señorita? Perhaps I am being indiscreet. It's really not for me to say."

I took Marta's hand. "*Por favor*, Marta. This is important. I need to know what Señor Firenze planned. Believe me, I won't say a word to anyone."

Marta looked around carefully before she replied, "When we come to the privacy of your room, we will talk."

The path wound down a hill to the beach. The rush of the ocean grew louder and a warm breeze caressed my face as we continued our walk. "Is it far?"

"No, Señorita." She pointed to a boulder ahead. "Just past the rock. It's close now."

I was feeling suddenly lightheaded. I slipped and grabbed Marta's arm for support.

"Are you all right?" Marta asked with concern. "It must be the heat." Her eyes shot ahead to the palapa roofed cottage. "There it is." She took my elbow and led me further. "We're close, Señorita."

When we reached the door, she took out the key and inserted it into the lock. Swinging the door open, she looked expectantly at me.

I leaned against the door frame, unable to move.

"*Dios mio!*" Marta exclaimed. "Let me help you." She guided me in. "I think you should sit, Señorita. You don't look well." She led me over to the bed and helped me down. "Would you like some water?"

"No, *gracias*." I steadied myself. The room was starting to spin. "Tell me about Señor Firenze, Marta. What was he doing that Señor Alvarez didn't want?" I tried to focus on her face but everything was becoming hazy. Her voice sounded hollow to my ears.

"Gambling—a casino, Señorita." Many of us here do not want them. The criminals will come and ruin everything. Señor Firenze had no scruples." Marta's eyes darted to me. "Perhaps you will feel better after a nap. I should leave. If I see your *novio* I will tell him that you are here."

I had more questions. Why was she going? "Wait!" I whispered urgently. Somehow, I couldn't speak any louder. She had to tell me more. My pulse was racing—I could hear the thud of my heart. I wanted to go after her but my legs were frozen. Was I still sitting on the bed? If that was so, why was my body lifting up higher, separating from the other part that still sat on the bed? As hard as I tried to bring myself back down, I remained suspended—floating.

Harsh, rasping breathing. Someone was there. I listened. But the wheezing came from somewhere inside of me. A heavy pressure squeezed my lungs. Stay calm, I warned myself.

I was back down on the bed. I breathed deeply, attempting to get a grip on the situation. It would all be better if I rested, I assured myself.

Grasping the cover, I pushed it aside. My hand froze. Blood was everywhere. Red blotches on the white sheet! I gasped. Trying to get off the bed, I backed to the edge. I needed to tell them. Surely they would change these. Eying the sheet apprehensively, I tried getting up but my legs wouldn't move. My skin felt itchy—tiny wispy hairs touching my legs. No, I was wrong. It couldn't be blood—the red blotches were moving. Squirming beetles. My eyes riveted on the red insects. They wiggled towards me. I screamed.

Suddenly they stopped their advance and flattened back into red spots. Tentatively, I touched a blob. It was still moist. I brought my finger to my nose and smelled it. An unpleasant sweet smell. It was blood.

I wanted to touch them again just to make sure but my fingertips were starting to feel numb. I was so tired. Too tired to sit anymore. I let myself slide down on the bed, resting on my back. The stained sheet repelled me but I lacked the energy to move. I felt powerless.

Something hard pressed into my skin. With a supreme effort I forced myself to wiggle aside and pull it out. I brought the metal object up in front of me. It was a picture frame containing a small black and white photo of a man...a man I knew.

Dean grinned malevolently back at me. His face grew larger and zoomed in closer. His lips curled back into a snarl. Sharp fangs emerged, blood trickling from the corner of his mouth. "No!" I cried out. Throwing the horrific frame away, I sank back down limply, closing my eyes.

The door rattled and banged but I was too tired to respond. I felt myself leaving the bed—lifted by a strong force. I opened my eyes to see swirling red—the room rotated around and around. It wouldn't stop whirling. The phantom placed me back down on the bed. Frightened, I cringed, hiding my head beneath the cover. My numb body entered a dark cavern—a deep hole going nowhere. Inside, I felt alone and afraid. My body trembled. Engulfed by monstrous arms, smothered by the pressure, I struggled to breathe, but the dark thing wouldn't let me go. I kicked out against it…and then, nothing.

* * *

I awoke with a start. The room was still. Outside I could hear the birds shrieking loudly. My stomach felt queasy. Sitting up, I brought my hand to my mouth just as some bile surged up my throat. I leaned over the bed and wretched—fluid dribbled onto the tile floor. It wasn't much, a few clear, yellow tinged drops. I lay there energyless. My stomach settled. Feeling better, I sat up and glanced around the room.

Although the bed was large and had a comfortable mattress, the room itself was fairly primitive. The wooden slats of our window were partially open, letting in bright light from outside. Above me, a loop of mosquito netting was tied to an overhead beam. Candles had been placed on the bedside table. That's when I spotted the note. I reached over and picked it up.

Babe. Thought I'd let you sleep. Going to the cenote. I think I can get something out of Sam. Wolf

The paper dropped on the bed as I rubbed my temples, hoping to ease my headache. I couldn't believe what I had just experienced. Dean had been here and it had felt real. I shuddered. Whenever we had been alone, Dean had managed some sort of lecherous double-entendre. Something came back to me—the blood. I swiveled about and grabbed the cover, shoving it aside to look at the sheet underneath. White and clean. No blotches of red. Had I dreamed it all? There was no way it could have happened. Dean had been a slimy human being but he wasn't a vampire, I thought, recalling the fangs.

My eyes shot over to my purse. I searched for my cell and took note of the time. It was past four. I'd slept for more than an hour. I found a tissue and searched for the spot where I'd vomited. Crouching down on the floor, I saw tiny drops and wiped them up. I wondered how long I had been here. Long enough for Wolf to have come and gone. It must have been a bad dream or sun stroke. I trekked over to the bathroom and splashed some water on my face.

I switched on the light and peered at myself in the mirror. My face was pale and drawn—in need of a complete makeover.

Retreating back into the bedroom, I picked up my purse and dug out my makeup bag. Repairs were crucial, especially with a viper ready to stick her fangs into my hottie. If they were alone at the cenote, she'd be coming in for the kill. I needed to hurry. Wolf was in danger.

Done with the touch up, I glanced at my halter top and shorts. A quick change and I'd be ready to battle the serpent. Thank goodness I had the foresight to bring a bathing suit. From out of my bag, I found my string bikini.

Bikini? My Hormone Voice snickered. Girl! What are you thinking? Reality check! If you think you had troubles holding on to that sea god before, wait until he sees the snake goddess in all her glory. Now compare that with you in a bikini. Yes, skimpy, I know. Most women would hesitate to wear it but a sexy bikini is still clothes, remember?

Hormone was right. Sam would be there flaunting all her wares and I'd arrive in a bikini. What a dork I'd seem. Well, so what? Wolf was the recipient of my recent enthusiastic passion and exemplary lovemaking skills. She, on the other hand, was a dim memory in his complex, romantic history involving numerous beautiful women. I had the upper hand and I'd keep the advantage. I smiled confidently and, tote in hand, headed out the door.

It was sunny. I was beginning to feel a lot better and thinking clearly. That nightmare was way out of the ordinary. In fact, I was beginning to realize someone had it in for me. The out-of-body experience, the blood, and the beetles were not a normal sunstroke reaction. Having indulged a bit, I knew about drugs, but this, I wasn't so sure about. My first guess was roofies, the rape drug, with the numbness and the blackout.

I was standing there mulling this over when I heard voices. Around the bend, a man and a woman were coming towards me, yes, nudists—not even fig leaves. They saw me and smiled as though intending to go around the weirdo with a bikini, but I started speaking, eyes high on the tops of their heads. "Hey, I was wondering if you knew which way it is to the cenote?"

"Cenote?" the man repeated in a dozy voice.

"Al," the woman piped up, "she means the cave pond." She glanced at my bikini and chuckled. "First day here is it, honey?"

I nodded.

The rotund guy smiled broadly. "Follow us, sweetie. It's not far. We'll point you in the right direction."

The path was wide enough for two, not three, so I trailed closely behind. The sight of two almost identical round asses was a bit disconcerting. If Wolf and I married, would our butts start looking the same? He was tall and I was petite, but we both worked out regularly—could that happen? I shot a glance back at my own derriere to see if it was looking more like his. It could be a good sign if it was. I grinned, thinking of his squeezable ass. I couldn't wait to touch him all over.

Walking along the dirt path, I caught glimpses of powdery sand through the bushes. Before long, we came upon a fork in the path. Al turned around and motioned. "Go that way, sweetie. Maybe we'll see you at dinner." He waved, not waiting for a reply and he and his lady friend trundled off.

Trekking gingerly along the path, I proceeded with care. Cozumel didn't have snakes but this was the mainland. If I were a snake I'd find a nice warm rock to lay out on and soak up the sun. I glanced up at the boulder alongside the path and half expected to see a snake. I didn't see one there but a bit further along I did.

Worse than any water moccasin, she was the tall brunette type of viper—exceptionally poisonous. Perched naked on a boulder by the edge of a pool of water, leaving nothing to the imagination, she sat comfortably on a towel, looking down at a broad shouldered, delicious man, as tasty as chocolate soufflé.

They couldn't see me yet because of the thick foliage, so I eased myself closer, peeking through the leaves, careful not to step into anything but close enough to see them and hear what they were saying.

Wolf was standing waist deep in the clear water of the cenote. The viper was leaning in to him, tantalizing him with her nudity.

"So you're a rich woman, Sam. Why bother going back to Canada?"

Was he crazy? He was encouraging the reptile to stay?

Sam brought her hand out and ran her long pointy claws down his cheek. "Want me to?"

"What's so interesting in Woodbridge anyway?"

Sam's lips turned up slightly at the corners. "Who ever said crime doesn't pay?"

I couldn't see Wolf's expression but I knew what he was thinking. It's like someone mentioning Jersey. "So the family is involved?"

"Dean wouldn't have had all that extra cash otherwise."

"He was money laundering?"

"I think so but I can't be sure. I didn't have access to all his accounts." She swept a loose strand of her wavy hair back from her shoulder. "This resort would have had a casino if Dean had got his way."

"Casinos aren't legal."

"If Diego wanted it to be."

Wolf nodded. "And if Firenze put money into it."

"But now that Dean's gone, Sam's a rich girl," she said smugly.

"Was it worth it...sleeping with him?"

"That was business, sweet man." She pushed her puppies into his face. "How about some pleasure?"

I shifted nervously and trod on a branch.

Sam straightened up. "What was that?"

"We're in paradise, babe. It comes fully loaded."

If I stepped out now I'd seem like a jealous, insecure girlfriend. I knew he was fully loaded but did he have to remind her of that obvious fact?

Sam's laughter tinkled. "I think we're wasting our time talking. Why don't we go back to my cottage?" As if the suggestion wasn't enough, she swung her foot out and slid it slowly up and down his arm.

Wolf glanced down to her foot before his eyes journeyed upwards to her face. "I came here for a swim."

"That's a thought. Hm-mm. Water does have its pluses." Sam lowered herself in.

Call me stupid and impulsive but it was time for me to claim ownership. "Hey, Wolf," I called out, "are you there?" before I stepped into the clearing.

I couldn't help but notice how mystical it was, with the shimmering stalactites reflecting gold from the sun, the turquoise water and two perfect human specimens swimming in the cenote. Wolf and the viper were both confidant swimmers, unlike me.

"Hey, babe!" my sea god, called out causally as if it was the usual thing for any man to be hanging out nude with his ex wife.

Wolf stood in the water, studying me in amusement. "Not ready for the total experience?"

Sam stopped swimming and leaned back on a rock, eying me appraisingly. "Wolfie," she said between giggles, "just where did you dig her up? The girl's positively Victorian."

I shot a look down at my skimpy bikini. If I was Victorian, she was a candidate for Caligula's court at it's perverted height.

Sam said something only Wolf was meant to hear, before she glanced at me. "It's perfect in here, Adele. Come on in."

I could believe that the part about it being perfect. With Wolf in the water the temperature must be off the heat scale. But I was vaguely suspicious. She didn't like me or want me there. What was she up to? Sliding up to the edge of the cenote, I climbed down the rope ladder and cautiously dipped my foot in. It was warm enough to take the plunge. I slid in, with a slight gasp as my body hit the water. Ten feet out Wolf stood and waited. I swam over and cautiously brought my feet down. My toes grazed the sandy bottom. Wolf reached out for me. Touching him brought fire to my core.

"The cenote is beautiful…" I gazed into Wolf's sapphire eyes as he pulled me in closer. It took every bit of my being to carry on a conversation. "Is this it—or does it go on?"

Wolf kept his focus on me. "There's more," he said, in his husky voice.

Somehow I didn't think he was speaking about the cenote. Silently, his eyes met mine. His lips sensuously caressed me while the light touch of his fingertips on my back heightened my desire. Our kiss was electric. Pleasurable tremors shot down my aroused body.

Wolf's hands slid along my hips and hugged the curve of my cheeks. His touch was magic. I pressed against his hard body, aching with need. He sought out my neck and nuzzled the hollow of my throat, sucking gently on my skin.

From somewhere behind me I heard a noise. I gasped as water splashed into my eyes. I backed away.

The next instant Sam popped up between us. Reaching over to my bikini ties, she tugged on a string. My top slid down. "Oops! Hey, didn't you know, Adele? This is a nudist resort." She snickered before she swiveled to Wolf. "Ew, honeypot, you need to help me. I have such a cramp. How about an itsy bitsy leg massage?" She lifted her leg completely vertical. She must have been a ballet dancer at some time in her life. "Hm-mm?" Over her shoulder she said to me, "It'll be easier to tie your top on out of the water, Adele. Why don't you leave like a nice little girl, eh? Go to your room and let a real woman play."

I felt like an active volcano, smoking before the lava came to the surface. She had deliberately untied my bikini top to humiliate me. I reacted. They call it muscle memory when you've practiced the same defense moves over and over. It was a foot sweep and it connected with her standing leg. When she hit the water, I'm sure my grin must have been as wide as the Cheshire cat's in Alice in Wonderland.

Unfortunately I wasn't rid of her. She resurfaced, spluttering. Seething with fury, she spat out, "Bitch! I should drown you in this water!" Although she outsized me, something in my eyes must have made her reconsider. Glaring at Wolf, she snarled out, "Your taste in women is appalling!"

"I think you know the old saying—two's company," I said calmly.

Wolf laughed. "You heard her, Sam. The bars open. Check it out!"

Sam spit her words through her teeth. "You little runt! What Wolf and I have, you'll never have." She reached over and viciously yanked my bikini top. With the water already loosening the straps, the force pulled it right off my breasts. Before I could stop her she held it up and tossed it as far as she could in the direction of the overhang. It hit the water and floated momentarily on the surface before it sank. "You aren't woman enough for him." With that, she swam back to the edge of the cenote and climbed up the rope ladder.

Satisfaction doesn't begin to describe what I felt when I saw her trotting off down the path.

Wolf grinned. "I think you won that one."

"I'm minus a top..."

"Don't worry, babe. I'll get it." Wolf gave me a quick smile before he dove beneath the surface.

By the time I climbed up the rope ladder, Sam had disappeared out of view. I took out the towel from my tote bag, folded it, and sat down. With the hot sun doing its job, there was no need to dry off.

Wolf reappeared on the surface, a colorful scrap of cloth hanging from his fingertips. I sighed with relief. I was not ready to go topless yet. As he swam towards me my cell started a salsa tone. This one was Diego. Should I answer it? He was probably calling about the float tonight. I'd have to politely refuse him. I thought back to the kiss we'd shared and smiled.

You should see him, my Hormone Voice advised. You know Wolf always has some woman latched onto to him anyway. Make him jealous. Drive him crazy! He'll be forced to give them all up to have you.

True, my Logical Voice agreed, but remember how he gave Adie jewelry and a lease to that house on the east coast? He obviously adores her and don't forget he was her teenage crush. The guy's special but who's to say he won't get angry and take off with the viper?

Yeah? Well, no big loss if he does, Hormone argued. Diego is devastatingly handsome and he's generous. He gave her an exclusive condo and jewelry. The man's obviously head over heels.

That's as far as those voices of mine got. I answered the call. *"Hola."*

"Adelina, where are you?"

"I'm in Tulum at your nudist resort. Listen, Diego, I'm sorry but I can't join you tonight."

"You're with Du Lac?"

I detected some hostility there. Diplomatically, I added, "You always knew Wolf and I were dating…"

"Right," Diego said shortly. "Never mind that. This is important. Something's happening here. You need to return."

"Diego, I can't. We have a room booked for tonight."

"I think you'll want to."

"Why?"

He lowered his voice. "The police have a warrant to search your hotel room."

"What!"

"Don't worry, *cariño*. I'll send Churo to pick you up."

"Diego, why are they coming after me?" I asked quickly, seeing

Wolf swim up.

"They have something—and don't forget, you have a motive. Who knows what the murderer might have planted in your room?"

Wolf pulled himself up the ladder and sat beside me.

"Churo will be there shortly to get you. Wait at the lobby." I heard the phone click on his end.

"You don't look good. What's going on, babe?" Wolf handed me my top. "Was that Alvarez?"

Absentmindedly, I pulled it over my breasts, only slightly distracted by his eyes watching me, and tied the strings. "The police have a warrant to search my room. I have to go back."

"And Alvarez knows this because…"

I shot him a look.

"His cousin is the chief of police."

I nodded. "That's my guess." I stared out at the cenote. Tiny fish, the size of large minnows, flitted past us in the clear water. "He's sending Churo. I'd better go and change." I stood up.

Wolf frowned. "Call him back. Cancel Churo. I'll go with you."

"No, I feel bad enough that you lied to protect me. If they see us together, they'll be more inclined to think I had an accessory or that you did it and I helped. I don't want that on my conscience." I stroked his cheek. "You stay."

Wolf wrapped his arms around me. "Okay, we'll do it your way. I'll check out the other suspects while I'm here." He kissed my forehead gently. "Phone me later. I'll fill you in on what Sam said about Firenze."

Gathering up my things, I smiled. "No need. I overheard the important stuff before I joined you."

That got a grin out of Wolf. He pulled me closer, his lips almost on mine. "I'm so focused on your other abilities," he whispered, "I forget sometimes that you have great detecting skills."

I would have liked to have made love right there in that perfect paradise until we both fell over in exhaustion, but I needed to make it to my hotel before the police arrived. If someone was setting me up, they would make sure I looked as guilty as sin.

Wolf drew my head into his. Our lips touched once more and liquid fire rushed down my body. I pulled away and gazed up at him. "Was that so I don't forget you?"

"No," Wolf grinned, "that's so you'd remember every part of

me." Reluctantly loosening his hold, Wolf took up my hand and we started down the path.

There was something I needed to mention. Possibly Wolf had seen an intruder. "Someone drugged my drink today."

Wolf looked at me with concern. "That makes sense now. I couldn't for the life of me wake you up." He shrugged. "Then I figured you needed it, so I went off to meet Sam."

"I had a scary nightmare—blood, Dean, and a horrible out-of-body experience."

"Roofies?" His eyes met mine. "Did someone try to…"

"Have sex with me?" I shook my head. "I don't think so. I had my clothes on when I woke up and I felt nauseous."

"He could have dressed you and left." Wolf hesitated and stopped walking. "Was there any…"

"Semen? No—didn't see anything like that. I'm sure there was some other reason…" The path had a gap in the bushes with a stupendous view of the ocean. Waves lapped gently on the shore and in the distance a few people were swimming. "It would have been beautiful here with you."

Wolf ran his hand down my cheek. "Think positively. This mess will be cleared up and we'll be together soon. You're not in this alone."

8

Wolf's words echoed in my mind. I watched powerlessly, as Sanchez instructed his officers in his clipped Spanish. Tearing the room apart bit by bit, they tossed my belongings on the bed and the floor as they searched the dresser drawers, my suitcase, and closet.

Grinning maliciously, Sanchez approached me. "Your safe, Señorita. I need your key, please."

I dug in my tote bag for my key and presented it to him. I was nervous. By the time I had arrived with Churo, they were there already, waiting. If someone had planted something, I was too late. My mind raced. I had a bad feeling in the pit of my stomach.

The hotel room wasn't that big. What could they have hidden in here that incriminated me and tied me to Dean's murder?

After they finished, the expression on Sanchez's face told me he was less than pleased. I, on the other hand, was thinking things were looking up. The tension in my shoulders was beginning to vanish when I heard a hubbub at the door.

A woman with a smoky voice spoke authoritatively to the officer at the door. Whatever she said worked. I was surprised to see my visitor. Lourdes entered followed by Alejandro, my stylist.

"Amiga," Lourdes said quickly, kissing both my cheeks, "Carmelita sent me with your costume. It's a brand new one. We must hurry. Alejandro will do your hair." She swiveled to Sanchez. "We need this space immediately. Señor Alvarez is waiting downstairs."

Her remark hit Sanchez hard. He had a pained look on his face like someone had just tightened pliers on his genitals. "Señor Alvarez?" he repeated nervously. I thought I heard him say, "*Mierda!*" under his breath, which anyone in his position would say if he thought he was in big doodoo.

"Okay," he said with resignation, "we'll leave." He called out to his men and they shuffled off to the door, waiting for him outside in the hall. About to go, he peered at my tote. "One more thing," he said to me. "Your beach bag, Señorita, *por favor*."

Taking it from my hands, Sanchez brought it over to the bed

and after taking out my towel, dumped the contents. He frowned and took up the bag again, this time sticking his hand in the zippered compartment.

"Please," Lourdes said, "we need to get her ready, now!"

"One moment." When I saw his triumphant glance, I knew this was not my lucky day.

His hand held a small bottle of pills. "I will be going now, Señorita. I trust you don't need these?" Not waiting for my reply, he turned on his heel and strode out the door.

* * *

An hour later, I was on the float, waving to the crowd with my handsome sheikh, Diego, beside me. His arm draped around my shoulders, Diego flashed his Hollywood smile at the admiring ladies in the crowd. On the lower level, Carmelita and her models were tossing out chocolates wrapped in purple ribbons.

Carmelita was getting her own share of hoots and whistles from the guys. A dead ringer for Matthew McConaughey was making her bend down to loop a strand of gold beads over her head. When she straightened up she threw him a kiss and the guy looked like he'd seen an angel.

Tilting my chin up, Diego said, "Open," before dropping a soft truffle between my lips.

I thought I'd died and gone to heaven so satisfying was the chocolate. I savored it a moment, letting it linger in my mouth before I swallowed.

"Do you approve?"

"Mm—mm. Do I ever." I sighed. "Very much. There isn't anything better."

Diego gazed into my eyes. "If that's what you really think, you need to spend more time with me and give that selfish bastard, Du Lac, the boot."

"I don't want to think about Wolf right now, Diego. Let's talk about the pills. I couldn't see a label on them. Did you ask your cousin what they were?" I tossed some chocolates down to some children who jumped up to catch them. One of the boys waved his fist full of candies at me. I waved back. They were so cute with their big brown eyes and happy grins.

"Herman was elusive at first," Diego said slowly, throwing a strand of gold beads to a lovely Latina in the crowd. "But he

104

knows what side his bread is buttered on. Let's talk about this later…"

I glared at him. "Now, Diego, if you know, you have to tell me."

Diego's lips drew into a line. "Apparently it's ketamine, the same drug found in Dean's body. They thought he had been using marijuana by the odor in the room but the autopsy also revealed ketamine in his bloodstream. You know what ketamine is, *cariño*?"

"No."

"A club drug. The person ingesting ketamine gets feelings of immobility, numbness, and the k-hole trip that the addicts love."

"K-hole?"

"An out of body experience. Some people hallucinate."

My mind flashed back to the nudist resort. "Omigod!"

"What?" Diego glanced at me curiously.

"Someone at the nudist resort drugged my lemonade with ketamine."

"What are you saying—one of the investors?"

"I'd bet on it." I stared at him. "And now you're telling me Dean was also drugged?"

"Or he chose to be. Some people like it. You know, as well as I do, that Dean was a user." He sighed. "Another reason it's better he's dead."

I met his eyes. "You didn't have anything to do with that, did you?"

Diego turned away, picked up some beads, and flung them into the crowd. "I made a mistake when I let him in on my venture. The man was a loose cannon. I wasn't happy about his ideas."

"The casino?"

Diego's eyes narrowed. "You were aware of this? Who told you?"

I shrugged my shoulders uncomfortably. "I must have overheard it at the nudist resort."

"One of the investors?"

"I can't remember who told me, I wasn't really paying attention."

He nodded. "Of course you weren't, Adelina. And you shouldn't be. You are way too beautiful to be concerned with the boring details of business."

"But I do want to know what the police are thinking, Diego. Please…tell me."

Diego placed a bundle of beads in my hands. "Hernan sees a connection between the ketamine in your purse and Dean." He frowned. "Why was it in your bag?"

I stared at the beads a second before untying them and placing them on my lap. "I'm being framed, Diego."

"Framed?"

"The murderer placed them there—the same person who drugged me."

Diego glanced at me. "When do you think this happened?"

"Today, at the investors' meeting, my lemonade was drugged."

"Were they all there?"

I tossed out some beads to some children waving their hands. "Yes, except Sam."

"But she was at the resort?"

I nodded. "While I was drugged up in the room, she went with Wolf to the cenote. At least, I think she went with him. It's possible she met him there."

"And that would have given her the opportunity to place the pills in your bag."

"Her or any of the others. I blacked out, Diego." I frowned. "It's only a matter of time until they come for me."

Diego stroked my hand gently. "No one will arrest you, Adelinita. I told Hernan you would be with me. Carmelita has made sure you have enough clothes and necessities at my beach house."

I turned to him in alarm. "What are you saying? I'm in your custody?"

Diego's brandy eyes studied me. "Better my custody than the San Miguel jail. Right?" He ran his fingers through a strand of my hair. "Surely, being with me isn't that bad?"

His hazel eyes with the green shimmering flecks were mesmerizing. I felt tingles of arousal as I scanned his sculpted bare chest and flat abs. If he ever lost his position of influence in Cozumel, he'd have a job waiting for him with Calvin Klein.

"I need to find out who's behind this. Doing that might be difficult if I'm staying with you."

"Perhaps under normal circumstances but remember we have Eduardo. He is very skilled with the computer and the internet. He will research the investors for you while you enjoy the Carnaval. As well, he can find out anything you need to know for a return trip with your tour group. When you return next year, you will be secure in your knowledge of the customs of Cozumel."

"Are you saying he'll report anything he finds to me?"

"He'll do whatever I say. When we get back to the house, you can tell him who to investigate. Okay?"

Diego was just humoring me. I doubt if he took me seriously. But maybe Eduardo could help me get out of this fix. He might be dangerous, not exactly someone you'd want to meet in a dark alley, but I had the feeling he wasn't anybody's fool.

The float ahead of us stopped as a group of American partiers squeezed through. The merengue dancers in silky blue outfits took that opportunity to circle around for another encore.

"Chocolate, Adelina?"

My ears perked and I turned to Diego expectantly.

"Close your eyes, *mi amor*," he whispered in my ear, "and open those pouty lips..."

It was beyond my expectations—creamy-smooth, delightful chocolate, even better than the last truffle. I opened my eyes. Almost as delicious as the man sitting beside me. In case you're wondering, was I forgetting Wolf? I bit my lip. That was the problem. I could never forget that man. When we were together so many years ago, out on that little boat up north, I had to stop myself from giving him my yet unexplored body. He was a sensual guy, even then, and had been extremely hard to resist.

"*Mi amor?*" Diego eased another chocolate between my parted lips, awakening me from my daze. The chocolate was thick and sinfully decadent. My tongue curled over it and pressed tightly until my body heat started the melting process. I captured and sustained the flavor as long as possible and then I swallowed.

When Diego's mouth met mine, the noise of the crowd became a distant hum. My senses went wild as his full lips invited more and when his tongue played at the roof of my mouth, I wanted him. My fingers ran through his curls—silky yet thick. When those tingles started in my V-zone, I was more than ready to throw caution to the wind and step up our contact.

But no, I had platinum highlights in my dirty blonde hair—I was a stealth blonde, not a real blonde, I told myself firmly. I had to forget about Diego's sizzling looks and remember Wolf could be mine. But Diego's lips wouldn't take no for an answer and my flesh was weak. I languished back against the pillows and let him stroke his hands down my arms as he nibbled my lip. If that rowdy Carnaval crowd had disappeared, I would have taken that opportunity to pull him down for more. Except I had this annoying voice blathering on in my head.

You need to nail Wolf, Logical advised, and quickly. He's a highly sexual man. He's out there with that viper right now. Don't forget how he was aroused in that cenote. For all you know she still turns him on. Can he be trusted not to satisfy himself if you're not there? Don't you remember how they were together? He was way too comfortable naked with her.

If you ask me, Hormone piped up, Adie should have gone nude. Wolf would be fantasizing about her right now if she had. She's way too conservative.

Are you out of you mind! Logical shouted. Anyone wearing that skimpy bikini is definitely not conservative. Adie is a classy woman, unlike that slut. Besides, that's what Wolf likes about her—she's a non-conformist.

When the crowd below started cheering, I came to my senses. What was I getting myself into, anyway? Sure Diego was devastatingly handsome but I wasn't the only one who thought that. He had women...lots...always had. And for sure, Delores wanted him badly. She wouldn't be the only one, either.

I pushed Diego away. "Come on, we need to do some serious bead throwing."

He smiled in amusement. "We've got to show them more than that." He motioned for music and we had a pulsating merengue to dance to. Diego must have majored in body rubbing 101 in university. Gone was his previous scorn about this crazy dance. Hadn't he said it wasn't his thing? But here he was, giving the crowd a display they wouldn't forget and neither would I with his leg rubbing between my thighs and his hands on my hips.

The spectators shouted when I spun him around and I reciprocated by sliding slowly behind him along his firm body. I smirked, thinking it was a good thing sheikhs wore loose pants, and for a few minutes I completely forgot about the trouble I was in.

Of course it hit me with a wallop a while later in the limo—the trouble, that is. But not right away. Diego's brandy eyes electrified me with hidden messages before his tongue entered my parted lips. On a scale of one to ten his kiss hit ten with a jolt. My body was melting as quickly as butter on a sizzling grill. It took every ounce of will-power to push this scrumptious man away.

I sank down into the soft leather and questioned my sanity as the limo entered the main street. Why was it that whenever I had one of these two men with me, I had difficulty thinking? That was supposedly a male problem—an obsession with sex.

"Adelinita, you are so beautiful." Diego sucked my ear, his breath warm on my skin. Through the thin material, his hand found my breast, the tips of his fingers tantalizing my already taut nipple.

Oh, yes, I wanted him. Who wouldn't? And sex could be just the thing I needed to relieve all this tension. Diego's hand slid under my flimsy bra, smoothly stroking my skin. I sighed with the sensation. Leaning back, I was swept into a heat wave. Fire blazed inside of me and an indescribable ache consumed my body. The shimmer in Diego's eyes said it all. He was feeling what I was. There was no mistaking the lust. Yes, I was the sheikh's harem girl— the touch of his hands lifted my body high on a magic carpet ride of pleasure.

When the car suddenly jerked on a speed bump, it brought my fantasy to an end, especially when I spied Churo's broad face watching us in the mirror. What exactly had he seen? I flushed, thinking it was probably way too much.

Warm and comfortable against Diego's strong body, I had to mentally pinch myself to focus on my tenuous situation. Abruptly, I sat upright, pushed him away, and repositioned my bra.

Diego glanced at me in amusement. "You will enjoy yourself here, Adelina. Relax. You are way too tense. Don't worry about the police. Soon we will find the murderer and your troubles will all be over." He stroked my hand. "Besides, they can't do anything as long as you're with me."

But I was not convinced. It was clear Dean's rumor about our affair gave me a motive for his murder. My jaw tightened. The police must think I killed him because he was trying to destroy my relationship with Diego. They were all afraid of the powerful Santiago Francisco Bolivar Alvarez. What sane person wouldn't be? With his connections and henchmen, no one would betray him. And they assumed I was his mistress, after all, not just a tour agent. If my situation had been threatened, I would have had no choice but to remove the threat. They must have concluded I killed Dean to protect my position as Diego's mistress.

The car came to a stop. We had arrived. I was Diego's prisoner on my way to jail. It was a beautiful jail, but a jail, never-the-less. I'd been to Diego's beach house before but never in this capacity. Once we turned off the main road we entered a driveway that went on endlessly until finally we stopped at a gatehouse. Upon seeing the limo, an old man pushed a mechanism that opened the gate.

"What kind of security do you have, Diego?"

"No one will be able to get at you here. You are perfectly safe, Adelina."

I shook my head. "I don't question that. I was merely wondering about your estate. Do you have guards?"

"Of course. Motion activated cameras on the driveway, entrances, and of course there's Diablo."

"Diablo?"

"Eduardo's doberman. He takes him around the grounds a few times in the night."

I frowned. "A guard dog."

"Very necessary. But there's no need for you to be afraid. I'll introduce you to the beast. He isn't a problem." Diego took up my hand, kissing my wrist as he met my eyes. "I want you to be happy here, *mi amor*. This whole Firenze murder can bring us closer together if you'll allow it."

When the limo pulled to a stop, Churo assisted me out. Coming over to my side, Diego placed his hand at the small of my back and we walked together. With only a sheer harem costume on, the cool breeze blowing in from the sea made me shiver.

The lanterns in the trees illuminated our way and with the added silvery light from the moon the tiny stones in the path shimmered like diamonds. From all around us the scent of the flowers, sweet and heady, filled the air. Our walk through the garden was like a trip into an enchanted forest.

By the time we opened the front door, I was again reminded

how impressive Diego's beach house was. From the heavy oak door to the immense stucco house, I was awed by the size of the property and what was on it—a pool, a six-car garage, and tennis courts by a perfect stretch of beach on the ocean.

A middle-aged lady in a dark blue dress rushed up to greet us. Casting a surreptitious glance at Diego's bare, sculpted chest, she smiled and said enthusiastically, *"Buenos noches,* Señor Alvarez."

I knew exactly what she was thinking. It was running through my brain at break-neck speed, too.

Whoa! Logical shouted. Get a grip, girl! You're not a 'ho'.

Oh, shut up, you Victorian! Hormone giggled. Wake up and smell the coffee. Women have needs too. Get this hunk of burning love in bed ASAP.

"Louisa, I'd like to introduce you to our guest, Señorita Sturm."

"Buenos noches, Señorita." Scrunching her face, she inspected my flimsy costume before she remembered her manners. "Welcome!"

"Gracias, Louisa." I assumed she was familiar with Diego's female companions in various states of undress but I doubted if many of them sported harem wear.

Having only been here to enjoy Diego's pool parties, I glanced around curiously. This wing of the house was new to me. The paintings on the yellow ochre walls caught my eye. Heavy oak frames enhanced the subject matter which varied from landscape to portraits, but the skill of the artist was apparent even at a glance. "This art is beautiful."

"Diego Rivera—a Mexican artist, Adelinita. His work gives you the feel of the land, doesn't it? In the salon, I have some paintings from a few European artists I'm sure you'll recognize." He turned to Louisa and instructed her quietly. "Tell Eduardo we need him in the salon immediately and perhaps you could prepare some of your delicious quesadillas for us, Louisa?"

"Si, Señor Alvarez." She grinned widely. I will bring them in to you and the señorita as soon as they are ready." She took a last eyeful of Diego in his sheikh outfit before she headed down the corridor.

"Come, *mi amor.* You need to relax." Diego brought me into the room on our left. The elegant couches were gold, the walls a deep cherry, and the paintings were an eclectic mixture, right out of the Louvre—Matisse, Chagall and a small Van Gogh. A square oak coffee table inlaid with copper had been placed in front of a couch near a cozy fireplace. In the corner of the room, a large Oriental vase held long-stemmed, yellow roses.

"I thought with it being a chilly night we might enjoy some tequila by the fire." He led me to the couch and I sat down, leaning against a pillow.

It did look inviting. "A few days in Mexico and I can actually believe it was cool tonight." I laughed. "People back in Canada, with the snow piling up, would think I've lost my mind. Funny, how that happens—suddenly thinking it's cold when it must be in the mid seventies."

"I like the idea that you've acclimatized to Cozumel. You do have a condo here and you told me how much you liked it, didn't you?" Diego brought his hand to my forehead and slowly slid his fingertips to my bangs to brush them away as his hazel eyes searched my face.

Why did he have to touch me like that? And more importantly, why did my body love it so much? "I do. It's lovely." A luxury condo, Italian furnishings and designer clothes all mine, courtesy of Diego. "It was generous of you, Diego—too generous. It's wrong for me to have it."

Diego placed his hand on top of mine. "No, *mi amor*. You know I owe you. The condo is merely a token of my gratitude."

The trouble was it made people here believe I was Diego's mistress. But Wolf knew it wasn't true…

No, Wolf thinks you're his but don't forget men are possessive of their women, My Logical Voice warned. With this tasty man, you are extremely close to taking a dangerous plunge.

Two snifters and a bottle of tequila had been placed on the table. Diego started to speak as he poured me a glass. "I know you've tasted the best tequilas before." Diego smirked. "You're certainly not a virgin when it comes to tequila anejo."

"I think you made sure of that," I said dryly, not amused at his humor. On his yacht, after too many drinks, I'd been too close to having had a delicious bite of Diego.

"I can't forget that first kiss—sweet, yet wickedly so, with your mouth tasting of one of my favorite tequilas. I don't think it was this one though, *mi amor*. This is Partida Anejo Tequila, aged eighteen months in American oak barrels. What's unusual is that their blue agave comes from their own plantation. They allow ten years from shoots to harvest for the agave to mature and hence, they are ensured a ripe rich tequila. You will see it has an exceptional bouquet, zesty even." He raised his glass to mine. "*Salud!*"

I clicked his glass and repeated, "*Salud!*"

Diego flashed me a Hollywood smile. "Try it and see if your palate is as good as I think it is. Let's see if you can discern the flavors."

Glancing at my glass of premium tequila, I wondered if I could. Always up for a challenge, I swished the rich, golden hued tequila around in my glass before I sipped.

"So?"

"Fruity…very smooth."

"Captivating." Diego studied me with those hazel eyes so similar to the tones of the tequila.

My body responded. "Honey…" I said softly.

"Yes, *mi amor*?"

I felt my cheeks grow hot. "I mean there are honey flavors."

The corners of Diego's full lips turned up ever so slightly. "Perhaps you need to drink more before you make a judgement."

I tipped my glass back once more. "Bananas, I think."

"Correct. Did you taste the almonds?"

I sat back against the couch, and smiled, pleased with myself as I detected something very subtle. "Mm-mm and chocolate."

Diego laughed. "Excellent! I'm impressed! I thought you might like that. It's been a least an hour since your last chocolate fix."

I sighed, thinking back to the truffles. Yes, I admit it…I'm a chocoholic, happily addicted. No group meetings for me, ever. Even if they had them, I would never quit. Luckily for me, I was here in the land of the Mayans…the people that had discovered cocoa beans and chocolate. No wonder I was so obsessed with Mexico. To me, chocolate equals pleasure—endorphins released in the brain that intensify every single sensation. It was as powerful as any drug. Which brought me back to those not-so-pleasant thoughts about my ketamine trip.

At that moment, Louisa appeared with a tray of quesadillas, plates, and napkins. On her heels, a trim, dark-haired man entered.

He took the seat across from us and got right down to business. "Señor Alvarez? You have an assignment for me?"

"Have a quesadilla, Eduardo," Diego directed. "No need to rush."

I focused on his face and tried not to stare at the jagged scar that marred his lean face.

"Thank you, Señor Alvarez, but I have eaten."

"You brought your notebook, Edurado?" Diego lifted a quesadilla to his full lips and bit in. "Ah-hh, Louisa has outdone herself." He glanced at me. "What do you think, *mi amor*? Do you like yours?"

I nodded, chewing the buttery soft cheese wrapped in a tortilla. I swallowed. "Amazing!"

Diego smiled. "Louisa is a godsend." He fixed his gaze back on Eduardo. "We need a report done immediately. Señorita Sturm will give you the names of the people in question. We have reason to believe someone is framing Señorita Sturm for the murder of Dean Firenze."

I picked up another quesadilla and bit in while Eduardo took out a pen and small black notebook from his jacket pocket. By the time he looked up to begin, I had finished yet another. Feeling a lot better, I concentrated on considering the suspects. Could I eliminate anyone? I could hardly ask him to investigate his boss, though, could I? "Dean's wife, Terry and his stepdaughter Janine," I said, pausing, and waited for him to stop writing.

Eduardo's eyes flicked up. He eyes glowed darkly as he looked me over. "*Si,* Señorita Sturm?"

"Dean's son-in-law, Jim Langly, and his mistress, Samantha Stevens." I felt vaguely uncomfortable at his intense stare. I glanced away to gather my thoughts. "Oh, and his brother, Dale." I turned to Diego. "Is there anyone else?"

"What about Du Lac? He would've been insanely jealous if he thought you'd slept with Firenze."

This little tidbit caught Eduardo's attention. He stared at me appraisingly.

I grimaced. "Wolf? And what about you, Diego?"

"Adelinita, he's claimed you, I haven't." He grinned mischievously. "Not yet, anyway."

I shot him a look. "I don't expect you to understand, but Wolf and I have a very special relationship."

"And as I said before—I'm a patient man. Sooner or later, Du Lac will bury himself."

An interesting way to phrase it. I sat back and watched Eduardo scribbling away. I began to think he knew more than he let on. Maybe he did. In fact, he could be the murderer. This could all be a tactic to appease me. This led to another question. If he was the murderer, someone had sent him. Carmelita or Diego?

"You know, there is someone else we should investigate."

"Who?"

His eyelids were heavy-lidded and the vibes I got from him were hotter than burning oil. In fact, I'd say Diego was entirely focused on the subject of murder suspects. I had to remind myself why we were gathered here. Pulling my thoughts together, I said, "Juan Jose, Terry's new boyfriend."

Diego nodded. "Good thinking, *cariño*. Got that, Eduardo? Work on it tonight. I want some answers by tomorrow. I expect a report for both *Señorita* Sturm and myself, by, let's say, ten. We will have breakfast at nine, shall we, *mi amor*?"

I nodded and sipped my tequila slowly. Glancing at Diego, I had to wonder if he had other plans besides breakfast together.

"How are you feeling, Adelinita? Do you feel better now that Eduardo is doing the homework?"

"I do, thanks, Diego." Nevertheless, I couldn't help but feel boxed in. My freedom was out of my control. "Would you mind if I said goodnight? And Diego, you did mention there are some things for me to wear?"

"Everything you need. Carmelita and her designer brought over her latest samples and the ensuite bathroom is all equipped with feminine necessities." He stood up and took my hand. "Come, *mi amor*, I'll show you to your room."

I had seen the upper floor from the outside of the house, but had never imagined such a grand staircase. Climbing the stairs slowly with Diego, I glanced down at the splendor of the house below. The marble floors and the ochre walls combined with the white pillars were Spanish style at its finest.

The upper floor was similar, but here the butternut-colored walls were adorned with impressionistic paintings. A Degas ballet dancer was one I recognized. Diego loved art and with his money he could afford to buy the best.

We made our way down a hallway. The doors were on the left. Although some of the house was used for business meetings, this wing looked solely residential. All bedrooms, I assumed.

Stopping at the third door, Diego opened it.

"Am I the only one up here tonight?" I was hoping to diplomatically probe into the whereabouts of Diego's bedroom.

Diego flashed me a smile. "Don't be frightened, Adelinita. I'm in the next room. The old wing is under renovation. That's why we're both up here." He switched on the light. "Do you like it?"

I surveyed the cool green walls and the warm cherry furniture— a large four poster bed and a matching dresser. "It's lovely," I said, leaning against the wall.

"The bathroom is that door to the right and the closet is over there." He waved to the other side. "This room has a balcony—in fact, we share one." Diego suddenly forgot about the amenities. Stepping in front of me, he blocked my view of the room. His hand caught up a strand of my hair. Thoughtfully, he threaded his fingers through. "We don't have to be apart, Adelinita." His hazel eyes sparkled green. "You're safe with me. I wouldn't force you to do anything you wouldn't want. You know that," he said, his mouth so close to mine. Lips that demanded passion.

With his arms wrapped around me, he pressed his mouth firmly to mine—his tongue playing a tempting game. I was caught in a whirlpool of pleasure that seemed too good to discard.

Diego brushed my hair back and nuzzled my ear, tracing the contours before nibbling my lobe. "Adelinita…" His breath was soft as a breeze. Tender kisses trailed to my shoulder. "I don't want you with anyone else," he murmured before his lips gently sucked my skin at the nape of my neck. The air sparked. Delightful tremors thrilled my body. I glanced at his wavy dark hair which brushed my skin so sensuously and wondered how those soft curls would feel when we made love. Caught up in his hot, feathery kisses, I pressed against him.

But was he the man for me? Diego liked to please. I could be happy with a man who satisfied and held me in esteem—treated me like a queen. But could I trust him? For all I knew, he'd arranged this whole thing with Hernan. Eduardo could have killed Dean because of the man's interest in me. Diego wouldn't have hesitated to send him and if there was a business reason such as gambling at the resort as well, he'd do the expedient thing. Rich, powerful people have a different set of values. And now I was his prisoner. A bird in a gilded cage. This was not what I wanted. I pushed him away. "Diego, no. Just hold me. I don't want anything more."

He didn't answer but he brought me closer to him, and held me close. "We'll find the killer, Adelinita. Don't worry. Eduardo is good at what he does. In the morning he should have some answers and then you can relax."

"Thank you for keeping me out of jail, Diego." I know I should have told him the truth about finding Dean dead, but I had doubts. "You believe I'm innocent, don't you?"

Diego nodded. "You're not the vengeful type." He brought his hand behind my head, and wove his fingers through my hair. "One last kiss?"

"That's the first time you ever asked."

His changeable eyes studied me. "We have as long as you want, Adelinita," he said, before his lips met mine in a warm, lingering kiss. It was the type of kiss that tossed me into a soft, blissful breeze.

But when his glance shot over to the bed, I shook my head regretfully. "Goodnight, Diego."

"So soon?" he asked, his voice husky.

It took all my resolve to say, "Yes. Could someone knock on my door at eight-thirty, so I could get ready for breakfast?"

"Of course, my sweet one. Goodnight. May your dreams be happy ones."

When he left I made my way to the closet to find something for bed. Sliding the door open, I couldn't believe my eyes. It wasn't even close to my birthday and here I had everything I ever wanted in one closet. Dresses, tops, skirts and jackets, all in chic designs. Carmelita's collection favored purple and gold—the Carnaval colors.

I couldn't help but be excited by the fabric choices either. Silks, cottons and jerseys but what about sleepwear? Against the opposite wall, I spotted a heavy cherry dresser. I decided to check it out. Opening one drawer, I saw an amazing assortment of bras and panties and in the next, silky and lacey lingerie. I tugged out a blue outfit. Way too sexy for the maid to see. This was definitely an appetizer for a man. My fingers stroked a silky red number. I couldn't resist. This was the one.

In the bathroom mirror, I held it up against me. This little piece of silk would be mine tonight, but first I had to clean off all my makeup. Everything I could possibly need was here on the counter—wipes, cleanser, moisturizer, body lotions, and my favorite perfume. How did Carmelita know about that?

After I wiped off all the glitter I glanced up, half expecting to see Wolf behind me. An ache in my core reminded me of our brief encounter. He was like a magnet and I was like a tiny piece of iron filing that couldn't resist his powerful pull. I shook my head. There were too many memories with that man for me to easily forget him.

In the shower, I was eager to feel clean again. The shower's massage jets shot straight into my tensed up muscles. I was lacking for nothing. My favorite shower gel and a variety of hair products filled the shelves as if someone had secret knowledge of my bathroom at home.

A while later, I dried off and applied body lotion. The scent wafted through the air—chocolate. I felt an emptiness in the pit of my stomach. It was déjà vu without the man in the mirror.

He had urged me to update him. It wasn't chill to pursue the man, but I had to believe this was justifiable, considering the circumstances. From out of my bag, I took my cell and speed-dialed. It rang and went to voice mail. "Wolf," I said, "Sanchez found ketamine in my bag. Someone planted it there when I blacked out. I'm at Diego's house." I considered the animosity between Diego and Wolf. "It would be best if you stayed away." I pressed end.

Why hadn't he picked up? I rubbed my lip reflectively. Sam? Was she with him? There was no point in dwelling on that. Negative thoughts only destroy my chi.

I glanced at the flimsy piece of silk that fell midway to my thighs. Feminine and delicate, the berry silk gave my skin a pinkish glow. My blue eyes sparkled back at me.

Switching the light off, I hopped into bed and fell asleep, dreaming of a wickedly handsome pirate with dark rimmed eyes and unruly hair.

9

Light filtered through the pale cotton sheet covering my eyes. The knocking woke me but I was still in that hazy half-dream state. "Come in…" I managed.

I heard the door swing open and someone step in. As the maid approached, I said, "Thank you. Tell Señor Alvarez, I'll get ready." I closed my eyes and waited for her to go.

She shuffled to my bed and set something on the table.

"*Gracias,*" I mumbled.

Instead of leaving, the heavy woman settled herself on the edge of my bed.

That was nervy. I had assumed Diego's staff would be better trained than that. "I'm awake, Señorita. It's alright for you to go." You can't imagine how furious I was to have this woman tug the cover off my head. "What the…" I sat up with the sheet falling to my waist.

"*Muy linda!*" Diego grinned mischievously. "How lovely and tousled you look, Adelinita. Too bad, I wasn't responsible for the disarray."

I felt like shrinking into a pea size ball and sliding back under the cover. My face was puffy with sleep and nasty looking, not to mention having absolutely no eye makeup on. "Diego," I said in a tiny voice, "I thought we were meeting for breakfast downstairs."

"Ah-hh, *cariño*. I thought I'd surprise you." He reached over and grabbed a couple of pillows. "Let's put these behind you." Sliding the pillows behind my back, he propped me up in front. "This should be just right for you. What do you think? Are you comfortable?"

I noticed the tray he had set on my bedside table with covered dishes, coffee, and orange juice in fluted glasses. "You brought breakfast? How wonderful, Diego."

"Something for us to share, but first, I think you need coffee." He turned to the tray and handed me a mug. "It should be just the way you like it. At least I hope so." He grinned. "Milk, for less calories and half a cup of sugar."

"Milk, yes," I smiled at his sugar dig, "sugar only when I don't have sweetener handy. You know me so well..." I sipped the coffee and regretfully found it still a touch bitter but it was the thought that counted. "Thank you, Diego."

Diego watched me from over the rim of his mug. He set his mug down and said, "I can see it's not quite right."

"Oh, no, Diego, it's great."

"I told Louisa to buy some sweetener but she forgot. By tomorrow you shall have your coffee exactly the way you like it." Taking my mug away, he placed it on the table. "Now, here's something Louisa prepared for you at my request." He waved at a covered dish. "She's a talented chef—studied in Paris, but usually I have her supervise rather than cook. Today is special, however, with you staying here with me." He perched the breakfast tray on my lap and took the lid off of the dish. "Hope you like Eggs Benedict?"

What's not to like? Such a delightful way to serve eggs— poached with peameal bacon on an English muffin and topped with hollandaise sauce. Diego sure knew how to make breakfast an experience.

"But first," he handed me the fluted glass with orange juice, "mimosas for us."

"*Salud!*" He clicked his glass to mine.

I'm not a morning person and this was all a bit overwhelming. I tipped back my mimosa and regarded Diego. "Breakfast in bed with champagne. Very thoughtful of you."

His eyes swept down. "Entirely selfish, on my part. I assure you."

I glanced at my lingerie. While the underwire lifted my breasts into a perky position, the lace that trimmed the neckline revealed more than I wanted. To divert his attention, I asked, "Aren't you eating with me?"

"I had something earlier. Here," he handed me utensils, "go ahead. I'll just sit here and watch."

That's what I was afraid of. I tried sitting straighter to avoid creating more of a visual display for him but hunger prevailed and I dug in. "It's excellent," I said, between mouthfuls.

"I stole Louisa away from a local French restaurant." As he tipped back his mimosa, Diego's brandy eyes sparkled. "Churo made the drinks."

"A man of talent." Tipping back my glass contemplatively, I asked, "Should I hurry? Is Eduardo waiting?"

Diego smiled lazily. "No need to rush, my sweet. Our first morning together should be special."

I ate the egg breakfast slowly, amazed at the taste.

"Her sauce is exceptional, isn't it?" Gathering up a napkin, Diego shaped it to a point and brought it to the side of my mouth. "Just a..." he wiped something away, "there. Much better."

I felt rather embarrassed about my sloppy eating habits and a little taken aback by the way Diego was cleaning my face. Taking up my fork, I had another delicious mouthful.

"May I have a taste?"

"Of course." I scooped up some eggs for him. My fork entered his mouth. I watched as he swallowed.

"She has outdone herself." Diego snatched the fork from my hand and took up the last morsel. "Let me..."

This time it was my turn to be fed. I ate and leaned back on my pillow.

"How careless of me, Adelina. I've spilled a little."

I glanced down and saw a speck of Hollandaise on the rise of my breast. "Oh!"

"Let me help..." Diego leaned over and licked off the sauce.

Soft curls brushed my skin. It felt so pleasurable, yet I was determined to stop him. This was not going to happen. "You'll have to convey my compliments to Louisa and to Churo, as well," I said, nervously trying to cover up the quivers he'd released. "They certainly prepared a special breakfast. I had no idea..." I babbled.

Diego abruptly snatched up my plate and utensils, setting them back on the table.

"Mm-mm. That was delicious," Diego said softly. "Can you imagine what it would be like if we were both eating?"

The heat in my cheeks was nothing compared to the fireworks sparked in my core.

"Finish your drink, Adelinita. I have something for you." He took my glass and said, "Close your eyes."

What entered my mouth was soulfully sweet. A luscious strawberry coated in thick, creamy chocolate was deposited between my lips. I let it rest on my tongue, moving it lightly against the roof of my mouth and holding it there a moment before I bit in. The juices of the strawberry harmoniously mingled with the rich, decadent chocolate—a resplendent chorus of flavors.

"And now it's my turn." The bed moved as Diego stretched out alongside of me, reached around me and kissed me, thrusting his tongue in to taste. "M-m-mm, more?"

Not waiting for an answer, he pushed another chocolate-covered berry into my parted lips. As I savored the wondrous flavor, Diego's lips wandered lower to my cleavage, teasing me further with each hot caress. Breakfast had never been like this. Delicious kisses and tasty food—a shock to the system. But the floor show that followed blew me out of the water.

From the doorway, a woman shrieked. Looking over Diego's shoulder, I saw his assistant, Delores. In a clingy low-cut dress, her breasts heaving significantly, she rushed into the room. Dark eyes sparkling with anger, curls flying wildly about, and tears streaming over her high cheek bones made her more attractive than ever. She was one gorgeous female even with her eyes shooting daggers.

Cool as a cucumber, Diego sat up and said calmly, "Perhaps you should have knocked, Delores, but since you are here, please come and meet my friend, Adelina."

Her face flushed, Delores swept up to Diego and soundly smacked his cheek. I don't think he was expecting quite that sort of reaction but when she steamed out of the room, his lips twisted.

Glancing back at me, Diego said, "I'm so sorry, Adelinita." He shrugged his shoulders in a typical continental fashion, and said, "Spanish women are overly emotional. Please excuse the drama. Why don't I meet you in the salon, where we were last night? I'll have Eduardo report to us there."

I nodded, a little stunned by the scene I had just witnessed.

When the door closed behind him, I got out of bed and padded over to the shower and turned on the taps. Shrugging off the slinky piece of silk and setting it on the chair facing the mirror, I let the water refresh me, pondering the strange scene I had just witnessed. Was it possible Delores and Diego were lovers? Had he gone out to comfort her?

I was upset. Wakeup calls were not supposed to be like that. Slowly to the sound of soft music would have been much more agreeable. The sexy man was a good idea too, but I definitely drew the line at raging jealous women invading my bedroom. I stepped out of the shower and dried off, mulling this over. An attractive man like Diego would have numerous admiring women but her reaction had to be the act of a jealous lover. So he'd been holding back that little secret. How naïve I'd been to assume he was in love with me. I should be grateful that she had interrupted something that could have led into much more than breakfast.

Ruefully, I applied makeup, wondering how I always managed to read people wrong. I thought Diego cared about me and maybe he did, but not any more than for his other women. I was just the blonde in his collection. Well, I could roll with the punches. After all, I wasn't here to be his lover. My mission was to find out who was framing me.

My hair combed, I checked for clothes. Spanish women didn't wear shorts, so there were none of those. I decided on a denim mini-skirt, a flimsy turquoise top with a scooped neckline, and a matching bra and panties. The wooden box on the dresser was filled with intricate jewelry in silver and gold. The sheen of the white silver attracted me. Mexican silver glows brightly with its own light. I picked out a chain with an oval piece of turquoise suspended from the center link and predictably saw a pair of matching drop earrings. The other drawer contained the ring— turquoise surrounded by flattened silver feathers.

Now to find the salon. In a house this size that could be a challenge. I proceeded cautiously down the hall to the stairs and paused there, hoping Delores was far gone. I was sure the woman wouldn't hesitate to give me a wallop for good measure and considering the power of her strike, I'd have to block her and be careful not to hurt her. No use ending up in jail for two charges— murder and assault. The police probably wouldn't mind me murdering an unpopular tourist as much as me knocking the lights out of a local professional woman. I could see myself on the enforced diet prison plan. Pounds would fall off rapidly with a diet of gruel de maiz. And if prison didn't kill me, chocolate withdrawal would.

Eduardo was speaking intensely to Diego when I waltzed in. Both men stood up.

"*Cariño,* how ravishing you look!" Diego extended his hand to help me into the love seat, where he snuggled close to me, his leg tight against mine. His eyes lingered on my necklace that nestled in the valley between my breasts. "A quality turquoise. Carmelita picked a good piece." He brought his finger to the jewel and examined it. "According to the Maya, it protects the wearer."

"And it's especially lucky for me since it's my birthstone." I was all too conscious of his warm finger stroking my skin beneath the pendant. With his steady gaze on me I was no longer sure we were speaking of the turquoise. It was lucky I was sitting—my knees were turning into jelly. The glimmer in the depths of those changeable eyes of his made me feel like I was the center of his world.

A discreet cough from Eduardo on the opposite couch brought Diego's examination of the necklace to an abrupt halt. "Ah, yes, Eduardo. You have a report for us?" He reached over to the table where snifter glasses and a decanter of a bronze liquid had been placed. Pouring out a bit on the liquor in each glass, he handed me one. "This is Bowmore, one of my favorites. It's a fine vintage—aged eighteen years. I thought you might enjoy it."

"Thank you ." Scotch was not something I liked or had much experience with but after that unexpected drama with the delightful Delores, I could see the necessity of having a calming dose of scotch. Diego was probably more in need of a sedative than I was but I had the police to contend with.

"I have photo copies." Eduardo handed us both a sheet and waited for us to read it. "As you can see, I started with the most obvious suspect—Teresa, aka Terry. She gains a sizeable fortune and is spending her time with one Juan Jose Montenegro."

"What did you find out about him?" I said, clicking my glass to Diego's.

Diego admired the bronze hues, ignoring Eduardo's frown. "Tell me what you think about it, Adelina."

I let the scotch trickle down my throat. It was better than I'd expected. "It's very smooth."

"Complex flavors, *mi amor*, some floral—some smoke. I wasn't sure you'd like it since it is an acquired taste but I can see you are pleasantly surprised."

"It's good. Something in there really appeals to me. I'd swear there's a chocolate flavor, too."

"I'm in awe." Diego grinned widely. "You are so right—once more, I should add."

I tipped back my glass again. "This scotch is unique but I doubt if it will ever replace a daiquiri in my books."

Diego laughed and patted me on the knee. "All right, Eduardo—continue. Señorita Sturm asked about the guard. What do you have on him?"

"He's from Nicaragua. I'll need more time to investigate why he came here."

"You have connections there?"

Eduardo nodded and wrote something in his notebook.

Diego set his sheet down and opened a cigar box. "What of the mistress, Samantha, the ex wife of Wolf Du Lac? You have very little about her."

"Went to school with Janine. Married and divorced Du Lac. She manages Firenze's Woodbridge Branch in Canada. I have reason to believe she was involved in illegal activities."

Sam had mentioned something like this. "Such as?" I asked.

"Casinos attract drug money. What's better than laundering the money in a government endorsed casino?" Eduardo's deep-set eyes peered at me from under heavy dark brows.

"I think you'll have to look thoroughly into Dean Firenze's activities, Eduardo." Diego clipped a cigar. "You don't mind, do you, Adelina?"

I shook my head.

He lit it and drew it in. "The Cohiba goes so well with the scotch." He smiled in satisfaction as he puffed it out. "There's nothing like an excellent Cuban cigar, is there?" He threw that remark out, not really looking at me.

Eduardo nodded, probably wishing he had been offered one.

Diego glanced at me. "I am being rather rude. Would you like one? I forgot how women have been smoking them too, lately." His eyes crinkled in amusement.

So he thought I wouldn't. Another one of his superior male ploys to put me in my my place? "Sure, why not?"

Diego grinned. "I didn't know you indulged, *mi amor.*"

"There's a lot you don't know about me, Diego."

"Point taken. Why don't we share? Would that be agreeable?"

I took the cigar from him and drew it in. It had a mild earthy taste. I was surprised. Not unpleasant at all. I puffed without inhaling and call me crazy but this cigar tasted of coffee and chocolate. Was it better with scotch? I sipped a bit.

"What do you think of it? This one is relatively mild."

"Tastes a bit of leather but not unpleasant, eh?"

"Chocolate."

"I'm impressed, Adelina. You are an outstanding female. Not only can you smoke a cigar but you can detect the subtlest of flavors. And isn't it fantastic for us to share this pleasure?" He kissed my cheek. "It makes us on an even footing doesn't it—when we can enjoy these things together?" He took the cigar from me and had a puff, gazing into space. Eduardo and I looked at him but he sat silently smoking.

"Señor?"

Glancing at Eduardo, Diego said, "This possible mafiosa connection worries me. It makes me wonder why you failed to inform me about this earlier."

"But you hadn't asked me to investigate Firenze until now."

Diego puffed slowly. After a moment he nodded. "True, but I have many business dealings and numerous partners. As my employee, I would expect you to anticipate what needs to be done before I involve myself with an unsavory associate."

"My apologizes, Señor Alvarez. I had assumed—"

"Never assume, Eduardo. This man had shares in my resort. I hardly want any association with the mob." He tipped back his scotch. "I am disappointed in you."

"I apologize and will be more careful in the future."

"I would hope so. Now, let's get on with it. What about the daughter, Janine?" He handed the cigar back to me.

At this, Eduardo smiled maliciously. "Found her on a porn site."

"Interesting." Diego rubbed his lip reflectively. "What exactly did you find?"

I clutched Diego's hand. "That can't be!"

"It took some work but her picture matched up. I took it from a video on the net." Eduardo pulled up an eight by ten glossy for us. Diego and I studied the photo. Her face was in profile. The girl had an upturned nose and pale skin. The freckles could have been hidden by a heavy coat of foundation.

Eduardo spoke up, "Admittedly, Señorita Sturm, it's hard to tell it's her with the darker hair. The photo's old—taken a few years ago."

Diego laid the photo on the table. "It's her, I'm positive of that...good work, Eduardo."

I couldn't believe what I had just seen. Could it really be Janine?

"I doubt if this a professional shot." Diego patted my hand conciliatorily. "It happens all the time, *mi amor*. A young teenage girl falls for some guy and he tells her it will be sexy," he shrugged his shoulders, "and the next thing she knows he splits up with her. He's a sleazy sort—decides the DVD would make a good cash cow. She probably doesn't know she's out there on the net." He glanced back at Eduardo. "What else?"

"She was wild—drugs, marijuana, coke—you name it."

"Find anything out about her husband?" Diego took the cigar from me and put it to his lips.

"Langley's a technical genius, but socially," Eduardo shrugged, "somewhat backward. He's from Toronto originally, so I would think for a normal single of his age, he would have been out clubbing in the city but apparently this boy tends to be a home body. No girlfriends as far back as we could trace."

Diego stretched his arm around my shoulders and gazed at Eduardo. "Bears a closer look. He did gain from Firenze's death, although, I suppose, indirectly."

"My operatives are digging and if there's anything to be found we'll have it soon."

I pushed my hair back from my neck. "Toronto must be where he met Janine."

Eduardo shook his head. "No, it was a resort area in Canada called Port Elgin. You know of it?"

I nodded. "On Lake Huron." I thought of a romantic sunset I had shared with Wolf many years ago.

"Firenze introduced them at his cottage and shortly afterwards hired Langley for the Toronto office."

"You don't think it's a love match, do you, *cariño*?"

"Janine wanted a divorce right after they were married. But that all changed once she found out that she'd lose her share if she divorced him. She wasn't happy about that, but he seems to like the idea of being married to an heiress."

Diego puffed on the cigar. "Langley came to the resort with her, didn't he?"

I nodded and picked up my glass for another sip.

"And what about Du Lac? He stayed behind to be with the wealthy Samantha, didn't he?"

"I told him to stay," I said sharply. "I didn't want the police to think we were conspirators."

"That was wise. But Du Lac is no fool. I'm sure he realized it wouldn't be in his best interests to be anywhere near the police, would it? Perhaps he realized how easily Firenze's wealth would become his with his ex so interested in him."

"That's crazy, Diego. Wolf would never kill anyone."

"Sam is a rich woman. Money is a motive."

Internally, I denied that but in the back of my mind I recalled his suggestion for Sam to stay on in Cozumel. Was he planning to ditch me and get it on with her?

"Anything else, Eduardo?"

"No, *señor*."

As Eduardo stood to go, Diego reminded him, "You are to stay close to Señorita Sturm in my absence. Is that understood?"

When Eduardo left, I asked, "You're going somewhere?"

"Unfortunately, I have to, *mi amor*. Keep your cell with you. I'll call you later about the parade." He glanced out the window. "Perhaps you can pass your time sunning by the pool. Louisa will prepare you lunch. I've left her instructions." He ran his fingers through a tendril of my hair. "I hope to be back later this afternoon if all goes well. *Mi casa es tu casa*."

"Thanks, Diego. You have already made me feel like it's my home. I'll go up to change."

Diego leaned over and whispered, "Have a good afternoon, *mi amor* and know that you will be in my thoughts."

I intended to kiss him lightly on the lips but he pushed the back of my head into him and wove his fingers into my hair before his lips met mine. The kiss was anything but platonic. Just as I felt like pushing him down on the couch and tugging off his shirt, a quiet cough broke the moment.

"The car is ready, Señor Alvarez," the massive man at the door said quietly.

"Ah-hh, Luis. You do pick the most inopportune moments. You

remember, Señorita Sturm?"

"Of course, *señor. Buenos dias,* Señorita Sturm. I hope you are enjoying your visit?" Luis kept his face expressionless, but I had to wonder if he thought Diego's dilemma was amusing.

Diego helped me up and held my hand a second longer and kissed my wrist before he released it. He whispered, "It was very clever of you to think of sharing the cigar. Your mouth tasted delicious…mm-mm. See you later? I shall rush to be back with you."

We parted in the hallway where I continued up the stairs alone. At the landing, I glanced down and saw Diego and Luis heading out the front door. I remembered I needed to contact Wolf.

In my room, I searched for my tote and found my cell, but when I tried to text found the battery too low. This was frustrating. My charger was back at the hotel. Being in Diego's custody, I felt a little awkward about asking Louisa. I'd wait. Diego had said he'd be back in a while. In the meantime, I'd get into a bikini and sit by the pool.

If anyone had seen me at this moment they would have wondered why I looked like the cat that swallowed the canary. But why shouldn't I? I'd just kissed a very desirable man and even though my future was uncertain, I did have Eduardo the computer whiz searching for the real killer. But most important of all, I knew I would have a selection of bikinis I could never afford as a lowly tour group operative. Terribly shallow, I know, but there had to an upside to being a prisoner.

I headed to the dresser and pulled open a drawer. My fingers trailed through a colorful heap of string bikinis until finally I selected a pink and purple print. It looked flattering, I thought, as I critically gazed at myself in the mirror. I glanced down to make sure that tiny piece of material was tied tightly and then looked for a wrap. Carmelita hadn't forgotten a thing and in no time I was out at the pool with a paraeo wrapped around my waist, looking for a prime spot to lie on.

The day was bright, sunny, and getting hotter by the minute. The clear water in the kidney-shaped pool looked extremely inviting, and in fact, it would be one way to get out of Eduardo's line of vision. I dropped my towel on a chair and took off my paraeo, ready for a swim.

Eduardo slouched down in a lounge chair at the shaded end of the pool. Taking his boss's orders seriously, he eyed me from behind a pair of mirrored glasses. The harsh smoke from his cigarette drifted over with the breeze from the ocean.

Feeling uncomfortably warm, I made my way to the ladder, sat at the top, and stretched out my foot into the water. It was cool but most likely because the air temperature was not only hot but extremely humid. I glanced over at Eduardo. For all I knew he could be asleep behind those shades but I wouldn't bet on it. If he'd been told to watch me, Eduardo would do his job to the letter.

Gathering my courage, I sank deep into the water. My body shuddered in shock as I hit the refreshing water, but as I swam, I began to feel invigorated. I touched the rim at the far end and headed back to my starting point, repeating this several times until my arms tired.

Pulling myself up the ladder, I heard voices.

"Hola, amiga*!"* In a red sundress, Carmelita appeared on the deck. She dazzled me with a show-stopping smile. She was gorgeous with her shoulder-length light brown hair and willowy figure. Dark glasses covered her eyes. "You are so athletic, *cariño.* Diego will need to step up his gym routine to keep up with you. However," she said, perusing my body, "it does pay off. My models would do well to stop their dieting and start exercising." She giggled. "Lazy bitches." Handing me a fluffy, white towel from the basket near the lounge chairs, she perched on a chaise lounge and stage whispered, "He can't keep his eyes off you. The pervert must not have had a woman for a while." She smiled mischievously. "That side cleavage will have him in cardiac arrest."

Hastily, I pulled my top on before I took the chair beside her. The warm, ocean breeze felt pleasant on my damp skin.

Carmelita called out, "Eduardo, get us some water, *por favor.*"

I could see he was not in the least bit pleased with this directive. The corners of his mouth curved downward, but he did as she wanted and strode over to the bar.

"Clever way to get rid of him." I watched Eduardo busy himself getting glasses and ice.

Carmelita smirked. "He knew he couldn't very well refuse." She leaned in closer. "Did you finally succumb to Diego's advances or are you seriously in trouble like my brother said?" She snickered. "Or both?"

"They had a warrant to search my hotel room and came up with some pills planted in my purse. Someone wants the police to think I murdered Dean."

"So my brother thought he'd save you. That's one way to get rid of the competition. Next thing he'll have Wolf arrested." When she saw my expression, she added, "Just joking, amiga. He wouldn't do that." Seeing Eduardo with two glasses of ice water, she said loudly, "*Gracias*, but they need lime. You don't mind, do you, Eduardo?"

He set the glasses down and with his lips twisted in a grimace he returned to the bar.

"Don't worry, Adelina, we'll get you out of here for a while. Lourdes has reserved a table for us at the Museo. There'll be dancers performing all day. You won't have to be with him. We'll make him sit elsewhere. I doubt if a macho guy like that will want to sit with us females anyway."

An idea popped in my head. "Could I borrow your cell? Mine died."

Carmelita glanced at Eduardo returning with a dish full of lime slices. "If it's private I wouldn't say anything in front of him."

"No, it's not." On my cell contacts I found the number, as Eduardo placed the dish on the table.

Carmelita handed me the tongs for the lime. I plopped a slice of lime in each of our drinks and thanked Eduardo. He nodded and sat down on a nearby chair.

Taking the cell from Carmelita , I clicked in Janine's number and let it ring. "Hey, Janine. I was wondering if you can join me at the Museo? With Carmelita and Lourdes."

"Sure, when?"

I looked at Carmelita significantly. "Half an hour?"

She nodded.

"We'll be there for a while. No rush."

"Okay, see you, girlfriend."

When I heard the click on Janine's end, I turned to Carmelita. "That all right with you?"

Carmelita twirled her swivel stick. "She might have some interesting observations about the investors."

"Um-mm. That's what I was thinking. I need to find out who's framing me. If I can eliminate her, I'll feel better."

Carmelita grabbed my hand and squeezed it. "We'll get something out of Janine. You and I both know you didn't kill Dean. Someone is being very clever setting you up like this." She waved to Eduardo. "Hurry with those. We need to leave."

Eduardo protested, "Señora, you can't go anywhere with Señorita Sturm. Señor Alvarez said I must watch her."

"Of course, Eduardo, and you shall." Downing the last bit of water, Carmelita stood up and said imperiously, "Why don't you get the limo ready for us? Señorita Sturm needs to change."

Sipping the icy water, I watched this exchange, intrigued by Carmelita's skilful maneuvering.

Not to be outdone, Eduardo whistled and a huge Doberman came bounding out from the garden. I hadn't known he'd been there all this time. Good thing, too. With teeth pulled back, he eyed me like a thick grilling steak.

Eduardo grinned when he saw my expression. "Tequila!" Interestingly, with this word the snarling stopped. The hound from hell appeared decidedly less in attack mode.

"Sit, Diablo." At his master's orders, the dog plopped back on his haunches.

"Put out your fist for him to smell."

I have a great affection for my body parts. I wasn't quite ready to part with my hand, not just yet.

"Do it." Eduardo patted the hound's head. "He'll be your friend. You'll see."

Easy for him to say. But I gritted my teeth and extended my fist for Diablo to sniff. Nerves of steel. That's what it took.

Diablo hesitated and then gave my fist a lick.

"Now scratch him under the chin."

I would need a strong daiquiri when we got to the restaurant. Extending my fingers, I scratched Diablo under the chin.

Carmelita laughed. "Diego would be proud of you, amiga. Diablo hasn't had a snack yet this morning, has he, Eduardo?"

Eduardo nodded. "Señorita Sturm is a brave one. Señorita Lourdes didn't do so well with him."

Carmelita smiled. "Well, we did warn her she needed to be properly introduced to Diablo before she went out on the beach.

But no harm done, Eduardo. She knows better now."

"What happened?" I asked.

"When Lourdes went down for sun, Diablo followed her. He must have been attracted to her scent. Came right up to her and started licking her thigh. When she started screaming, Eduardo came down to rescue her." She remarked slyly, "I think he does that with all the pretty women, don't you, Eduardo?"

Eduardo smirked.

Carmelita set her drink down. "We'll see you at the limo in a half hour. Come, Adelina."

* * *

The Museo Restaurant was crowded but once the maitre d' caught sight of Carmelita he hurried over to show us to our table. Lourdes was already there with Janine and when she saw us she waved wildly, practically knocking her glass over. They had ordered a pitcher of strawberry daiquiris and by the look of it, were three sheets to the wind.

"Hey!" Janine called out, as we approached. "We've had a head start so you two better drink up."

I'd been to the museum but never to the restaurant on the upper floor. A pleasant, cooling breeze blew in from the sea. Out in the distance, cruise ships and ferries dotted the turquoise waters of the Caribbean. Down on the street, a troupe of dancers decked in blue satin costumes, the ladies in plumed headbands, began to line up for their performance. The street was buzzing with onlookers holding cameras while little children pressed against their parents, trying to get a better view.

"How'd you get here so fast?" Pouring myself a glass, I glanced at Eduardo seated at a small table against the wall. He lit a cigarette and stared back.

"Well, as it happened, I was down the street shopping at Cinco Soles when you phoned. I was just ready to take a break. Where've you been? I tried your room when I got back and you weren't there. I phoned a few times."

"Something happened."

"Oh?"

Lourdes, sensing some good gossip, leaned in closer.

"They had a warrant to search my hotel room and now I'm in Diego's custody."

"What?" Lourdes leaned forward. "Because of those pills they found in your bag?"

"That's crazy!" Janine rolled her eyes. "So what if they found some drugs?"

Lourdes nodded in agreement.

"The thing is they weren't mine. Someone planted them in my bag to link me to Dean's murder."

"That wouldn't seem to be enough to arrest you, amiga," Lourdes said in disbelief.

"Apparently, they're the same pills Dean took." I sipped my daiquiri slowly before I added. "He was stoned on ketamine."

"What's ketamine?" Carmelita tilted her head and gazed at me. "And why would that be important? Can't anyone buy it?"

"If you know someone like a vet who can hook you up with it, but ketamine is different, let's say, than ecstasy. This stuff left Dean immobile, allowing the murderer to cut his throat."

"O-oo!" Lourdes gasped. "And the police think you did it," she asked incredulously, "because he slept with you? That's your motive?" She giggled. "If I had killed everyone I slept with, who knows if there'd be any good-looking men left in this town."

Carmelita yawned dismissively. "Quit bragging, *chica.* You've never slept with Ricardo." She smiled. "He only has me in his heart."

"Hah! What about your Fede? Shouldn't you be more concerned with your husband?"

Carmelita laughed derisively. "The pond scum has probably slept with every woman in San Miguel, Playa, and Cancun and frankly my dear, I don't give a damn."

"That's the attitude, Carmelita." Janine held her glass high. "To friends!"

We clicked our glasses.

"Amiga," Carmelita said to Janine, "fill us in on the naughty stuff. I want to know if Samantha got what she wanted." When Lourdes raised a questioning eyebrow, she added, "I'm not talking about her investments. What happened with her and Wolf?"

"You mean the blond guy you were with, Adelina?" Lourdes perked right up. "He's so hot."

Carmelita barged in, "Sexy doesn't begin to describe him, Lourdes. Wolf is sweeter than honey. I'd say he's on par with a creamy Belgian truffle."

Visions of my sea god in his naked splendor popped into my head. "A man like that makes you forget you have a mind."

Janine laughed. "Brings on those blonde moments, eh? Wow, with both of you blond, you must be in heaven when you're together."

"Pleasure heaven." I smiled in satisfaction.

Janine poured herself another daiquiri. "Wolf was with Sam for dinner. Who knows what happened later."

That worried me. Samantha was a deadly viper capable of anything. I took a sip of my daiquiri and glanced down to the street below. I did a double take when I saw Jim cozied up to a slim tall man. "Did you know Jim's out there, Janine?"

Frowning, she got on her feet and peered out. Plastering a smile on her face, she turned back to us. "He said he'd come out here after he took a nap."

Lourdes tilted her head and studied Janine. "He likes to nap in the morning?"

"He sleeps all the time."

Lourdes giggled. "A real ball of fire. I wouldn't think you'd like a man like that? You look like a woman who likes some heat in her man."

Janine sighed. "Unfortunately, the will says I stay or I wait 'til I'm thirty to pass go."

"And in the meantime, he gets to spend your loot," Carmelita added, studying Jim and his companion. "He seems very friendly out there."

Janine's jaw clenched.

Sensing Janine's discomfort, I asked, "Is Wolf back?"

Carmelita looked surprised. "You don't know? Diego distracted you that much?"

I felt heat rise to my cheeks. "Diego has been great helping me, but you know Wolf and I are friends. It's just that I left the hotel in a hurry, didn't charge my phone and now it died."

Carmelita dug in her purse and took out her phone.

"Here, use mine. Call him."

With all of them looking expectantly at me, I punched in Wolf's number and waited. A husky voice said, "*Hola.*"

"It's me."

"You okay?"

"I'm at the Museo Restaurant with friends. Are you back?"

"I'm in Playa, baby. What happened? Alvarez with you?"

Three pairs of eyes watched me. "No, not right now. I had to borrow Carmelita's phone. Mine died."

"You can't speak, can you?"

"Not really."

"I should be there later. Dinner tonight, or are you with Alvarez?"

"Don't know."

"I need to see you, spicy woman."

"Mm-mm," I was thinking the same thing. The cadence of his voice brought on strange restless yearnings.

"You teased me unmercifully in that cenote—so much woman in a skimpy bikini."

Tingly sensations awakened my core. I shifted restlessly in my chair.

"It was beautiful there. But not for long. When you left it rained and it kept on raining and in fact, it's still raining now." He paused. "I felt like that inside after you'd gone."

I sighed, thinking the same. An emptiness that hadn't ever been filled.

"I went through the motions at the meeting. We need to get together, babe. I want to be with you."

"Mm-mm," I said in agreement. His lean strong body was made for loving. I could imagine my hands running over his skin, kissing every part of him and finally returning to taste his sensuous mouth.

"Adie?" His voice sounded distant. "You there?"

"It might be difficult tonight."

"Alvarez? You staying at his house?"

"Yes and..."

"The police? They giving you a hard time?"

"Um-hmm."

"Bad?"

"Yes."

"Alvarez do anything about the police?"

"He sure did."

"And now you owe him," Wolf said quickly.

"Worse."

"Shit."

"Um-hmm."

"I found out something. Tell you when I see you. Got to go. Stay strong."

"Bye, Wolf."

"Kisses."

I leaned back in my chair, closing my eyes a moment— imagining the two of us in that mirror with chocolate body butter smeared all over our hot, sweaty bodies. With a sigh, I opened my eyes and gave the cell back to Carmelita.

Lourdes clasped her hands together, her expression dreamy. "Wolf's romantic, isn't he, Adelina? You are so lucky to have a man like that."

I smiled, lost in his words.

"Well, what happened? Did he tell you about Sam?" Janine broke the silence. "Is he cheating on you?"

Lourdes piped up, "That's stupid, Janine. How can she tell something like that on the phone? You know you have to look into a man's eyes to see if he's lying!" She glanced at us for confirmation.

Carmelita nodded wisely.

"You were there, Janine. Did Sam say something?" I asked.

"She didn't have to. I know her, Adie. She's workin' him."

"But you and Jim left early?"

"Yup. Said he had to do something," she said, her eyes on the street.

I followed her glance. Dancers dressed in green spun around in a lively salsa in front of a captive audience but it was Jim and his friend that held my attention. He reminded me of Wolf—tall and athletic. There was something intimate about the way the taller man leaned down to Jim.

"It must be a problem," Lourdes said solemnly, "being married to a gay man."

Janine shot her a look. "Only if he blows my money."

Carmelita flashed a smile. "So he buys a few trinkets for his boy toy. No harm in that but watch it if he buys him cars and diamonds. Now that could get expensive." She waved down the waiter who hastened to our table. "*Huevos rancheros*."

"Waffles, *por favor*," I said. It wasn't Mexican but sometimes it's good to forget about calories and enjoy something decadent.

"That sounds good," Janine said, with Lourdes nodding in agreement.

Carmelita rolled her eyes. "You're a bad influence, Adelina. Soon these two will look like they've visited Ixchel. I don't care about Janine but please not my top model."

Janine looked puzzled.

"Ixchel is the goddess of the moon, the sea and fertility," I explained. "Mayans thought Cozumel was the center of the earth where Earth children multiplied like bees from a hive. Women rowed twelve miles from Playa to pay homage to the goddess."

"And you're the lucky recipient of her jewelry," Carmelita quipped. "*Chicas*, Adelina had both Diego and Wolf give her these fantastic pieces. I was so jealous. Ricardo needs to be more generous if he wants me to cater to his needs."

This time Lourdes rolled her eyes. "Ricardo worships the ground you walk on when he's not with his dragon wife. She's the…"

The waiter interrupted her story, setting our orders in front of us.

With the daiquiris being so powerful, I needed the food to sober up. I had two potential suspects in front of me after all. "Carmelita, I need to do some research for work. Do you think," I jerked my chin towards Eduardo, "he'd let me go to the square?"

Carmelita giggled. "*Si*, but you'll have to walk with him or he'll take you right back to Diego's. Think you can handle it?"

I forked up a mouthful of waffle. "I think I'll have to, unless you can come along too?"

"Can't. Have to get some clothes ready for my show tonight at the Hotel Maria." She dug in her purse and handed me some tickets. "Here are a couple of tickets if you want to come with someone. Oops, I forgot. You need to be with Diego or Eduardo, don't you?" She shrugged. "Well, keep them anyway. You might be free by then. Diego's got Eduardo working on it, doesn't he?"

"He gave us a brief report this morning but I'd like your take."

"On what?"

"Dean."

"I told you the story." She pushed back her bangs. "The man was annoying me and I sent Churo to straighten him out."

Lourdes raised an eyebrow.

Carmelita wiggled in her seat. "It's true."

"Everyone thought you were having a fling with him," Janine said sweetly. "The perv was red hot for you after Adie refused him.

"*Mierda!* Who told you that?" Carmelita glared at Janine.

"The man was a player. Not at all my type. Tell her, Lourdes. You know how much I adore Ricardo."

"I'm not the only one who thought that. Sam said he was about to dump her because of you."

Carmelita clenched her jaw. "That's crazy. I merely flirted with Dean—nothing more." She cut into her eggs.

"And then when he got crazy you sent someone over to fix him."

Carmelita brought her knife up. "You're *loca*, Janine! I didn't cause his death, nor did Churo."

Janine's eyes narrowed. "You're a Bolivar Alvarez," she said, her voice edgy. "Diego is like the godfather! If Dean irritated you bigtime, that man," her eyes flicked to Eduardo, "would make sure he wasn't a problem—permanently."

"You know what, Janine?" Carmelita's voice rose an octave. "Just because I'm a Bolivar Alvarez, doesn't mean I'd arrange that scumbag's murder!" She leaned forward, glaring at Janine. "You and Terry have the most to gain and you know it!"

This whole thing was getting out of control, with them both yelling. "Why don't we forget about Dean and his murder. Sorry I brought it up. These waffles are delicious."

"You're right. This is stupid," Janine said. "I apologize, Carmelita. Let's forget about that creep," she stood and started refilling our glasses, "and party."

Somewhat mollified, Carmelita took up her glass and sipped it slowly. "You're right. No need for us to argue on this glorious day. We must not let a little thing like Dean's murder break up our friendship. Why don't you tell us your plans now that you have a small fortune."

"Rio," Janine smiled, "Europe maybe, and definitely Malaysia."

"And Jim," I said, meeting her eyes, "is he included?"

"I think he should go back to Toronto." Janine poured syrup on her waffles. "He's needed at the business."

"What exactly does he do?"

"He was Dean's right hand, CEO. Yeah, I know, looks way too young, but he's a genius, you know."

"By the way, girlfriend," I said, in between forkfuls of waffle, "was meaning to ask—what happened with you and Juan Jose?"

Janine grinned mischievously. "You name it—it happened."

"Ooo-oo," Lourdes moaned. "He's so hot. Have you seen his tats?" she asked me.

"No," I said, "what and where?"

"An eagle on his bicep and way low on his abs, a cobra. Isn't that cool?"

"If he's so hot, why did you let your mother have him?" Carmelita remarked tartly.

Janine clenched her jaw. "Dean said if I married Jim I wouldn't need to work."

"Dean made you ditch Juan Jose?" Carmelita's eyes widened. "That is so old fashioned."

"Let's say there was no way he was having JJ as his son-in-law and he knew I liked money too much to give it all up for love. Besides, I thought maybe I could still see JJ."

I cleaned my sunglasses with the edge of the table cloth. "Why would Dean go to such lengths?"

Lourdes moved in closer, sensing some dark secret.

Janine lowered her voice, her eyes flitting nervously from side to side. "All I know is, JJ is dangerous—more dangerous than you'd ever imagine. Dean didn't want him near us."

"Whoa," Lourdes breathed out the word, "a bad boy. Terry is so lucky."

"I wonder if he's wicked in bed." Carmelita raised an eyebrow and stared at Janine.

Janine smirked.

Lourdes picked up a corn chip and dipped it into the salsa. "So convenient that Dean died."

"He didn't just die, Lourdes," I said, "he was murdered—his throat cut."

"And Hernan thinks you did it, Adelina," Carmelita pointed out. "Did they find the knife?"

"Not as far as I know. The murderer must have gotten rid of the thing."

"Unless he was stupid." Carmelita shoved her plate away. "You know the killer could have been with him. First they smoked some weed and..."

I eyed her. "How'd you know about the weed, Carmelita?"

Carmelita smiled mysteriously. "All his women knew how much he liked the stuff. He got stoned all the time. Said it made him function better. Did you know he had an attention deficit disorder?" She signaled the waiter and he brought over the bill. "Charge it all to my account." Carmelita stood up. "If you want to go to the square, Adelina, I'll tell Eduardo." Smiling in a queenly fashion, she directed with her chin. "Come Lourdes. *Adios, chicas.*"

10

We sat at a small table. Music from a mariachi band playing in the park filled the air. In front of us, quiet protestors in afro wigs and blue print dresses waved signs at the patrons of the Mexicano Restaurant.

"What's that all about?" I said, watching them marching back and forth.

"The environmentalists are not happy about the sand from the east coast being moved to the west coast resorts."

"Hm-mm. A lot of us are not happy."

Eduardo's jaw tightened. "I am working on your situation, Señorita Sturm." He snarled. "As you pointed out, there are many suspects in Firenze's murder. It's not simple." His eyes lit on something outside my view. "*Caramba!*" He grabbed my arm tightly. "Don't look now, but there's a man that could be Firenze's double sitting at the bar."

I pursed my lips thoughtfully. "Dale. It must be him. He's a dead ringer for Dean. I saw him out at the resort. Did you find out anything more about him?"

Eduardo lit a cigarette. "No."

The waiter placed a bowl of salsa on our table and looked at us expectantly. I dipped a corn chip into the red sauce.

"What are you having?" Eduardo asked impatiently.

I hesitated after the daiquiris at the Museo.

"How about a margarita?"

"I'm not sure I should drink anything."

"Señor Alvarez would not like it."

"All right, I wouldn't want to get you into trouble. A margarita *sin sal,* please." I stared at Eduardo. "You are very careful to do whatever Señor Alvarez wants."

"I'm not a fool, Señorita Sturm. I take my job seriously."

"Glad to hear it. Take a look and see if he's with anyone."

Eduardo glanced fleetingly over to the bar. "A big *hombre.* Mean looking."

I rolled my eyes—this coming from someone who ate nails for

breakfast.

When the waiter returned with a margarita, I took a sip. Frosty, green and powerful—in other words, a perfect margarita.

"You drink those without salt?" Edurardo scoffed.

"I don't like salt in my diet."

"You're *loca*...crazy. The tequila needs the salt."

"That's your opinion and you're entitled to one."

My Logical Voice added, Yes, you are. I'm sure someone appreciates your stupid opinions, Slugface.

Of course, I didn't say that. I'm not suicidal. A guy like that would probably, at worst, whip out his knife and slice my throat or, at best, pound me one. I had a feeling his punch would be a lot worse than Delores' backhanded slaps. Eduardo was wiry but there was a steel-like strength in those muscles.

"I'll go over and see if I can overhear anything. You stay here." With that Eduardo strode over to the bar. Posturing in a macho fashion, he checked out the females at a nearby table before he engaged the bartender in conversation.

I wasn't sure if Dale would remember me. After all, I had only had a glimpse of him myself at the nudist resort. I looked totally different today in my flimsy turquoise top, miniskirt, and high heeled silver sandals. Wouldn't it be better for me to be there, listening in? That's what I told myself as I headed over.

The bartender glanced at me as he dried a glass with a towel. "*Si*, Señorita?"

"A margarita *sin sal,* please." On my tiptoes I pulled myself up onto the barstool beside Dale. It was stupid to order another drink after the first, but what else was I to do? I avoided looking anywhere near Eduardo, who was standing beside the massive man in the white linen suit. My nose twitched from the smoke drifting my way.

"Pardon my friend, pretty lady. He's forgotten his manners." Dale glanced at the thug. "Mario, put out that cigar. You kin see the littl' lady doesn't like it." He jerked his chin up. "Wachya name, honeh?"

"Adie." I tried not to freeze. He looked so uncannily like his brother. But with his American accent I knew he wasn't. "Where are you from?"

"Here, there, and everywhere." His eyes shot to my cleavage.

"Nice outfit," he said softly.

Mario seemed to like my cleavage as well, but after Dale gave him a warning look, he stubbed out his cigar and directed his gaze to my face.

"What kind of work do you do, er...?"

"Dale." He extended his hand. "Gonna be here long? Ah mean, in Coz?"

"For a few days."

"On vacation?"

"Sort of. I'm doing some research on the Carnaval."

"Sounds like mah sort of job. You alone?"

"Sometimes." I gave him a wicked look. Bond girls —move over! Adie Sturm was getting the goods on this dude.

Dale's eyes swept over my body, starting at my chest and slowly wandered down to my legs, where they stopped for a second at my silver sandals before they made their way back up to my face. "You married?"

"Not yet. What did you say you did in the States?"

"Um-mm." Dale chuckled, glancing sidelong at Mario. "Didn't say, did I, gorgeous? But if you have time we could have some lunch, watch the action, and get to know each other." He turned to Mario. "See you at the hotel?"

"But," the big man protested, "we haven't gone over the figures yet!"

Dale patted the gorilla on his heavy shoulder. "No *problema*, as they say in Mexican."

I coughed. "No rush. I wouldn't want to interrupt your business. Go ahead, I'll wait."

Mario nodded and pulled out a leather notebook. "Here's what we got for the last quarter, Mr. Firenze."

Dale frowned as he surveyed the columns. "Ah think we could do better. What do ya have for Vegas?"

Mario flipped a few pages and showed Dale the book.

I tried to peak, leaning into Dale's arm. The smile on his face grew wider when he felt my breast nudging his arm.

"These ain't bad." He glanced over at me. "Ah'll be done in a minute, honeh." His eyes flicked to the book. "Get some info on the new site. We'll meet up in the hotel in two hours."

A loud vibrating noise sounded and everyone looked over at

Eduardo. He tugged out his phone and after a few words, left his beer and strolled over to the back of the restaurant to speak in private. I strained to hear Mario as he muttered something under his breath, but I couldn't quite catch the drift of it. While Dale was flipping through the notebook searching for information, I stared at him. It was like being with the ghost of Dean Firenze. I couldn't help feeling a little strange about it.

I was halfway done with my drink by the time Edurardo came back. I looked away in case he was anxious to go. It wouldn't do to leave Dale without further investigation.

"Let's get a table." Getting off his stool, Dean jabbed Mario on the arm with his fist in one of those guy-bonding things. "Seeya, okay, bud? Later."

Mario grinned back. A diamond embedded in his front tooth glittered in the sun.

Dale placed his hand at the small of my back and steered me to the table nearest the park. "Pretty place, eh?" He pulled out a chair for me.

"I guess you must have spent some time in Canada," I said, sitting down.

He took the chair next to me, looking puzzled.

"Eh. That's what Canadians say."

Dale squinted. "A smart blonde."

I smiled. "It happens."

Dale tweaked my cheek. "Nice to have that combination— brains and beauty. Sometimes, I miss talkin' to a female."

"Enjoy the moment, then."

"Smart ass."

"I can be."

His dark brown eyes examined me carefully. "Something tells me you aren't quite what you seem. Tell me why we're really having this conversation."

I smiled seductively at Dale. "Because you're a man and I'm a woman. Isn't that reason enough?"

The waiter came over to our table and said, "*Buenos tardes, Señoros.* What can I get you?" He looked at me.

"Water."

"Bring us *dos* margaritas, yeah, two." Dale added, "You're joining me, Adie. I'm not drinkin' alone."

This was a dilemma. The man had information and I needed to get it. If I stopped drinking, that would mess things up with Dale. Problem was I'd already had a few drinks.

"A hot babe like you shouldn't be so serious. Let's have fun, eh?"

"Is this your first time here, Dale?" I said, running my fingers down my strap and letting them trail down to my breast.

His eyes followed my fingers before they shot back to my face. "The island, yeah," he paused a second, "but ah've been to the Mayan Riviera a few times. Was hopin' to set something up there."

"Like what?"

The waiter brought over our drinks. I had a sip of water first. I didn't need a hangover later and at the same time it would give me a break from the effects of the margaritas.

Dale brought his glass up to his lips and looked at me. "Drink up, honeh. Party time."

I put my glass down. "Not sure I can drink this. I've had enough."

"You drivin'?"

"No."

He handed me my drink. "In that case, like ah said, it's party time. Where you from?"

"Toronto. You know where that is?"

"Um. Ah knew someone that lived there."

"Doesn't live there anymore?"

"Died."

"Sorry to hear that."

"Can't say ah am. I know I should be, but ah ain't." Dale stared out at the park.

"Relative?"

"Why'd you say that?"

"I always find relatives the worst."

"You're right. They are."

"Close?"

He nodded. "My brother. I was three years older. Had a business together for a while but ah didn't like the way he operated."

"What did you do about it?"

"Ah split for Vegas. He stayed in Toronto." He shifted to me.

"What kind of things do ya like to do?"

"Well, when I'm on vacation, I like to play blackjack but," I deliberately pouted, "Cozumel doesn't have any casinos."

"You're right, honeh. That's what Mexico needs. Makes it fun, doesn't it?" He tilted his head and gave me a direct look. "You have nice eyes."

I smiled and said softly, "Thanks," with one of those sultry looks from under my lashes. "You've been to Atlantic City?"

"Yeah, did business there. What about you?"

I sipped my margarita. "I liked Vegas better. Warm desert breezes—very romantic with the right man." I was trying to flirt but in the back of my mind I was making sure he wasn't Dean's ghost.

"Lots to do there besides the gambling. You said you were alone on this trip?"

"For now."

He put his hand on mine. "Not any more you're not, honeh." The ghost of Dean winked at me. I giggled.

He looked at me in amusement. "Why don't you finish that one and I'll show you my hotel?"

I was buzzed, not stupid. "I'm having too much fun with you to go anywhere. But your drink is almost done."

As if on signal the waiter appeared. "*Mas,* Señor?"

"Sure, make it *dos*."

Any more drinks for me and the place would start spinning. "You have any other brothers or sisters?"

Dale's mouth curled down. "Had another brother, a year younger. He died."

"Died! Him too?"

"The three of us were goin' to Detroit. We all got wasted. Dean was driving. Derek was in the back lying down. No seat belt. Never made it to the hospital."

"I'm sorry, Dea... Dale. No wonder you're angry."

"Yeah, ah am. Dale was a druggie and even after that accident, he didn't change. Maybe got worse."

"You said Dean died. How?"

"Someone slit his throat."

"That's awful!" I had a sudden playback of the blood seeping through the towel covering Dean. The margarita started to rise up.

I closed my mouth and willed it to go back down.

"That piece of shit deserved it."

"Where did it happen? Toronto?"

"No, here."

"Cozumel?"

"He and his wife were stayin' at the Primavera Hotel." He set his empty glass down. "You don't wanna talk about this."

"I don't mind. It's bothering you, isn't it?

Dale's dark eyes burrowed into mine. "The way he was murdered was brutal. Someone came up from behin' him and cut his main artery."

"Why?"

"Why do it or why do it like that?"

"Both."

"Dean screwed people left and right." He took up his glass and drank deeply before he continued, "It could be he screwed the wrong people."

"Like?"

Dale frowned. "There's some people you don't cheat. Could be they decided to make an example of him."

"Why Cozumel?"

"Perfect place. Blame it on the Mexican hoodlums." He glanced at my half-empty glass. "Drink up. Enough serious talk. A sweet babe like you needs to relax." He whispered in my ear. "I have strong sexual needs."

"You do?"

He nodded.

"Me too."

"I know. I can tell."

"How?"

"You have that look in your eyes that speaks sex. It's a 'take me if you dare' look."

So that was why Diego thought I'd go for a chocolate-coated-him.

We were interrupted by a discreet cough. "Excuse me," the waiter said, "but there's a phone call for you, Señorita. If you'll follow me, please?"

"Sorry, Dale. My cell died and I left this number for a friend to reach me." When I got to my feet, I was very much aware of the potency of the margaritas I'd consumed. Navigation with my four inch stilettos was definitely a challenge as I made my way around the tables and up the steps to the next level. I steadied myself with my hand against the wall, puzzled by the phone call. Who would know I was here?

11

The waiter directed me down a narrow hallway to a small office. When I entered, Eduardo was inside, standing with an older man, whom I assumed to be the owner of the restaurant.

"*Buenos dias,* Señorita Sturm. I am Alberto Perrara. I hope you enjoyed my restaurant?"

I shook his hand and said, "Adie Sturm. *Si,* very much."

Eduardo interrupted abruptly, "Señorita Sturm, we must leave. We'll go out the back way."

"Why? I'm getting Dale to tell me about Dean."

"Don't be stupid. Firenze can't wait to get you in bed."

"You heard that?"

"I didn't have to. It was obvious."

"Okay, Eduardo. We'll play it your way. I guess I got everything I could out of him." I twirled around to go, but my balance was slightly off and I grabbed the little owner to steady myself.

"Señorita, are you...are you all right?" He stuttered nervously as I pressed close to his chest.

"*Si.*" I flushed. In embarrassment, I stepped away.

The short man grinned broadly. "You are very beautiful, Señorita." He gave me a card. "Give that to the waiter next time and you will have a free dinner."

I stuck it into my bag and smiled. "*Gracias,* Señor."

"Enough!" Eduraro hissed through gritted teeth.

Señor Perrara took my elbow and with Eduardo's arm around my waist, I was escorted to the back door. "Come quickly, before he discovers you are leaving!"

"*Hasta Luego!*" Perrara called out and waved.

I gave him a smile back before Edurado hustled me out into the street. From there it was a short block to where he'd parked the limo.

"You moved the car, Eduardo." I squinted into the bright sunlight at the silver Mercedes.

Eduardo scowled. "Had to. I didn't think I'd be able to carry you back to the Museo Restaurant."

I giggled. "You're smarter than you look, Eduardo."

"If you weren't Señor Alvarez's woman, you'd be learning your lesson right here and now."

"Which would be…"

"Who the man is here."

These Spanish guys were so medieval. No, I was wrong. Diego was way too cosmopolitan to think like that. "Well, I guess you'll have to practice your macho stuff on some primitive female out of touch with the twenty-first century. There might be one in Coz but I wouldn't bet on it."

Eduardo scowled, opened the door for me, and shoved me into the car seat. Regardless of what I thought of him, I knew he was working hard to uncover information about the investors. I had to ease off. It wouldn't be wise to alienate him at this point.

As he drove through the side streets to get back to Avenida Raphael Melgar, he informed me in a more reasonable tone, "Señor Alvarez phoned. He was concerned as to why you weren't answering your cell."

"I couldn't. My phone died. My charger is back at the hotel."

"I see." His eyes flicked back at me from the mirror. "Señor Alvarez said he's unable to return tonight, so you won't be required on the float. He wanted me to remind you that tomorrow is the big night of the Carnaval—Fat Tuesday. He has invited guests to his float."

"Who?"

"The investors with his company."

I sank back in my chair. "That's good. It'll give me a chance to find out more about them. Don't forget you're checking out Juan Jose."

Eduardo glanced at me over his shoulder. "If you stay in your room tonight, and give me no further cause for concern, I will do some research, but remember, I am also in charge of security. I have rounds to do."

"Well, think of it this way, Eduardo. The sooner I can prove my innocence, the sooner I'll be out of your hair." I fixed my eyes on the back of his head. His hair was cut in a military crew cut. If I were in his hair, I would easily fall out. I giggled. "Were you ever in the army, Eduardo?"

He grunted something which I took to be a yes.

Hm—mm. That accounted for his rigidity. He was the kind of guy who ordered his girlfriend around. Treated her like a slave. I recalled the fashion show tickets I had. Fashion shows weren't just for women and gays. A real man, like Wolf could enjoy the models and at the same time be attentive to the woman he was with.

Surprisingly, my wild man had attended a fashion show and we'd had a great time together. Carmelita had put on quite the performance for the Days of the Dead Fashion. So, yes, Wolf was capable of doing something that would have been intimidating to a lesser man, if he was with a woman he liked.

My Hormone Voice added: He doesn't just like you, Adie. Get real! The man would climb mountains for you. But, before you get a swelled head, don't forget he also has a viper latched onto him— one that's injecting her venom into him as I speak.

Shut up, my Logical Voice snapped. Wolf is only digging into Sam's story. He'll get here. He's worth waiting for.

Wolf isn't psychic. He doesn't know where she is, does he? Hormone argued. She'll be forced to explore the Diego option. Hormone snickered. It's a sacrifice, but what's a girl gonna do?

By the time we arrived at the beach house, I was feeling the after effects of those margaritas.

"Come, Señorita Sturm." Edurado helped me out of the limo and guided me up to the front door. "Louisa has dinner ready for you." He shouted, "Louisa!" tapping his foot impatiently while we waited.

Flustered, Louisa appeared, her hands clasped nervously as she eyed Eduardo. "*Si,* Señor?"

"Take Señorita Sturm to her room and make sure she has everything she needs. It would be preferable if she has dinner up there. Stay with her. I have things to do."

"Wait, Eduardo, there's something else I need to tell you."

"What?" he snapped, glaring at me.

"Jim Langley. I found out he's gay. You need to find out what he's buying for his boyfriend. Don't you see? If he needed the money, he would have done the crime!"

"A man is only capable of so much in one day. I'm sure the police won't arrest you by tomorrow. Things take time here in Mexico. Do some womanly things. I'm sure Señora Alvarez left some nail polish for you. Paint your toenails." He added sarcastically, "That should keep you busy."

"Good thinking, but I have a better idea," I said with a grin. "Señora Alvarez gave me two tickets for the fashion show. Why don't we go together? You'd love..."

Eduardo's eyes shot daggers. If looks could kill, I would be on a slab—dead.

Afraid I'd pushed him over the edge, Louisa pulled me along up the staircase. "You look tired. Let me help you, Señorita Sturm."

This was not such a bad idea. Although my speech was smooth enough, my body had stopped obeying my brain. I allowed her to slowly guide me to my room.

Once inside, she remembered to breathe. Color returned to her cheeks. "Señorita, it is not wise to tease Eduardo. He has what you call a short fuse. Let me help you change and then I shall bring you some supper."

Help was most welcome, especially as I became acutely aware of my unsteady high-heeled saunter over to the bed. I barely made it before I caved and plopped down. Heaven knows that wasn't my only problem. My parched throat felt like I'd trekked through the Sahara for the last two days. The miserable after-effects that comes from too much alcohol.

"Water?" I croaked.

"You have a mini-bar in this room, Señorita. Did you know? I will bring you a drink. Wait here." She trotted off to the far side of the room and retrieved a bottle.

It was easy enough to sprawl on the bed and have Louisa do the energetic stuff. She hadn't been forced to drink in the pursuit of justice. While I sipped the chilled water, Louisa selected lacy blue lingerie and a matching, silk robe. I was impressed. The lady had good taste. It was that same outfit I had hesitated to wear my first night—a V-necked baby doll and a lacey thong. She turned away politely while I changed and then handed me the short silky peacock-blue robe. Louisa was pleasant enough company and she didn't seem to be in a hurry to leave. Could be she was glad to be hiding up here with me, no more anxious to encounter Eduardo downstairs than I was.

Smart woman. The guy was in a foul mood and I had the feeling he was fed up with babysitting me.

But I wasn't any happier with my situation. With all the tidbits I'd heard this afternoon, I still wasn't any closer to determining who Dean's killer was and to make matters worse, I was alone tonight without either of my delicious hotties. I couldn't even do any Carnaval research cooped up in here. I would be bored out of my mind. How I longed to be out of here. I glanced out the window into the light of dusk and thought I saw a flashlight.

Louisa followed my gaze. "It's one of the security guards, probably Javier." She shuddered. "Or it could be Eduardo doing his rounds with Diablo. They do them every hour. Believe me, I feel as much a prisoner as you tonight. Normally, I leave right after supper. I don't know what's wrong with Eduardo. It's not as if you'd be running off, is it?"

"No, you heard him, I'll be painting my nails—womanly stuff."

Louisa's lips curled upwards. "I'll get you your dinner."

"Will you join me?"

"I shouldn't."

"Bring something for yourself. I'd like your company."

Louisa smiled briefly. "Thank you, Señorita. I'll be right back."

I watched her shut the door behind her. Thoughts jumbled in my brain. Someone I knew murdered Dean and was trying, successfully, I might add, to set me up. Why me?

Maybe I should start there. Who hated me? Obviously, there was Samantha. With me out of the way, she would have the money and chance at Wolf. I pushed my hair away from my neck and lay back down on the bed.

Sam could have done it. In fact, what would have been more perfect? I recalled Janine with Sam that night. Stoned for sure— both of them. So she smokes some weed with Dean and then murders him. Later, she appears with Janine as an alibi. She incriminates me, saying she didn't see me with Wolf. That way she clears him.

My thoughts raced to the nudist resort. Sam could have placed the ketamine in my bag and then gone off to meet Wolf at the cenote. What an ingenious plan. But there was only one thing that didn't quite fit.

Louisa knocked before she swung the door open. She was carrying a tray loaded with covered plates and she placed it on the table. "I brought some garlic soup and some fish. You like fish?"

"Um-mm," I said, getting up slowly.

Louisa raced over. "Let me help you, Señorita. You are quite pale."

When she had me seated at the round table, I lifted a lid and at the sight of the soup my mouth watered. "Mm-mm. It looks fabulous. You are a very talented chef. I haven't told you how much I enjoyed the breakfast you made."

"Gracias, Señorita. You are too kind."

"Did you bring anything for yourself?"

"Soup, as well. Is that all right?" Louisa took the seat across from me.

"Of course. I hate eating alone." I lifted the lids off the soup and pushed the bowls closer to us. *"Salud."* I raised my icy bottle of water.

"Salud! It's too bad Señor Alvarez has been delayed in Cancun. But I'm sure the party tomorrow night will be spectacular."

"From what I've seen so far, the Carnaval rivals the Mardi Gras." I spooned up the soup. "Delicious, Louisa."

She smiled. "Garlic is not the food of love but it's healthy."

"True." Where was my hot lover, anyway?

Seeing my expression, she said quickly, "Sorry, I shouldn't have said anything, especially when there isn't a man here with you tonight." She perked up. "You must know Señor Alvarez has romantic thoughts about you, and he will be sad he is unable to be here." Her eyes took on a dreamy expression. "We all think Señor Alvarez is *muy guapo*. Do you?"

"Mm-mm, he certainly is a sexy man but I'm not the only one who thinks so."

She paused, her spoon raised. "You mean the rich lady, Señorita Karges?"

The name was familiar but didn't ring a bell.

"Barbara Karges from Texas."

"Oh, yes." I thought back to November, my last time in Cozumel. I had met her. "A tall redhead?"

Louisa nodded.

"Do you know if she was invited to the Fat Tuesday fiesta on the float?"

"She had an invitation along with many of Cozumel's society people. All the guests were to receive a costume from Señora

155

Alvarez. Her designer and his staff have had to work hard to make these so quickly." She smirked. "Luckily the material is scanty for the women and well the men—they had better be in good shape to wear only those *pantalones*."

"How will he get everyone on the float?"

Louisa grinned. "He has three floats reserved for Fat Tuesday. Señor Alvarez wanted his clients and potential investors all to be there." She leaned forward and whispered conspiratorially, "Is it true Señor Du Lac is your *novio*? I heard he will be there." She clasped her hands together and sighed. "He is very handsome, your Señor Du Lac."

I nodded. "I wanted to go to the fashion show with Wolf but I can't now. I'm stuck here with that man outside." I studied Louisa. "Would you like the tickets?"

Louisa beamed. "You would give them to me? You are indeed generous, Señorita Sturm."

I set my spoon down and walked over to my tote bag, took out the tickets, and handed them to her just as rapping sounded at the door. Going over, I swung it open. I was surprised to see Eduardo standing there, notebook in hand.

His eyes took in my short silk robe and high heeled slippers. "Waiting for me?" he asked, a glint of undeniable lust in his eyes. He peered over my shoulder and noticed Louisa. "You still here? It's not necessary for you to stay any longer."

Louisa shot me a worried look. "The Señorita did ask me to join her."

Eduardo frowned. "I'll come back later."

"You have some information for me?"

"Why don't we speak after you're done with your supper?"

"No, I'll be busy, remember—painting my toenails? Why don't you come in and give me your report?"

Eduardo's eyes journeyed up my legs before he glanced over at Louisa who had turned back to her soup. Coming in, he sprawled himself out on the sofa, his legs hanging over the edge, and waited for me to return to the table.

"Go ahead," I said, sitting back down.

"Langley recently bought two Jeeps, neither one of which was for his wife."

"Anything else?"

"A square cut diamond—a man's ring. That's all I have on him. But I did find out something about the security guard, Juan Jose."

I shoved my bowl away and took the lid off the fish. "He was from Central America."

"Right—but I'll get to that. First…you know he was involved with Janine Firenze before he became Teresa Firenze's lover. That is strange, wouldn't you say? Also, I found out our friend is forty-six and has only been in Mexico for the last year."

"He looks way younger." I thought back to that super buff bod that was only thinly disguised by his black uniform. In fact, the uniform enhanced his svelte appearance. Men in uniforms—hm-mm. There was something very sexy about that.

"Was he here, working at the hotel?"

"Since the time he met Janine Firenze. Before that, who knows?"

"A coincidence you think?"

Eduardo studied my legs a moment before he replied, "Perhaps I am too suspicious but he's made sure his past is untraceable. In my opinion, he's a man to be reckoned with. Nicaragua is like many of these Central and South American countries. It has a history of violence."

I started on my fish, thinking about what he said. "So he might have been involved in some sort of subversive activity?"

"It's possible."

Louisa covered the empty soup bowls and placed them back on the tray and got up.

I was worried with the looks Eduardo had given me. "Please stay."

"Louisa has a family to go home to. Javier and I will be here if you need anything."

The housekeeper glanced at me and said, "Strange those lights we saw outside."

"We were outside," Eduardo said dismissively. "You should know that."

I got up and walked over to the window. "There were several flashlights, weren't there, Louisa?"

Eduardo shot up from the couch to join me. "Where?"

I glanced back at Louisa, who said quietly, "Near the entrance. I was about to go down and tell you about them."

"You stupid woman!" Eduardo growled at Louisa. "Why didn't you say anything about this before? I'll go down and check the grounds." He marched out, slamming the door behind him.

Louisa carried the tray to the open door and paused. "I hate that man!"

I grinned. "But you spoiled his plan."

Louisa giggled. "I did, didn't I? Now hopefully he won't bother you tonight."

"I'll keep the door locked."

"Don't worry. I'll take the key from his chain before I go. Even if he wants to visit you tonight, he'd have to break the door down and that wouldn't look too good to Señor Alvarez."

I stopped in the midst of helping Louisa load the tray. "Do you think he'd really try?"

"The man is capable of anything. I'm sure he'd fabricate something to explain himself to Señor Alvarez if he had to. I have a bad feeling about this. I don't want to leave you with him."

"Thank you, Louisa," I said, touching her hand. "I'm sure I'll be all right."

"*Buenos noches,* Señorita. You must lock the door. I don't trust him—the way he looks at you." She headed out into the hallway and I closed the door behind her.

And then, I did as she suggested—locked the door.

12

When I'm stressed I feel the need to do something physical but they hadn't given me any workout clothes. I needed some busy work while I thought about my situation so I trundled over to the washroom and came up with a base coat and a bright red nail. For a badass, Eduardo was smarter than I'd thought. He'd suggested getting out the nail polish as a joke but I know for a fact nail polish was a good thing—for me and for my man, Wolf. He loved my feet and especially liked bright polish on my toenails. And applying it was always somewhat therapeutic. Besides, red made me feel brave. It was the color of the warrior.

Taking everything over to the table, I settled myself down on the couch, restlessly shifting to get comfortable. I was definitely on edge and needed a distraction. Some mindless television? I grabbed the controller and switched on a police investigative program with Spanish subtitles. That would do, I thought, pushing the toe-separators in place. Starting the painstaking task of applying nail polish, I kept an eye on the door. Zoning out for a while, I watched the heroine getting in and out of trouble.

When the show ended, I could no longer avoid the problem. Even though I had secured the door, I was worried, having seen the look in Eduardo's eyes. He would be difficult to stop if he was determined to force himself on me and I was in this room with a dead phone.

After removing the separators, I made my way to the balcony and slid the doors open. The salty breeze from the ocean fanned my hair away from my face. I let it, enjoying the feeling of oneness with the sea. The moonlight lent a ghostly glow to the trees. From above, the stars sparkled, and one by one, popped out into the dark canopy of the sky.

My eyes searched the grounds for Eduardo's flashlight. He'd be somewhere out there with Diablo making his last rounds, leaving Javier to continue for the night. My time was running out. I had to get out of here, but first, I needed a weapon. I glanced back into the bedroom. My eyes lit on the fork left behind on the table. Small yet effective.

I clicked back in my high-heeled sandals. Not very appropriate for an escape, but without my cross trainers, I needed to protect my feet. The same could be said for the silk robe and lacy lingerie, but still they'd be better for climbing down than any of the long slinky dresses I'd found hanging in the closet. Hastily, I picked up the fork and dropped it into the pocket of my robe and went back outside.

Glancing to the far side of the balcony, I could see Diego's room—the curtains of his windows partially drawn, the room shrouded in darkness. He wouldn't be a concern tonight. My eyes searched the grounds for the presence of Eduardo or his helper but this time I saw nothing. "Where are you, Wolf?" I said out loud, in frustration and angry with myself for even wanting his help. I was proud of my independence. After all, I'd gotten myself into this mess alone and I should get out of it alone. But there was something else inside of me that cried out for that man. I shook my head. I could and would handle it myself.

A dark cloud blocked out the moon, but in the distance I could see the crests on the waves, sparkling silver. My mind wandered back to Wolf. The water was my sea god's home. He was a swimmer, a diver—a man strong, fearless, and untamed. Years ago as teenagers, I'd first experienced that extraordinary chemistry between us. Tonight he'd said he'd return to me. That was impossible. Eduardo would never allow him to speak with me. I was stuck.

In frustration, I pounded the railing with my fist. "I need you!" I called out to the breeze.

"Beautiful," the wind whispered back.

I'd assumed the margaritas had worn off but hearing voices was too strange. Peering down into the shadows of the trees I heard noises—maybe a bird. More rustling and crackling branches made me think of coati—raccoon-like creatures with long sharp fangs and nasty temperaments, something like Eduardo.

A movement. Something glinted silver in the light of the full moon. "Hello?" I called out softly but no one answered.

My imagination must be playing tricks. Back to working out my plan. I gritted my teeth in annoyance. I should have confessed and gone to jail. Wolf would have helped me. He'd know some trustworthy lawyers. But as soon as I imagined the jail, I knew I was better off here. Let's not forget, men ran them. Perverts were everywhere but they were especially sadistic in jails.

I had to solve my own predicament. If it came to a fight with Eduardo, I didn't have a chance. The only plan was to escape. Glancing down, I estimated twenty feet. "Damn!" I swore in exasperation. How would I get down? Then it struck me. Sheets. Isn't that what people did in fires? If I knotted them together, I thought, glancing at the pillars on the balcony and tied one around, I'd be able to manage it.

A board creaked. I nearly jumped out of my skin. I would have screamed but a hand covered my mouth to stop me. My attacker squeezed tightly against my back. Self-defense starts with the element of surprise. I bit him. He released me with a jerk, muttering something sounding like "shit" but before I could react he whispered urgently, "Don't scream! It's me."

I twirled around to face my assailant. "Wolf! Are you insane? What are you doing here?"

He laughed softly. "Is that any way to greet me?" Brushing my hair away, he brought his hands to my face. "Don't pretend you don't want to see me, baby. I heard you call." His sapphire eyes glittered magically. "You looked so sexy in the moonlight. It was almost as if you were nude with the light from the bedroom shining behind you." His sensuous lips torched mine with an intensity that made me melt with their heat. Against me, his body felt warm and hard. His face was shadowed but his blond hair gleamed silver. My hands reached up behind his neck and I held him tightly, his unruly hair brushing my fingertips. I dug into the ruffled waves, aroused by their silken texture. At the same time I was afraid he was just an illusion and if I released him, he'd disappear into thin air and I'd be left here alone.

He brushed my hair aside for his lips to lightly caress my neck, his tongue feathering down to my shoulder, while his hand stroked me through the delicate fabric, trailing from my waist to my hip, fingertips resting on the cheeks of my butt. "Have I told you how much I love your tush?"

"You mean more than the rest of me?"

"Every part of you is beautiful but I have a particular fondness for your luscious ass." His hand moved to my thigh, and his fingers slid up and down. "And these strong, smooth thighs. They're calling out to me."

The warmth of his hands sent a jolt down my body and his words reminded me of how much I wanted him. I'd been deprived too long. There was no one like him. His body's scent of soap and ocean breeze lured me and I felt like tugging off that shirt to stroke his taut six-pack. But something nagged me.

"You stayed at the nudist resort longer—another day. I suppose Sam was there with you?"

"Um-hm."

"What do you mean by that?"

"She decided to stay."

"After she knew I was gone?"

He grinned.

"She came on to you, didn't she?"

"Let's say she has fond memories."

"And?"

"You said you wanted me to investigate."

"And I'm sure you did!" I snapped irritably. "She is more the show than tell type."

"She was cooperative." Wolf grinned. "Just trying to help, Adie."

"Really?" I asked sharply. "Why did you tell her to stay on in Cozumel?"

"You heard that?"

"Why, Wolf?" I insisted.

"I had to make her think I was interested in her. That way she'd tell me more."

"And did she?"

"I think I got everything I needed."

I clenched my jaw. "Needed? And what was that exactly?"

"Long story best left for later. Let's talk about Alvarez. Was he successful?"

"In finding Dean's killer?"

"No, in getting you out of that lacy outfit."

"This one?"

"Ah, there were others? Of course, how stupid of me. One for each night."

"Wolf, as much as I'd like to speak about my extensive lingerie collection, this is not a good time. Eduardo will be done with his rounds soon and if he sees you he'll lose it."

"Tricky bastard."

I thought back to the look in Eduardo's eyes. "Worse than that."

"Lucky I found you."

I stared at him in puzzlement. "How'd you know where I'd be?"

"Louisa." Wolf stroked my cheek gently. "She told me about Eduardo. You weren't planning on staying here, were you?"

"No," I admitted, "but I don't want anything to happen to you. Eduardo wouldn't hurt me but he'd kill you."

"Really? I think what he'd do to you would be worse. The man is an animal, Adie. Louisa told me how he was buzzing around. You really don't want me to leave you alone here, do you?"

"I don't want him to hurt you, Wolf. This is my problem, after all."

Wolf grinned. "Let him try."

I stroked his cheek. "Thank you for coming here so quickly. How did you find me?"

"You were standing on the balcony. I wasn't sure which room you were in until you came outside." He looked out at the gardens. "I think we've discussed this enough. Time to go. You agree?"

"Okay."

"That little number is an incredible teaser but not exactly the thing for a breakout. Why don't you go change into something else?"

"Wish I could. They didn't given me any regular clothes. Nothing suitable for an escape. How did you get up here, anyway?" I gazed at the oak branches that touched the house. "I was about to tie some sheets together to get down but you're thinking we should climb down the tree?"

Wolf glanced from the oak to me. "You won't have to." Pulling his black shirt away, he revealed a heavy thick belt, or was it? From around his waist, he pulled out a rope. His teeth flashed white in the dim light. "Remember the rope climbing we did?"

I frowned. It had been a long way down into that cenote and I would never have attempted it without him. "You mean you want me to hold on and we'll get down using the rope?"

"I'll tie it to the railing. Go get anything you want to bring with you. Hurry!"

Wolf was right. There was no time to lose. I rushed back into the room, grabbed my tote, and threw in some things before I scurried back as fast as I could on my high heeled sandals.

Outside, Wolf stood silently, looking in the direction of the gate where I could make out a flickering light.

"How'd you get in?"

"From the beach."

"But the dog, Diablo. Didn't he come after you?"

"Louisa told me he likes steak."

"But after he finished?"

"Ground some valium in." He pulled out a plastic package from his waistband at the small of his back. "This is for the return trip."

"It must have been uncomfortable for you with all that meat tucked in. Why don't I stick it in my bag?"

He glanced at my cloth tote. "How were you planning to bring that anyway?"

"Easy. The strap will go over my head and shoulder." I grabbed the steak and tossed it in along with my sandals and adjusted the strap. "I'm as ready as I'll ever be."

"Wait a sec." He slid his body from the balcony, gripping the rope with his hands and legs. "Adie, I'm ready for you. Make sure your legs are locked around my waist and hold on tight."

It was frightening. I tried not to look down—heights scare me. But when I was sure I was secure on Wolf's back, I whispered, "Ready."

Our descent seemed endless, Wolf inching his way down the rope. Finally he warned me, "Dropping, now. Ready...roll!"

My karate training prepared me—I tucked and rolled. I was so glad for the soft carpet of grass, rivaling the lush terrain of golf course at the Primavera Hotel. I looked up to Wolf extending his hand out to me. "Do we need the rope?"

"No, we'll do without it. Even though those shoes won't be great, I think you should put them back on. They'll give you some protection."

I tugged out the sandals, slipped them on, and was about to lift the strap of my bag over my head when Wolf took it from me.

"It'll be easier for me to carry. You've got enough to deal with." He glanced at my metallic high-heeled sandals. "Watch out for the rocks."

"Don't worry. I've got years of experience with stilettos. Rocks are the least of our worries."

"Come on, babe," Wolf said, taking my hand, "we'll head to the beach."

Although we could hear the surf, I had the feeling it wouldn't be that easy to get there. The gravel path was lit by the moon and an occasional lamp in the trees, but the palms cast shadows, making our trek precarious. We kept a rapid pace and at one point my foot slid out from under me but Wolf steadied my balance and I straightened up without landing in the underbrush.

"We're gettin' closer," he whispered encouragingly. "Hang in there."

The rush of the ocean became louder and I almost didn't hear them. Men's voices from the grounds and then I saw the lights. They were close. Too close.

"Wolf, go! It's me they want. Who knows what they'll do to you?"

Before he had a chance to reply, I heard a shot ring out. I hadn't thought they'd fire at us.

"Run, Adie! I'll be the decoy."

"No!"

Wolf gave me a shove. "I mean it, go. I'll see you at the gate."

I nodded and ran. It wasn't far. Stumbling on a stone, I righted myself and sprinted down the last length of the path. The wrought iron gate came into view, glinting silver in the moonlight. Getting over it would be another matter. I didn't have time to solve that problem. From behind, a black figure jumped out at me, knocking me backwards. I remembered to breakfall with my forearms hitting the ground first, saving my back from a painful hit.

He was faster than I had anticipated. I didn't have a chance to get up. Eduardo leaped on top of me, grabbed my wrists, and pinned my arms to my sides. His knees were tight against my hips, and he arched over me, his face inches above mine. "Good try, *bruja*, but I won."

I tugged my arms out and he allowed it, keeping a strong grip on my wrists. His face was close enough for me to smell his breath—a strong odor of unfiltered, Russian cigarettes. From the lustful look in his dark eyes, he found the dominant position even more stimulating. He had to lean forward to keep hold of my wrists and by doing so was off balance. He glanced down at my robe that had come undone. The strap had slipped off my shoulder and the deep 'V' of the camisole left only a patch of lacy fabric covering my breast.

"You shouldn't have run away. I am *muy fuerte...*virile. I can last all night. You would beg for more." He glanced at my breast again. "You know you want me. Say you do and all will be forgiven. I'll send Javier home and we will make love." He smiled. "But if you prefer, we could do it here. It might be even more exciting, tiger woman."

I squirmed and he focused on the swell of my breast. Releasing my wrist, he slid his hand over the fabric and cupped my mound.

While he fondled me, my free hand reached into my robe and grasped the dinner fork in my pocket.

"Tell me you want it, *bruja...*witch," he hissed, as a shot resounded through the trees.

His eyes flicked away. I jerked my hips up unbalancing him and twisted my body pushing him over with my knee. When his hand stayed tightly clasped around my other wrist, I brought the fork down into his hand. He groaned. My hand slipped out of his grasp and I rolled out. And now I had to finish the job. Coming up, I kicked the side of his head—hard. He grunted and sank down.

I hesitated. Where was Wolf? If he'd been shot, I'd have to go back for him. From down the path, I heard footsteps crunching on the gravel. I hid in the shadows, until I saw a tall, dark figure racing towards me. With his hair glinting silver in the moonlight, I knew it was Wolf.

I stepped out into the light. "Eduardo's down."

Wolf grinned. "That's my girl." He grabbed my hand and then pointed with his chin. "There's our gate."

Thick steel bars and I guessed seven feet in height, but it was better than the smooth, white wall. It would be even harder to scale for a vertically challenged person like me. I couldn't see any easy way over.

Wolf read my thoughts. "I'll boost you up and you drop down into the sand on the other side. Piece of cake, right?" He grinned in that way that made me want to punch him.

"Funny man." Climbing was not my forté. He should know that by now.

Wolf stood close to the gate and kneeled. "Get on my shoulders and I'll bring you up as high as I can. You do the rest."

Once I was on his shoulders it was about a foot more. I gripped the top rail and brought my legs up and over. It was dark and shadowy on the sand. I took a quick breath and jumped. Hitting the sand, I let myself relax and fall.

From the other side, Wolf started his climb. A blast from a whistle sounded from the bushes. The next instant a great black dog bounded into the clearing, heading straight for Wolf.

13

Diablo barked sharply.

Wolf whipped open the tote. Growling, the dog closed in on Wolf's leg.

Thinking rapidly, I yelled out, "Tequila!"

Diablo's ears perked and he stopped uncertainly, a low growl deep in his throat. "Good boy! Sit," I said, deliberately making my voice deeper, more masculine.

Wolf took that opportunity to toss down the steak.

Diablo sniffed the meat. Wolf started his assent and as he swung over the railing, Diablo tore into the steak. At that instant, Eduardo staggered out from behind the trees.

"Stop, Du Lac! If you take her, the police will find you and throw away the key. She's already in big trouble—you're making it worse!"

Wolf dropped to the ground. "We'll take that chance. Come on, Adie."

I slipped off my shoes and held them as we ran on the moist, packed sand near the water's edge. The condominium on the adjoining property had been ruined by the hurricane and only the pillars remained, ghostly specters in the moonlight. Here it was slower going. A coral outcropping blocked our way. It would have been impossible to scale the rocks with my shoes on, but having them off was just as difficult. Wolf steadied me from behind as I climbed higher but going down I slid on a frond of seaweed caught between the coral and when I tried to regain my balance, I slipped and knocked my shin. I cried out with the sudden pain.

"You okay, baby?"

"Bruised my shin, but I'm good." I tried to be positive, but felt sore, dirty, and tired. This was not the easy escape you see in the movies.

"Stay there. I'll go first," he said, before he jumped. From below, he stood on the sand, extending his hand up for me to grasp. I stepped gingerly in my bare feet while his hand helped me maintain my balance. I inched my way down. When I was close enough, his arms encircled my waist and he lifted me over the rocks onto the soft, powdery sand. Thank goodness for tall strong men!

"I wish I could tell you it's close, but we still have a way to go. The Jeep's parked at the beach club past the next two hotels."

Knowing there was an end to this would make the going easier. But that was only wishful thinking. Something scuttled across my toe. I gasped, clutching Wolf's arm.

"Just a sand crab, Adie. Be careful stepping here. The stones are sharp."

I knew what he meant when something jabbed the side of my foot. And that was the way it was, a prickly path of pain until we hit the beach fronting the next two hotels. Here the sand was raked to perfection and the ocean lapped quietly onto the shore. Both of these exclusive hotels had wisely chosen a bay with protective palms that kept the wind gentle and forgiving.

On a jetty a few people sat having drinks and chatting—their voices carrying over to us in the still of the night. We made it to the garden that bordered the hotel without a hitch.

It was a relief to be back on the grass. After I put on my sandals, we headed down the trail to the parking lot. On the far side, Wolf's black Jeep sat camouflaged under the shadows of the trees. From the main road it remained hidden. I had a feeling of urgency. By now, they'd be looking.

As I slid into the passenger seat, Wolf revved the engine. I glanced at his rugged features in profile, suddenly aware of how he sizzled. "Where are we going?"

Wolf glanced at me. "The safest place we've got." He backed up the car and rolled up to the entrance, his lights still off. Seeing no other vehicles, he switched on the headlights and we made a right onto the highway.

I urged my mind to think. "They'll be watching the ferry crossings to Playa. Eduardo has probably got his men on it."

"We're okay, for a day, maybe two."

"Diego's back tomorrow. He'll be angry with me for leaving."

"And pissed with me," he said, his jaw clenched, "but I wasn't leaving you there with that scumbag." Wolf glanced fleetingly at me. "You glad I came?"

"Made getting down that balcony easier," I said lightly, trying to chase away my lustful thoughts. He had been standing down below while I went on about wanting to see him. His head must be swelled the size of giant beach ball. Yet, I had to admit, a sexy sea god coming to my rescue was as romantic as "Romeo and Juliet".

"Good to be useful."

"You are…very."

The road was well lit and when he glanced over, his intensely blue eyes sparkled. "I'll have to make sure you get everything you need tonight."

My body flamed. That husky voice aroused me, like Pavlov's dogs salivating at the sound of a bell. But I wasn't about to let on. He could still have feelings for that viper. It was more important for me to think about my tenuous situation. Who killed Dean? "Wolf," I said, steering him away from making further innuendos, "Eduardo dug up some info. What about you? Did you find out anything from Sam besides her sexual preferences?"

"Took a while to steer her away from that subject," he drawled. "She kept going on and on with the details."

I jabbed his arm in annoyance. "What else did she say?"

"JJ had a fling with Janine but Firenze wanted her to marry Jim to keep up appearances. Jim's gay."

"I guessed as much from the way he looked at you." I stared at his long, tapered fingers around the steering wheel. What was it about long fingers that turned me on? "Eduardo told me JJ was from Nicaragua."

"Paramilitary man. One of the rebels from what Terry said."

"Terry?"

"Yeah."

"I'm surprised Sam let you talk to her. How did you manage that?"

"Told her I was coming down with something."

"And she didn't want to stay and tuck you in?"

Wolf flashed me a grin. "What do you think about JJ killing Firenze?"

"One way to get his wife and his money."

"He's strong enough."

"The motive could have been something else."

Wolf lifted an eyebrow. "What?"

"Dale said..."

"Dale? You spoke to him? When?"

"Carmelita and I met Lourdes and Janine at the Museo. After we finished lunch, Eduardo let me go to the square to see what was going on. That's where I saw Dale."

"And you struck up a conversation."

I nodded. "He said the mafia might have hired someone."

"JJ?"

"Could be. Another thing. He told me how he hated Dean."

"You can strike him off your list."

"Why?"

"Flights only come into Coz on weekends. Too hard for him to get here, murder Firenze, and be back again by Sunday morning in time for him to be picked up at the airport."

What he said made sense unless he came in from Atlanta. It would have been a difficult plan but not impossible. But somehow, I'd place my bet on one of the others. I sat back and watched the road. Headlights appeared in the distance. Seeing them, Wolf pulled onto the gravel road to El Cedral and drove down a few yards before he did a U turn and eased back out to the intersection. It was clear.

When Wolf zoomed off to the right, I asked, "Where are we going?"

"Your house."

"Ah-hh."

"Good idea?"

"You never told anyone you gave it to me?"

"No reason to. What about Alvarez? Did you tell him?"

"No, but Eduardo could find out. I think you should know Eduardo is a computer whiz."

"Besides being an all out bastard?"

"Right. Believe me I felt like hurting him when he started touching me, but he's dug up all kinds of things about the investors and if I'd heeled him in the throat..."

"He'd be dead."

"And no good to me."

"As well as giving you a ticket straight to jail for murder—this time for real."

"Damn it, Wolf. I should have."

Wolf reached over and stroked my hand. "I know he deserved it but you did the right thing. If the bastard finds out something to clear you, the police will arrest the murderer. Hernandez would believe him."

Up ahead, we could see lights on the road. "Shit," Wolf muttered when we saw the striped barrier and a police officer motioning for us to pull over.

When we stopped, the officer came around to the driver's side. Wolf lowered the window. "*Buenos noches,* officer."

"*Buenos noches,* Señor," the officer said, his mouth pinched into a straight line. "*Por favor*, come out of the Jeep. There is a problem."

Wolf's jaw tightened. He glanced reassuringly at me before he got out. Towering above the short cop, Wolf dug out his wallet and handed over his license. The officer perused it before giving it back. He pointed to the front of the vehicle and said something. Wolf strode back to the door with the cop accompanying him. I overheard the officer. "We need to go to the police station, Señor."

I knew what that meant—trouble, with a capital T.

Wolf opened the Jeep door, sat down, and started the engine. "The rental agency will fix the headlight, officer."

They engaged into an intense staring contest. I breathed a sigh of relief when the cop broke contact, trekked back to the barrier, shoved it aside and waved us through.

"How much did he want?"

"Didn't say."

"I was afraid he wasn't going to let us off. What was wrong?"

"A headlight burned out."

"He could have charged you for that."

"If I were a permanent resident he would have given me a warning, that's all, but hey, they think a tourist is a live one."

"Good thing you've lived here for a while. If it were me, I'd have paid."

"If you were alone in this car," he glanced down at my legs, "I think he'd have wanted something else."

"You must be kidding," I said in disgust.

"That's what it's like in these Latin American countries, babe. Way worse in places like Venezuela."

The Jeep shot around a bend which I figured must be the southern most point of the island. I knew the road continued north, now that we were on the east coast. With Cozumel being only thirty-two miles long, driving to any point didn't take long.

"Do you think he'll report this to the station?"

Wolf stroked my hand. "No way. It'd look bad for him. Police have to be friendly to the tourists here."

"Can you imagine what would have happened if we'd been brought in?"

Wolf glanced over at me. "It would have caused a rise at the police station."

"Because Eduardo's been looking for me?"

His eyes shot over. "Because Adie Sturm is hot in lacy lingerie."

I glanced down at the dirt smudges on my knees. "A little too grubby to be hot."

"Easily cleaned up." He grinned. "Wolf Du Lac, at your service, *ma chérie*. I will make you feel *très bien* in the shower."

French—the language of love. I could feel my temperature rise. "I'll bet you say that to all the ladies."

"Not all of them." Wolf smiled seductively. "This special service is reserved."

"For…"

Wolf took his hand away from the wheel and ran a finger down my cheek.

I couldn't take my eyes off of him. It wasn't just his sexy face, or his hard, lean body—he had a story behind his dangerously cool eyes. They flicked back to the road.

We were now on the wild side of the island, far from the maddening crowd of cruise ship tourists. The surf was high and rough and the heavenly beaches with their powdery sand were deserted. After passing a beach club, there was a huge expanse of ocean and beach with nothing else. And on the east coast there were no lights on the highway. "It's close, now, isn't it, Wolf?"

It was as if I hadn't spoken. Wolf gripped the steering wheel tightly, staring at the dirt road ahead.

"Wolf?"

"Soon, princess."

I studied his drawn face. "Is there something wrong?"

"No, babe, we're good."

Not convinced, I asked, "What is it?"

He reached over and squeezed my hand. "Chill, Adie.

Everything's fine."

The road wound away from the coast and then, at a grouping of palms, it branched off—a narrow dirt road leading up to a cliff. Wolf swung the Jeep into the driveway and as we got closer, the trees thinned and a white stucco house appeared in the distance.

When the Jeep came to a halt, Wolf let the motor run and sat silently staring at the house. I hesitated to speak. What had I done? "Wolf?"

"We'll get you there," he said softly.

He put the Jeep in neutral, pulled up the hand brake and slowly got out. Opening my door, I swung my legs out and over. Jeeps are high off the ground and as a petite woman, it's a stretch for my legs before I jump out and not too easy, especially in strappy, high heeled sandals. Not that I couldn't, if it's right into the arms of a sizzlin' man. I waited. Wolf moves quickly and silently. The longer I waited, the more puzzled I was. He always went over to my side to help me out.

I jumped down carefully and made my way over to Wolf. He stood leaning against the bumper, gazing at the house.

"Wolf?"

"We're here, princess. You want to see it?" His eyes on the house, he started up the road without me.

"Wait!" I called out, catching up to him. "Wolf, don't you remember? I did."

Wolf frowned. "When?" He ran his finger down my cheek, staring at me in confusion.

"November."

Wolf shut his eyes, rubbing his forehead. "Months ago." He nodded. "Yes, I'll never forget that day." He gave me his hand. "Come on, baby."

It had been hot and humid when we were still at Diego's but here, the night breeze was stronger and cooler. I shivered. The heat from Wolf's hand warmed me a little. "I'm cold, Wolf. Could you put your arm around me?"

Wolf draped his arm over my shoulders and with the hill getting steeper, our pace slowed. I was tired and he must have been more so, but when we came to the house surrounded by palms, it was as beautiful as I remembered. I felt energized.

From under a flower pot by the step, Wolf retrieved a key and opened the massive oak door. Once inside, Wolf switched on the light. The marble floor gleamed white as did the stucco walls, contrasting to the dark oak beams supporting the high-vaulted ceiling. "Did I tell you it was a mission, years ago?"

"It's a lovely house."

"The design is simple. You don't mind all the white?"

"No, with all the arches and high ceiling, it's simple elegance. Was it furnished when you leased it?"

"Partially. There's one room you've never seen." Stooping down, he scooped me up in his arms.

Strong, lean, and smoldering with a wild fire, all his own, Wolf's current flowed to me—our bodies intense conductors. A powerful force spread wickedly down to my thighs. I was captured—a willing victim, this time.

14

I clung to my sea god as he carried me into the spacious bedroom. When he gently dropped me down on a large four-poster bed, he gave me a rakish smile. My head sank into a fluffy pillow and I stretched out, my arms above my head, aware that this pose would get his full attention.

From the slats in the window, moonlight flowed into the room. Wolf sat down beside me, his face shadowed. "Woman," he stroked my leg, "you drive me wild."

My face flushed at the touch of his hand and heated my body. I reached over to switch on the light.

"No." He stopped my hand. "I have a better idea." From a dish on the bedside table, Wolf took some matches and lit a white cylindrical candle.

His task completed, he turned back to me. The flickering candle light softened the rugged contours of his face. Increasingly aware of his powerful magnetism, I was drawn to his full lips. Reflectively, I traced my lips with my finger.

Wolf's eyes followed my finger before he took up my hand and brought it to his lips. As he sucked each fingertip in turn, a hungry ache stirred deep inside me.

He released my fingers and gazed at me intensely before he spoke. "A man could get lost in those ocean-blue eyes—so unpredictable, like the hues of the Caribbean." He smiled. "Luckily, they're not turquoise tonight. If they were, I'd have to proceed cautiously. An angry Adie Sturm is a dangerous lady." He leaned over and said in a husky voice, "Come here, babe." He brought his hand to my robe and slid it off my shoulder.

"Should I be?"

"What?" he mumbled distractedly, as he pushed away a strand of my hair and kissed my shoulder, his lips lingering to caress me again.

"Be angry? Have you slept with Sam?"

"I think you know the answer to that. I'm yours, princess." Bringing his lips down on the curve of my neck, he softly said,

"Always," his words barely audible.

I sighed, and let myself fall back on the bed. His sensuous lips fell to the hollow of my throat, the tip of his tongue teasing my skin. Delicious shivers raced down my body. I tugged at the belt of my robe, undoing it. Wolf pushed the silk to my shoulders. As I lifted my shoulder slightly, he helped me shrug it off.

Resting on one elbow, Wolf's eyes swept to the lacy lingerie. "Blue like your eyes—eyes that send a message." He lay back down on the bed, his head propped against the pillow.

"What do you see?" I whispered, enthralled by his heavy-lidded gaze. I couldn't remember if he'd ever looked at me like that before. He was so different tonight.

Usually he was a laid-back sort of guy, but not when it came to passion. Like a panther that waits passively, he always took me by surprise with his spontaneous lovemaking. This was a change. And an opportunity for me to explore that magnificent body of his.

Liking the idea of taking control, I placed my hand on his thigh and stroked upwards. Lightly, my hand circled over the significant bulge in his jeans. I smiled, pleased with this new situation. After all he was Neptune—a man that other women lusted for.

From outside, the rushing surf played its own steady rhythm for us—a mystical tune that lent a dreamy, unreal atmosphere to our private hideaway. His eyes half-closed, Wolf watched me. Befitting a pirate more than an entrepreneur, his face was dangerously arranged in a way that oozed sexuality.

My eyes still focused on him, I slowly undid his belt buckle and pushed down the zipper. Bringing my fingers down, I reached to the opening. He groaned as I touched him. But before I could do more, he pulled me back up to his blazing lips, kissing my mouth slowly, until I was engulfed by his raging heat. Tongues met to swirl in a seductive salsa, beguiling each other in their passion. His hand ran over my hip to my cheeks, lightly brushing my skin until I ached, my body screaming for something as yet elusive. I pressed against him, desire melding like wine in a cask of arousal.

Pushing my strap away, he cupped my breast and brought his mouth to the soft mound, sparking my skin with his fire. His tongue licked and tantalized until my senses were mesmerized by his touch. When I could stand it no longer, his mouth wandered down the valley and licked his way to my waiting breast. Here he lingered, determined to drive me crazy.

I closed my eyes and wove my hand into the silky softness of his hair. Touching him lifted me up into a cloud of desire, where every part of me wanted more. When I moaned with the delicious pressure of his lips, he sat up, his eyes mirroring my arousal.

Impatiently, he pushed the lacy fabric down and I lifted up to allow it to slide down over my hips. A caravan of kisses journeyed down my belly, while warm hands swept my skin, tormenting my senses. Like a flower bending to the sun, I craved his touch but now I wanted to give him something back—feel his strength and let his masculinity consume me.

I pulled away to grasp his shirt, pushing it down past his shoulders. With one sleeve down, he pulled on the other. I shoved the shirt off, where it fell to the floor. Then I forced his T-shirt up, my hands caressing his taut abs as I pushed higher. "Lift your arms." As I shoved it over his head, a fire surged inside me. The sight of his muscular chest sent tingles to my core. If a passive role was his new game, I was ready to play. I wanted to take the lead and discover every part of his powerful body. I needed to taste him.

The scent of soap and balmy ocean breeze assailed my nostrils as I brought my mouth to his chest. He was delicious—sinfully smooth, like rich milk chocolate. While my hands stroked his abs, I nibbled his nipple lightly. I glanced up to see the fire in his half-closed sapphire eyes.

The room was warm but not overly so. Strangely his skin felt fiery to the touch. When my hands glided over his bicep, I finally understood. It wasn't sweat. This had a thicker consistency. When I brought my wet fingers to my nose, I knew what it was.

This was why he hadn't wanted the bedroom light on. Had I done so, I would have found his secret. Reaching over, I switched on the light. "Wolf, have you lost it completely! Why didn't you say you were wounded?"

He grinned lazily.

"You are insane." I stared him down. "Here you are bleeding and," I examined his bicep, "have an infection from the looks of it." With a mixture of blood and fluid oozing from his arm, I was worried. When I placed my hand on his forehead, my suspicions were confirmed. "No wonder you couldn't remember the last time we were here together. You have a fever, Wolf Du Lac."

"Ah, Doctor Sturm, what would you suggest? Bed rest?" His eyes crinkled at the corners. "Won't you join me? That way you can make sure I don't overexert myself."

"Very funny! Rest is the last thing on your mind."

"I rescued the fair maiden from the evil prince and his henchman and she doesn't want to show me her gratitude?

Fairy tales have happy endings." He grinned. "I'm ready for my reward, princess."

I had to admit with his face flushed with fever Wolf was as desirable as ever. I could only compare him to the cake my mom made for my birthdays. A moist chocolate cake, decadently layered with rich mocha icing—every piece I ate left me craving more. But he was injured. I had to get a grip and remind myself that lovemaking was not the medicine he needed. "We have to get you to the hospital."

Wolf shook his head.

"You have to go."

"Not a good idea, princess. They're watching the roads."

"This is serious. You don't want a blood infection, do you?"

"We're staying here." Wolf closed his eyes.

"Where's your cell?"

Wolf sighed.

"If you won't let me drive you to the hospital, I'm calling a doctor."

"I'll be fine, Adie. Take it easy." He tried to raise himself up on one elbow but his strength failed and he sank back down against the pillows. "Why don't you get the scotch from the cupboard in the living room and bring it here."

He was being annoying but I decided to go along with him on this one. From the liquor cabinet I took out a bottle and carried it back. I sat down on the bed, unscrewed the cap, and angled the bottle. "This will sting."

Wolf took the bottle from me. "No, it won't." He took a swig.

I gave him a look. "I thought you wanted me to pour some on the wound!"

"No need to go to all that trouble, babe." He pointed the bottle at me. "Scotch?"

I grimaced. "Wolf, that infection needs it more than I do."

Scotch had a medicinal taste in my books. It was more suited as an antiseptic.

"Take it easy, Florence." He picked a glass from the bedside table and poured in a dram. "This is Glenfiddich, the best single malt there is. Come, baby, a good Scotch is to be enjoyed." He clicked my glass and watched me sip it. "There. Much better. Why don't we put down our glasses and continue where we left off?" He reached for my hand.

I pulled away. "No way, Superman! I know you're big and strong, but even macho guys need help sometimes. That wound has to be cleaned. I don't suppose there is anything in the bathroom?"

"Shampoo, soap, a few cosmetics for you...that's it."

I should have expected as much. Guys. I sighed and set my glass down.

"Mm-mm," Wolf murmured, when I started to search his jean pockets but he didn't resist. His eyes closed, he rested with a little smile on his face.

I felt something smooth and hard. No it wasn't his package, although I admit I couldn't resist lightly caressing it as I searched. My eyes shot up to his face. I'd swear that smile of his grew bigger by the second. Inside his pocket I felt the hard plastic. Triumphantly, I pulled out the iPhone. "Well, since you won't go to the hospital, you leave me no choice."

Hurrying into the salon, I rushed to a table where I had last seen a phone book. Flipping through the directory, I came to a list of doctors. With the information given in Spanish it wasn't easy but I was able to eliminate the pediatricians and gynecologists with the Spanish similar to the English. Finally, I came across a Doctor Lopez Gomez, *Medico General*. The ad mentioned English spoken. That was good, except for one thing. What doctor would be open now—this late? When I saw her cell phone listed along with the office number, I was hopeful. I had heard that doctors in Mexico actually did house calls so there was a chance I could get her to come over and help this stubborn man.

I tapped in her number and waited.

"*Diga*," a female voice said.

"*Hola,* do you speak English?"

"Yes. What is it you want?"

"It's an emergency, Doctor Gomez. A man has an infected

wound and needs medical attention. Could you come here?"

"It is bleeding?"

"Yes, and infected."

"For now, stop the bleeding with a clean cloth. I must ask you something, Señora. You do understand that if there is a crime involved, the police will want to know."

"Yes, doctor, but let me assure you, there was no crime."

"What caused this injury?"

"I'm not sure," I said, stalling, "but I need you to come here to the house. Do you know where Bonita beach is?"

"*Si,* but if it is anything illegal…"

"No, you are perfectly safe here. It's only the two of us and he refuses to go to the hospital. He thinks it's fine the way it is." I lowered my voice and said confidentially, "You know how men are."

There was a pause on her end and she sighed. "*Si,* I often encounter this attitude. Where are you exactly?"

"A kilometer north of Bonita Beach. There is a white house on a hill. I'll turn the outside light on. You can park at the bottom of the hill, but you'll need to walk up. When I hear your car, I'll come down to meet you. How long do you think you'll be?"

"A half hour."

"Is there anything I can do for him?"

"Have him rest. You realize house calls are rather expensive?"

"Don't worry. Your patient has the money."

"*Bueno.* And your name?"

"Adie. Please hurry, Doctor Gomez."

"*Chao.* I shall see you soon."

I ended the call and glanced over at Wolf sleeping. I reached over to zip up his jeans but first I needed to push his package back in. Not easy. The man had considerable goods to tuck. The doctor had probably seen it all before but I didn't think there was any reason to raise her hormone levels.

15

Doctor Lopez Gomez had a no nonsense approach. "Señora, you will leave us. I would like to consult with my patient."

I didn't mind her concern but she was concentrating a little too much on my hottie. Her dark eyes traveled down the length of his succulent body and back to his lean hard face. She turned to me. "Perhaps you could boil up some water. That would be useful."

Clearly, she wanted to get rid of me. Heading into the kitchen, I set about finding a pot and matches. I was not fond of gas stoves, having nightmares of death by fire. Not a nice way to die, but neither was Dean's blood bath. It was etched in my memory and was sure to come back to haunt me in the lonely hours of the night.

As I filled the pot, I contemplated whether the doctor would keep the house call a secret. Eduardo would have contacts at the police station and it wouldn't be pleasant facing his wrath when he finally located me.

I turned the knob and heard the gas release. Quickly, I lit a match and brought it to the gas. After the flame shot up, I placed the pot on the burner and watched the water thoughtfully. I couldn't help but feel angry with Diego. Why had he left me with Eduardo? None of this would have happened if he had returned when he'd said he would. But it was all my fault that Wolf was injured. I was responsible for this mess. I prayed he'd be all right.

The water bubbled to a boil. Carefully, I took the pot off the stove and carried it down the hall to the bedroom. I sighed with relief when I saw she hadn't stripped him completely.

"Set it down there." The doctor pointed to the table. "It won't be necessary for you to stay. I'll take care of Señor Du Lac."

I glanced at Wolf, shirtless, slouched against the pillows. He seemed relaxed enough but when I picked up the scotch bottle which was considerably emptier than before, he stopped me. "Leave it, babe."

I strode into the living room carrying my tote bag. Dropping it down on the elegant yellow couch, I thought about the doctor. She was way too arrogant. There was no reason to treat me like that. Ever since Wolf had given me the lease to the house, I'd kept a change of clothes in the closet. Right now I was decently dressed in a top and skirt.

The doctor knew Wolf. I was sure of it. San Miguel was after all the only town on the island. The high society people were a clique. Wolf was a frequent guest at Diego's parties and I wouldn't be surprised if the doctor had seen him there. She knew Wolf had money.

It was the right decision to get a doctor but I needed to clear the air before either of us was arrested. From a little book in my tote, I found the number.

"*Diga*," a male voice drawled.

"Diego, it's me."

"Adelina, where are you?" Diego asked sharply. "Eduardo told me you'd left. That was not wise, *cariño*. Hernan entrusted me to keep you at the house."

"As your prisoner."

"Of course, Adelina, but it was entirely necessary," he said patiently. "You must agree?"

"Um-mm."

"Then why involve Du Lac?"

"I didn't ask him to come."

"I should have known you wouldn't jeopardize your situation with such a foolish escape." His voice grew steely. "Du Lac needs to mind his own business. I should call Hernan. He has gone too far."

"That's not how it was, Diego."

"No? Du Lac couldn't stand the thought that he'd lost you to me. He played the knight in shining armor, didn't he? I never thought he would jeopardize your freedom, but obviously, I overestimated his intelligence."

"Wait, Diego, it wasn't like that!"

"I'm on my way. My pilot is flying me into Cozumel as we speak. Where are you?"

"Safe. In fact, safer than I was at your house."

Diego sighed in exasperation. He spoke softly, as if to a confused young child. "Adelina, you had security people and I made sure you had everything you wanted. If you weren't happy, you could have phoned and told me what you needed."

"No, I couldn't. My charger was back at the hotel and my cell went dead. Anyway, it's not what I needed, it's what I didn't need."

"You're speaking in riddles, *cariño*. What has you so upset? Tell me. You know how I adore you."

"I know you care for me, Diego, and believe me when I say I like you too."

"Then won't you explain this sudden self-destructive behavior?"

"Diego, you must promise not to do anything rash. I don't want any more violence."

"More? Have you been hurt?"

"I would have been had I stayed, Diego. But, seriously, I mean it. I need you to promise."

"Of course, Adelinita, if it will make you happy. Now tell me what you're afraid to say."

"Eduardo was…"

"Yes?"

"He was interested in me."

Diego chuckled. "Any man would be interested."

"It was more than that."

There was silence on the other end.

"He forced himself on you?"

"He would have if I'd stayed."

"You are sure about that?"

"When I escaped from the house, he jumped on me and he…"

"He dared to touch you?"

"I kicked him and escaped but not before he…"

"That bastard needs to be taught a lesson."

"Diego, I don't want anything to happen to him."

"You're way too kind-hearted, *cariño*. He tried to rape you, didn't he?"

"He's smart, Diego. He can help clear me. If anything happens to him I won't be able to figure out who the murderer is."

"The man is a swine. He has betrayed my trust and yours. I won't let him get away with this, Adelina."

"Listen to me, Diego. This is more important to me. I have this gut feeling. One of the investors is the murderer and Eduardo is the only one able to hack into websites and find the information I need."

"All right, you win. I'll speak with him and make him aware of his betrayal. Don't worry, Adelina, he'll be back to work on that computer for you."

"Thank you, Diego."

"He'd better damn well find something or I'll regret my decision."

"There are some things that he's already uncovered that have narrowed down the suspects."

"*Bien.* Now tell me where you are. I'll come and pick you up as soon as the jet lands."

"It's late. You must be tired."

"I am, but Adelina, you have to be with me."

"I'm afraid I can't."

"Why not?"

"Wolf needs me right now."

Diego laughed dryly. "Du Lac's physical needs can wait."

"It's not like that. Trust me. I'll see you tomorrow. *Chao,*" I said quickly and clicked the phone shut.

"Senora," Doctor Gomez called out from the doorway, "I'm ready to leave. Wolf's wound is cleaned up and bandaged."

Wolf? She was on a first name basis?

"I've given him a sleeping pill for tonight and some for the rest of the week if he should need them. For the infection, he has antibiotics. I would suggest you let him sleep."

What did she think I'd do—jump the man and ply him with sex? "Of course, Doctor Gomez. I will make sure he rests. How much do I owe you?" I reached for my tote.

She waved her hand dismissively. "Wolf took care of that. Rest assured that I would not jeopardize his whereabouts. He told me it was your husband that did this. I hope he doesn't intend you any harm?"

My husband? I stared at her. "No, not at all."

"It's fortunate your vacation is ending tomorrow and you'll be leaving with him. The Cozumel police dislike firearms on the island."

"Don't worry, doctor. He thought Wolf was an intruder. He'd been drinking and…"

"So he didn't think you were having a liaison with Wolf?"

I shook my head. "It was a mistake. I don't think he knew he shot Wolf. When he wakes up he won't remember anything."

Doctora Gomez headed for the door. "I'll see myself to my car. Stay here with him," she said sternly. Before she let herself out, she cautioned, "Remember, let him sleep."

When the door clicked shut, I headed back into the bedroom.

"So, aren't you a bad boy," I eyed my lover languishing on the bed, "and a lucky one, too. I told her my deluded drunken husband is sleeping it off."

"Nice of him to let me see another sunrise."

"You sure got the doctor's sympathy. How bad is it?"

Wolf shrugged and then winced from his action. "Flesh wound. Nothing to worry about."

"Good. By the way, she called you by your first name. Does she know you?"

"Not really—said she saw me with Alvarez."

I sat down on the bed. "You didn't tell her anything, did you?"

Wolf brought his hand up and stroked my cheek. "No, you're safe."

"I have to go back to Diego's."

Wolf's jaw clenched. "Not tonight you're not. You're staying here until Alvarez gets back."

"I phoned him."

"And?"

"He's flying back tonight but I didn't say where we were. I think we'll be okay 'til tomorrow."

"Good." He smiled slowly. "Why don't you help me take off my jeans?"

"Mm-mm, a helpless male."

Wolf shot me a lustful look. "Not that helpless."

Then I remembered the doctor's parting words. "The doctor said you needed to sleep."

In answer, Wolf pulled me on top of him. "And I will—later."

With Wolf grinning like a Cheshire Cat, I couldn't resist kissing that delectable mouth. That irritating smile stopped once my tongue teased his lips and entered his mouth to play.

My senses tuned to his. The tender skin inside my mouth had his attention, his tongue beguiling me. I withdrew, my lips closed, and returned to nibble his lip lightly. His breathing deepened and he tightened his arms around me. Bringing his hand behind my head, he pushed my head towards his face and a scorching kiss took over. Time stood still. His lips triggered an overwhelming passion.

I slid my hands down his chest to his smooth taut abs, longing to touch every inch of his hard lean body. As I stretched over him, his belt dug into me. I unbuckled it and slid my hands down to his waist. His jeans needed to go. It took some effort to tug them off especially with Wolf watching me, the ends of his mouth turned up.

His underwear was a boxer-brief. I paused to admire the man before me. Very sexy slim hips, strong legs and what was that? At the front of his pinstriped cotton garment, a noticeable bulge caught my attention. Tempting. I couldn't help but glide my hand over the hard member threatening to escape. Maybe it needed help. I grinned. I slid my hand over his briefs once more and felt his package stir. Wolf didn't seem quite so in control now. Was that a groan coming out of those sexy lips?

With him lying so passively for me, a childhood fantasy came to mind. I would be the doctor and he would be my patient. Before I could tease him further, he gripped my hips and lifted me up so that my mouth was on his once again. His demanding hot kiss made me feel like I was the feverish one.

"Help me, take it off, baby." Wolf's eyes glimmered with lust.

I pulled away. "I think you need to listen to your doctor's instructions."

"Never mind the doctor. She doesn't know what's good for me."

"But I do, Señor Du Lac. *Doctora* Sturmez advises you to stay put. She is in charge and all her instructions must be followed."

"*Doctora* Sturmez?"

"Now listen to me. You obviously have a temperature. I must take care of this problem." I brought my hand to his forehead. "Yes, you feel very hot."

His eyes burned. "I am very hot—for you."

"I believe my patient might feel some relief if I removed his clothing."

Wolf nodded. "It might take away the fever."

"Lift up, Señor Du Lac." I tugged on the waistband of his briefs.

My patient was most compliant, raising his firm buns up in order for me to relieve him of his garment. What I then saw, was no surprise. An impressive erection—sea god quality.

Driven by a force stronger than anything I'd ever experienced, I energetically sat up, threw his briefs on the floor and struggled wildly to remove my top.

"Oh, *Doctora*, is something wrong. Are you feeling ill?"

"Yes, Señor. I'm afraid I've caught your fever."

"It might be wise to take off your bra. It must be uncomfortable," Wolf said softly.

"Hush, Señor Du Lac. I told you, I am the one making the decisions tonight. You are the patient. I will not remind you of that again—although, this time I must agree." Slowly, I undid the hooks, while his heavy lidded eyes watched, mesmerized by my action. Flinging my bra on the floor, I turned back to Wolf.

"Come closer, spicy *Doctora*. This patient is hungry. He needs to have a nibble," he murmured, his voice seductively husky.

I leaned forward, my chest to his face. He cupped my breast and guided it to his lips. His tongue swirled around my swollen nipple, and heat surged down my body.

That tiger inside me took control. "Get down. You need to relax. Let your doctor take care of you." I edged up to his shoulder where I traced the contour of his neck with my tongue and when I encountered his ear, the tip of my tongue traced the ridges. Gently I blew in. His rapid breathing told me my tiny nibbles on his ear lobe were just what the doctor had prescribed. When he groaned softly, I blew into his ear again until he shuddered with the sensation. At the same time my hands smoothed over his powerful chest.

I paused. His chest was coated with a thin film of sweat. Not unusual for a man to sweat during lovemaking but his role had been relatively inactive. But he didn't give me any more time to worry. He reached over to my shoulder and stroked my neck with his fingertips before he brought his mouth to my throat. I shivered with the sweet sensation.

While he pulled on the buttons on my skirt, my fantasy was forgotten. "This needs to come off, princess. Could you…" His voice faded.

In a dream-like state, I sat up and slipped it off. The warmth of his arms wrapped around me once more. My spirit enveloped, I floated high like a feather in a gusty breeze—my destination unknown. All that I knew was this was where I needed to be. When Wolf's hands suddenly released me, dropping loosely onto the bed, I was wrenched back to earth. I sat up in alarm and looked at my sea god. His eyes shut, he lay perfectly still.

"Wolf!" I exclaimed in alarm. His forehead was hot to the touch. I stroked his cheek, and even in my disappointment, admired his rugged features that exuded a raw sexuality. I had so longed to feel that special closeness between a man and a woman, but life often foils our simplest plans. As I watched his chest rise and fall with rhythmic breathing, I was somewhat relieved—the medication would help the fever. The doctor had drugged him up solidly. Dreamland was his. Sadly, there would be no loving for me tonight.

16

I awoke to the sound of the rush of the ocean and the warmth of his arm that had been thrown over me in sleep. Like spoons, we lay side by side.

The sunlight beaming through the slats beckoned me. I sat up carefully, moving out from under him. The balmy breeze fanned my skin. I was in paradise. Energized by my sleep, I had this urge to experience the bite of salt water on my skin.

Carefully, I got up out of bed and found my tote bag. From the outer compartment, I dug out my bikini. The bottoms were slightly loose and needed a little tightening. After tying up the top, I took another look at my hottie breathing deeply as he slept. With those eyelashes a dark wheat against his tanned skin, I was tempted to crawl back under the sheets and stroke every inch of him until he woke to return my passion but that would be selfish. The more rest he had, the better he'd feel. I would need to wait. Padding out to the back door, I trekked over the wooden deck and took the stairs to the beach. With the sun high and the rays strong, I hadn't bothered to grab a towel.

The turquoise waters of the Caribbean rolled in steadily over the powdery beach. A dark patch beyond the shore indicated an expanse of coral, about ten feet in. I wouldn't be going that far. The west coast was notorious for undercurrents. I'd step in, get wet and then, swiveling about I spotted a smooth coral rock—I'd dry in the sun.

The sunlight torched my skin. It was time to let the sea cool me off. I ventured in as far as my knees. The frothy brine shot into shore, wetting my feet, vigorously sucking the sand, before it reluctantly retreated. The surf slapped my thighs and the sand pulled me out to sea. I lost my balance and toppled down. I started to regret my impulsive idea. I had to get out. But it wasn't as easy as I thought it would be. The current tightened its grip, propelling me deeper. I needed all my strength to resist. Somehow, I had to get back into shore. I jumped forward, thinking I could combat the battering waves. Tossed forward, submerged in water, my hands hit the sand and I somersaulted towards shore. Willing myself not to panic, I held my breath. As I tried to get up the water pushed me down. Only a few feet from shore, I was in danger. With the surf crashing down on my head and shoulders, my best efforts to battle the sea were futile. Flung under the waves, I crawled on the sandy bottom, in an effort to resist the current's pull. If my strength gave out, I'd be here permanently.

Determined to make it, I poked my head up for air. Fighting my way in was exhausting. Suddenly, something pulled me up. Another tug and I was at the water's edge. The force that brought me there wrenched me further until I was yanked onto the sand.

"Thank God, Adie!" Wolf shouted into my ear above the noise of the surf. "I wasn't sure I'd be able to bring you back." His arm wrapped protectively around me, we rested on the sand, the sea splashing our legs. He tilted my head to him. "You okay?"

I nodded, breathless. Sand had invaded every crevice of my body—ears, hair, and under my bikini bottom. And my top? I brought my hand up to my bare breasts.

Wolf's eyes flicked down and the glimmer in those sapphire depths jolted my body, every nerve ending sparking with his glance. On the sand, my head fell back, and my mouth waited for him. Our lips battled, bruising in their passion. His hand caressed my breast, his fingertips kneading my nipple. I ached for him—my sensuous sea god.

"Adelina!" a man's voice called out.

We looked up to the house. On the top of the stairs, dressed completely in white, Diego stood staring down at us. A moment later he hurried to the beach.

"Are you all right, Adelina?" he asked, running up. "I saw you in the water, from over there." He pointed to the fence at the top of the walkway. "I guessed you were in trouble. The gate was unlocked, so I let myself in."

"Wolf helped me," I shouted above the rush of the surf. "I'm okay."

Diego's eyes narrowed, as he took in the two of us, sand-covered on the edge of the water, my arms folded over my chest. He unbuttoned his shirt and whipped it off. "Put this on."

"No need. I have her top," Wolf said, bringing it to my breasts for me to grasp.

"Churo is up there in the house, Adelina. I didn't think you'd want him to see you this way. Would you like me to help you?"

"Yes, thank you."

Diego quickly donned his shirt. Grasping the strings of my bikini, he brought them around and tied them firmly.

"I only wanted to get wet, not swim. I knew there might be a current. I just didn't think it would be so close to shore. An error of judgement." I glanced at Wolf. "I'm sorry for all this." My eyes examined his injured arm. "Your bandages are wet. We need to change those."

"Why don't we go back to the house, Adelinita?" Diego suggested gently. "Don't worry about Du Lac. Churo will change his bandages and you can get cleaned up." He smiled slightly at Wolf. "Her impulsive nature leads her into trouble. Thank God you were on time to save her. For that, I am grateful, Du Lac."

I grinned. "Makes two of us."

Wolf smiled back at me. "Make that three."

* * *

This was the first time I had ever driven in Diego's silver Porsche. Stretched back against the smooth leather, I commented, "This is a change. You decided not to take your limo?"

"Um-mm. I assumed Du Lac would need someone to drive his Jeep."

"You knew he was shot? The doctor reported it?" She had promised not to tell. I should have known not to trust her. "Is that how you found me?"

"No, the real estate agent who leased your house to Du Lac, works for me."

"But how did you know about his bullet wound?"

"Javier remembered shooting Du Lac before he lost consciousness."

"Wolf knocked out Javier?"

"He didn't tell you?"

"No, we were more concerned about Diablo at the time and later, well other things came up."

"I'm sure," Diego said tightly.

"Javier takes it upon himself to kill intruders, does he?"

Diego grinned. "He's a loyal beast."

"Who? Javier or Diablo?"

Diego chuckled. "At least I don't have to worry about him

going after my woman."

"And which woman would that be, the red-haired Texan or your passionate assistant?"

Diego reached over the gear shift and squeezed my hand. "No other woman has your allure, Adelinita." He sighed, placing his hand back on the wheel. "I am so sorry, *cariño*. I made a gross error, leaving you with that bastard, but he's," Diego smiled slightly, "very repentant."

"He is?"

"I think we can be certain he will confine his research to the computer from now on."

I glanced over to read his expression, but he turned his eyes back to the road before I could figure out how Eduardo had become so compliant.

"She's very smooth, isn't she?" Diego said lightly as we drove over a speed bump with barely a jolt.

"She?"

"My Porsche." He smirked. "And a pleasure to drive."

"I think you're having an affair with your car."

"She does have a pleasing temperament and such smooth lines."

"I'm sure she's comforting in bed, too."

"Her motor revs powerfully but, alas, no, *cariño*, she's lacking in that department." He gazed at me in amusement. "But were you a car, I'd think you'd have all the abilities of this Porsche yet exceed her in every way. You are beautiful, intelligent, and a warrior."

"Thank you, Diego," I said, rolling my eyes. "That does make me feel more appreciated—so much better than your Porsche."

"I'm serious, Adelina. You know I would fight for you, don't you?"

"I believe you. You have fought for me."

He brought his hand over the gear shift and squeezed my hand gently. "And I would again, if you needed me. You can be sure of that." He paused contemplatively. "There are battles to be won."

"Now you're speaking about Wolf?"

"No. I was thinking of you. A relationship calls for a meeting of the minds as well as a union of the bodies."

"And you have many women who want you."

"Any woman pales beside you, *mi amor*."

"And you want us to battle?"

"When a man and woman are together, they're always in battle. No one has to win, of course, but challenges keep that relationship alive."

"Such as the rivalry you have with Wolf?"

"Du Lac and I understand each other."

"Is he investing with you?"

"He finds the Nudist Resort a lucrative proposition."

"He does?"

"Du Lac likes a good business opportunity."

We had driven around the bend and up the coastal highway north on the touristy west coast. I could see a billboard for Mr. Sanchez in the distance, one of those places that kids like for a mini-Disney experience. When he swerved into a side road running along the beach, I was curious as to our destination, but I felt I had to pursue the subject while I had a chance. This could be important to my future or lack of one.

"You're glad he's dead."

"Who?"

"Dean."

Diego shrugged. "With Firenze's death, the investors have equal shares. Not one person has the power to solely direct what becomes of the resort."

"Except you."

"Hm-mm. Yes," he said, his lips curling upwards, "it is nice to have the controlling shares back."

"It's advantageous then that Dean's been murdered."

"Everyone is happy about that, Adelina."

"You weren't pleased that he wanted to take it in a new direction."

"You are quite the little pit bull, aren't you?"

"I do my best."

"I'm eager for your bites."

"You might not say that later."

Past the row of palms, the road split—the signs indicating in one direction the exclusive El Presidente and in the other, the marina. As we approached, there was a beautiful view of the harbor. Boats of all sizes dotted the turquoise water. Diego pulled in a parking spot and turned off the engine.

"Hungry?"

An annoying rumble from my stomach reminded me I had missed breakfast. "Mm-mm. We're having lunch?"

"We are. I believe you need a break from all the excitement you've been having, although," he flashed me an even, white smile, "nothing has to stop us from having a thrill of another type."

I could only imagine what he had in mind.

Diego laughed. "You should see the look on your face. It's not what you're thinking, *cariño*."

"I...ah," I said, a little flustered as to what he meant. That white shirt exposing his strong forearms, perfect cheekbones, and those dancing eyes were a combo that torched my embers and I wouldn't be a living, breathing woman with any passion inside her, if I had not considered sampling such a tasty feast.

"I thought we might go out in the yacht for a bit. It's such a beautiful day," Diego said, swinging his door open. Striding around the back of his car, he assisted me out of the low leather seat. The ride had been worthy of Ali Baba's carpet with the additional bonus of having a handsome prince driving. I had already guessed our destination, but I was thrown off by the welcome committee at the gangway—Luis, Eduardo, and Louisa. A dynamic trio to say the least. I wasn't sure how Eduardo would take to my arrival. I searched his face but he regarded me impassively, like an emaciated Buddha.

Diego took my elbow. "All will be well, *mi amor*. Louisa has lunch ready and we will be dining shortly."

At the end of the wharf, Luis took my hands and helped me step on board the gleaming white yacht. A table between two built-in chairs had been set at the bow, while a bottle of champagne chilled in an ice bucket.

* * *

I was stretched out on a chaise lounge in my bikini, taking in the last of the afternoon sun. Diego refilled my glass and handed it to me.

"Everything was delicious. Thank you, Diego."

"But you hardly touched the ceviche."

"It was good but I'm still feeling a little stressed. You don't know how it feels to know a killer is traipsing around Cozumel without a care in the world while the police think I'm guilty of murder. Food is not a high priority for me right now."

Diego stroked my shoulder and rested his hand there. "You need your strength, my love, or you will never be able to crush the enemy. He leaned in closer. "Mm-mm, I love the scent of you," he whispered, pressing his lips against my neck. Tender kisses caressed my skin. My body unwillingly responded. A nibble on my ear made me ache for more.

A noise brought his lips away. My eyes followed his glance to the stairs where Eduardo appeared.

"Here's something to cheer you up. Eduardo has news."

I shot him a look.

He whispered in my ear, "Believe me, he's seen the evil of his ways and is repentant. He's very aware of how he should behave." Running his fingers through a tendril of my hair, he looked lustfully at me with those brandy eyes. "He won't be any threat to you from now on, Adelinita." He bent over and let his lips brush my shoulder. "What soft skin you have."

"What did you do to him?" I asked, suddenly afraid of what powder keg Diego had lit.

Diego's eyes flicked to Eduardo hobbling onto the deck towards us. "He got off easy." Handing me a glass, he said, "Relax," and brought his hand down to the curve of my back, letting it rest there. "Drink your champagne, *mi amor*. I'm sure he's dug up something helpful if he knows what's good for him."

Eduardo stepped carefully towards us. A few feet away he stopped, as if asking permission to proceed.

Diego nodded. "Sit," he directed, motioning to a chaise lounge.

I noticed he wore socks with his sandals and his tanned face had an unnatural pallor. Glancing up from his paper, he avoided making eye contact with me. "Juan Jose was a paramilitary man in Nicaragua."

"That is nothing new." Diego's voice had an edge. "What else?"

"My contacts believe he's a hit man. An independent for hire."

"Go on."

"My inside source said the mob had a contract out for Firenze."

"Why?" I asked.

Eduardo's face looked drawn as he met my eyes. "He took money that wasn't his to take."

"Mierda!" Diego exclaimed. "I have mob money in my

resort?"

"Not necessarily. His crimes go back a year. Apparently they warned him but he kept skimming." Eduardo shrugged his shoulders. "Possibly they wanted to set an example. They'd like the idea of a hit here in Mexico. It would be blamed on Mexican gangsters. A drug deal gone wrong. That would fit with Firenze's MO."

"We should have investigated him earlier, Eduardo, before he became involved in the resort. Had we done this, much could have been avoided." Diego rubbed his temple with his fingertips. He glanced at me. "Do you have any questions for Eduardo, Adelina?"

"Jim Langley. I know he's gay and has a boyfriend. What sort of money has he been spending lately?"

Eduardo glanced down at his notes. "Apparently, he bought his friend a Mercedes and a matching one for himself, not to mention watches, jewelry—expensive clothing."

Diego shot me a knowing glance. I pursed my lips, thinking he was right. Langley was a major suspect. He'd have as much motive to kill Dean as the mob. If he'd been pressured to give the boyfriend gifts he'd would have done as Dean wanted and married Janine. As CEO, his job would have put him up in the six figures but maybe not enough for a guy with a demanding boyfriend.

Our discussion was interrupted by shouts from the gangway. We had visitors. Noisy ones. Don, Lourdes, Carmelita and a very handsome man I'd never seen before stood on the pier in front of the gangway. Three sheets to the wind, Don, a champagne bottle in each hand, was the first to jump onto the deck with Lourdes hanging onto his Hawaiian shirt. She giggled, trying to keep up with his long stride. Carmelita and the stranger were locked in a tight embrace and seemed oblivious to everything and everyone.

"Was I right or was I right?" Don shouted over his shoulder. "Told you your bro would have chilled champagne ready for us. Come on, you two, don't keep the dude waiting." He glanced at his bottles and said to Lourdes, "Just as well I brought these, darlin', one bottle is just a drop in the bucket or should I say ocean." He chortled at his joke. "Hey, Diego! How you doin' man? It's party time. You need to get in the spirit if you want to win today."

"Diego!" Carmelita called out from the dock, "looks who's here from Mexico City! I haven't seen him for so long, I had trouble recognizing him."

"*Pinche*," Diego muttered under his breath, "my apologies for the language, Adelina."

"Who's Carmelita's friend?" I whispered in his ear.

"Fede." Diego's jaw clenched. "Carmelita's sad excuse for a husband—a philanderer and all out bastard. I wouldn't be surprised if my father sent him away just to have a break himself. I assure you I did not plan this. It was my intention to make it a quiet afternoon for you, my love, and now we have visitors, one of whom I'd rather not see." He tipped back his glass of champagne quickly and drained the glass. Leaning over, he grabbed the champagne bottle and filled our glasses. "Take a good look at him. Hopefully, he'll be gone by tomorrow."

Carmelita was too far away to hear any of this but Don, placing the bottles near the ice bucket, shot him a worried look.

Diego plastered on a smile. "Welcome, my friends. Please join us." He waved a hand to dismiss Eduardo.

Looking rather relieved, Lourdes and Don plopped down together on a nearby chair and struggled to right the chair before they both fell off. But with Lourdes grabbing Don's leg they landed on the deck, she on top of him. When they'd picked themselves up, Lourdes decided the best course of action was to settle on Don's lap. Her skirt hiked high to her thighs, she snuggled close to him. "*Hola*," she called out to us.

"That's the spirit, darlin'!" Don chuckled, wrapping his arms around her.

"Hey!" If I wasn't mistaken, I'd say those two had taken their relationship to the next level."

"Hey, darling!" Don sang out. "We interrupted something, didn't we? Shit, Diego. Sorry, man. I know you've been achin' since forever to have a chance with Adie and now we—"

"Don...Don," Diego said lightly, holding his hand up, signaling a stop.

Don smirked knowingly. "When the cat's away the mice will play. Or should I say when the wolf's away? He's a force to be reckoned with..."

Lourdes poked Don in his middle. He stopped his banter and went white as a sheet. For a second there I was alarmed. He looked sick, but when he let out a belch, he recovered his color and smiled. "That's better. Thank you, darlin'!"

"Someone has to stop you from putting your foot in your mouth."

"I'd rather put yours in my mouth. Love sucking those beautiful toes."

Lourdes giggled and threaded her fingers through Don's abundant chestnut locks.

Dragging Federico by the arm, Carmelita, resplendent in a strapless neon-green mini-dress, tottered over the gangplank. "*Hola*! Isn't it lucky we came with champagne? Now we'll have a real party. Put our bottles on ice, won't you, *mi amor*?" Carmelita said to her husband.

I glanced at the man Diego despised and saw a Latino whose body language screamed macho arrogance. He returned my appraisal with one of his own. It edged on the impolite when his eyes swept up my bikini-clad body and lingered on my breasts. I glared at him and he had the nerve to grin roguishly back at me.

Louisa appeared with a tray of snacks. I say that loosely. Capers, shrimp and caviar with crackers, for emergencies, I assumed. Following behind the best chef in Cozumel, Churo carried in a tray of assorted cheeses. To finish off the parade, Luis entered, setting down a few more ice buckets holding champagne bottles.

"Lookin' good!" Don smiled brightly. "Louisa, you are a miracle chef. You must be psychic to know what I'd like."

"You are an easy man to please, Señor Carrera."

Carmelita swiveled around and pointed. "Look everyone, the band's arrived."

Four men with guitar cases appeared at the gangway waiting for permission to board.

"Come!" Carmelita motioned to them. "Diego, these men are so talented and popular. We are so lucky they were available. If anyone is thinking of getting married," she said pointedly to Don and Lourdes, "they need to be booked at least a year in advance. So, make up your minds quickly or you miss out."

"Crazy babe," Don said with amusement. "Lourdes would never consent to such a thing with an old California boy, like me, would you, darlin'?"

"Hm-mm," Lourdes said shyly, "you might not have enough

money, *cariño*, but you do have some other skills."

Fede broke out laughing. "You surprise me, Don. But Lourdes, your boyfriend couldn't afford to get married, unless he's getting some of Terry's windfall." He propped himself on the arm of Carmelita's chair. "Fortunate the bastard died, isn't it, amigo?"

"If ever a guy needed killin', it was Firenze." Don chortled. "I wouldn't be the only one here who would have gladly seen him in hell."

Carmelita held her glass out for Diego to fill. "Let's not talk about Dean, darlings. Thinking about that man makes me literally ill."

"Right you are, *mi amor*. You've suffered enough at the hands of that pervert. Why don't we talk of something more pleasant." Federico tipped back his champagne and fixed his gaze on me. "Who is this lovely creature, Diego? You are terribly selfish, keeping her hidden away on this yacht so that other men are deprived of such beauty."

Carmelita laughed. "Diego tries hard, but between business and that sexy man of Adelina's, he doesn't have a chance."

"Oh?" Federico continued to admire my breasts as he spoke. "What man is that?"

Lourdes sighed deeply. "Wolf Du Lac. Surely you know him?"

"Not personally, but I've heard he has excellent business sense."

"And he's Diego's latest investor, Fede." Munching on a cracker topped with caviar, Carmelita continued, "Adelina went with him to our resort in Tulum. The ocean, the beach and her very own sea god. Was it romantic, amiga?"

"I'm afraid my visit was cut short. The police were gathering evidence in my hotel room."

Federico raised an eyebrow. "Police?"

Carmelita explained, saying, "Adelina is being framed for Dean's murder. We're trying to figure out who would do this." Her attention wandered to the band that waited patiently for her signal. She waved her hand for the band to start.

Soft notes floated out to us. Their music reminded me of a desert breeze in the early evening. I began to relax as all thoughts of Dean drifted away. But Federico's remark shot me right back to earth.

"The police wouldn't suspect her without reason." He smirked. "Perhaps she's guilty."

"That's ridiculous! Adelina is not the violent type." Lourdes smiled. "But if she were, none of us would turn her in. Adelina is worth twenty Deans."

"Imagine…someone actually cut his throat. Ear to ear," Federico said with a grin.

I was listening and wondering how Federico would have liked to have seen the blood in that room. I was beginning to agree with Diego's opinion of Federico. Why was Carmelita with this guy? With all the times he screwed around on her, she was actually glad he was back?

Selecting a strawberry from the tray, Carmelita placed it between her husband's lips. He basked in her attention for a moment before he brought his eyes to Diego.

"So you're hoping your float will win?" Federico asked in a blasé tone.

"He has the best concept. Tonight will be an event worth seeing," Carmelita said quickly, seeing the black look on Diego's face. "All of Cozumel society on three Royal Investment floats!"

"Three? That is extreme."

"Can't you see it, man?" Don piped up. "Everyone on the floats will be a sheikh or harem girl."

"*Meirda*! I hope you eliminated the fat girls." Federico downed his drink. "A few hippos in sheer costumes would turn a judge's stomach."

Diego's jaw clenched. "Believe me, everyone will look splendid."

"You are being rather optimistic." Federico shrugged his shoulders. "But I suppose if you have a few beauties, it would improve your chances. Your sister is quite a looker, Don. Adopted, wasn't she?"

Don nodded. "My mom was tired of our all guy baseball team."

"So, the lovely Terry will be there?"

"Most certainly. Terry loves a party, as does Janine."

Carmelita reached over and patted my shoulder. "Be prepared for Sam, *amiga*. She wanted a special one done up in bronze."

"Adelina has no reason to worry." Diego tilted his head, studying me. "That gold outfit you have for her for tonight is even better than the last one."

"A new harem costume? How's it better?" I asked.

"A gold-sequined push up bra, a gold thong, and sheer pantalons. Carmelita's designer knew what would look good on my lovely Adelina."

"You have me in a sweat already." Federico stole another lustful look at my breasts. "I can hardly wait to go."

"Perhaps it would be wise of you to remind yourself that Carmelita is your wife and as such, should be treated with respect."

"Hardly something I'd forget, Diego. My wife is the Princess of the Carnaval every year in the minds of all the men of Cozumel. Beautiful, gentle, yet powerful. A Bolivar Alvarez goddess."

Diego glared. "She's a bit too kind-hearted for her own good, Fede. Always forgiving and forgiving you."

"Stop, Diego!" Carmelita interjected sharply. "Please, let's not get into any of that now."

"Yes, listen to her. Your sister's not an angel. She has her own share of sins." Federico rolled his eyes. "And those are only the ones I know about."

Don, trying to make peace, hastily shoved Lourdes off his lap and got up to bring the champagne bottle around for refills. "You two are equal in the scandal department, wouldn't you say? Hey, it's party time. Let's forget about Dean."

Bringing the flute to his lips, Federico paused. "Dean? What's he got to do with Carmelita? She wouldn't have had the bad taste to..." He paused and stared at Carmelita. "You slept with him?"

All eyes were on Carmelita. Her face was flushed a high pink and her eyes were wide, from surprise or embarrassment.

Diego said, "That is ludicrous, Don. Sure, he wanted her as much as he wanted Adelina or any number of gorgeous women, but Sam was his mistress and she made sure he obeyed her."

Federico stared at Diego. "Obeyed? Samantha is kinky?"

Diego smiled slyly. "Heard she likes to wear black leather boots. Whether she has other equipment, my source didn't say."

"You had her investigated, Diego?" Carmelita asked.

"It's my aim to clear Adelina."

"For which she would be eternally grateful." Don grinned. "What a devious plan. That's one way to best Wolf."

I shot Diego a look. Had he set me up to be my hero?

17

Janine was rocking against Wolf in what was meant to be a merengue but looked more like a Kama Sutra position. Her butt was pushed up into his boys and her hands stroked Jim's back as he bent over to dig up some beer from the case on the floor.

I left Diego's side and carefully made my way down the stairs. The roar of the crowd was deafening in its appreciation of the show. They were eating it up. It was late and the drunks were encouraging Janine. Seeing me didn't stop her either. Janine liked the attention from the crowd. When Wolf broke away from her to pull me close, she swiveled around, her face flushed.

"Get lost, Adie. He's mine!"

Her eyes had an intense glint. Could she be serious?

"Take Jim. I want a piece of this hot man."

Wolf laughed and handed her a beer. "Here, drink this, Jan. That's all you're getting."

"Not fair! You owe me some more dancin'."

"Later…" Wolf grabbed my arm and led me over to the other side of the float.

"That's dancing? You couldn't have paid me to do something like that."

"It wasn't my idea. Believe me all she said was she wanted to dance."

"And then Jim got into it?"

"Yeah, unknowingly. The chick is messed up."

The moist breeze picked up and tossed my hair. I swept it away from my eyes. "Janine is a little bizarre." I tugged on my Ixchel pendant, sliding my fingers over the smooth jade.

Wolf looked up at the dark rain clouds gathering above us and then back at me. "It's what she said more than what she did."

"Which was?"

"She told me she had a knife in her bag."

I checked Wolf's face. Was he putting me on? "Are you kidding me? What kind of a knife?"

He shook his head. "There's something wrong with her."

I looked over at Janine rubbing against Jim in time to the

merengue. "She's drunk or stoned, Wolf."

"Maybe…" He looked up to the top of the float where Diego was shouting out something undistinguishable and motioning for him to come. Sam and Terry had taken my spot and were standing on either side of Diego, waving to the crowd.

"Alvarez wants me up there. He said he wanted his investors to join him for the second trek of the parade." He glanced over at Diego's sister with a group of harem girls gathering T-shirts to toss to the crowd. "Stick with Carmelita, baby. I'll be back in a while. Okay?"

I nodded. Watching him climb the steps, I thought over what he'd told me. Why would Janine have a knife in her purse? I had to find out.

Next to a case of beer, Janine sprawled against a plastic palm trunk. She glanced up when I got there. Her eyes looked spacey. "Hey, Adie! Want one?"

"Sure." How could I bring up the subject of the knife?

Janine picked up a beer can. "Here, hon. Just took the tab off for you. Wouldn't I make a great waitress?"

"Thanks." I'm not a beer drinker. To be polite I took a sip. I was suddenly aware of how thirsty I was, but water would have gone down better.

"Drink up. It's party time."

I sat down. With all the dancing Diego and I had done this evening and with the high humidity, perspiration coated my skin. It would probably rain tonight, I thought, hopefully not while we were on the float. There wasn't a lot of cover. My glance fell to the carry-on Luis had brought for me. Looped through the handles was my precious Burberry umbrella. He must have thought I might need it. I was just glad I had some of my own personal toiletries and my cell charger. Even if I was forced to live with Diego, I could keep in touch with my guy.

I looked up to see Janine watching me. She set her beer down. "I need some advice, girlfriend."

I raised an eyebrow. Would this have something to do with the mysterious knife?

Pulling me closer, she whispered into my ear, "I think I've found the murder weapon."

"The knife?"

She nodded. "It's in my purse. I told Wolf but I didn't have a chance to explain. Jim came along. I was hoping to get some advice on what to do."

"Where did you find it, Janine?"

"In Jim's sock drawer." She stared at me. "He knew if Dean died, I'd inherit a good chunk of the fortune." She shook her head and looked away. "I'm afraid it's been him all along. He murdered Dean. That lover of his is bleeding him dry." She clutched my hand anxiously. "Don't you see? With Dean dead he could give his boyfriend everything he wanted."

My eyes shot over to Jim sitting on the edge of the float, slugging down some beer. With his hair slicked back and the dark eye makeup, he had a malevolent look about him.

"I'm afraid of him. If he knew, he'd…"

I nodded.

"Talk to him, Adie. Keep him occupied. If you do that, I'll make a break for it. I have to get to the police."

I gripped her arm. "Why don't I tell Diego? His cousin is head of the Cozumel police. If Diego contacts him, they'll arrest Jim."

She shook her head. "You don't understand. He's been sticking to me like glue. It's almost as if he suspects I know. If he thinks they'll arrest him, he'll run and then you'll be the only suspect. You'll never be free—not to mention what he might do to me to keep me quiet in the mean time. Remember if he kills me he'd have my share of Dean's fortune. Please, Adie, you have to help. Stay with Jim. At the next stop I'm jumping off."

I nodded. "Okay. I have your back." Moving in on Jim, I blocked his view of Janine. From the corner of my eye, I saw her sliding her legs off the float as it came to a standstill. Quickly, I picked up some beads. "Here, Jim." I tossed him a bundle. "They expect us to throw them to the crowd."

"Yeah, I know. I need a break. Just so thirsty after all that spicy food. Aren't you?" He tipped back his beer, and finding it empty, scrunched the can with his hand before tossing it into a bin.

My throat was parched. In my case it was from fear. Janine was counting on me. I had to distract him. Was she already off the float? Nervously, I had a sip and set the can down.

"Shit! What the hell? Where's she going?" Jim stood up and stared at Janine zigzagging through the dancers following our float.

Without another word he brushed by me and slid off the edge of our float.

I had to go after them. My eyes shot to the top of the float where Diego stood with the investors. He signaled for music and Terry grabbed his hand to dance. Behind them, Sam in her risqué bronze costume was already in Wolf's arms. There'd be no help from him.

My eyes darted to the crowd. Where had she gone? For a second I thought I'd lost her but in the lamp light, amongst the dark haired Mexicans, her flaming red hair glowed brightly like a beacon. My eyes focused on Jim. Since he was a head taller than most of the towns people, I could easily follow him as he headed across the street, pushing aside the smaller Mexicans.

Janine was a slender woman—not at all capable of defending herself. I couldn't let him catch her. And if she was right, he'd kill her.

I needed to help her but first I needed a weapon. Glancing about, I spotted my new umbrella. A leather handle and a sharp point. Sliding it under my arm pit, I stretched my legs over the edge of the float and dropped down. My high-heels hit the cement hard. Landing in a squat position, I kept my balance. Straightening up on my tip toes, I peeked over the heads into the crowd. Jim was on the sidewalk in front of McDonalds. Janine was not too much farther, just past a store selling beer. I had to get over there.

On the street a scantily-clad dancer grabbed my hands. She was a tough little cookie. I tried to release her fingers but she had a firm grasp, determined to have me join her group. The others in her troupe began lining up in a double row surrounding us. I was caught up in the wild tempo as she pulled me from side to side. Forming an arch together, the other dancers stooped under our bridge. When the last dancer whizzed by, I finally worked my fingers free from her grasp and escaped the merengue web.

I took off like a bat out of hell, right smack into the sidewalk crowd. The next float loomed over me. When the immense wheels ploughed forward, I narrowly missed being flattened.

Sweaty hot bodies everywhere. We were packed in tight like sardines. This was not a place for the claustrophobic. A dusky brunette elbowed my rib cage. Urgently she pushed forward. I beat her to the gap in the crowd and surged ahead. My new amiga decided she'd hitch a ride on my tail. Together we squeezed against the pudgy man ahead of us. He wasn't happy but left some room for us to get through. Sweat filmed my brow. I was worried. Where was Jim? Aggressively, I pressed against the tall man in front of me. He didn't move and nudging him didn't seem to help. We were at a standstill.

Swiveling his head about, he asked me something in Spanish. I motioned ahead with my finger. He nodded and poked a man in front of him. Rapidly he explained in Spanish that I needed to go forward. The heavy-set man grunted a reply which I took as a negative. He probably thought I wanted a better view of the floats. My tall friend argued. There was no way the stocky guy would budge for a tourist. My chest pressed on the tall man's back and my butt snuggled against the brunette.

An unexpected gap opened up and I caught sight of Jim. Approximately ten heads down if I counted in a straight line. Janine was still safe.

My lady line-buddy took that as green light. She poked me. I squirmed my way up to the obstinate guy and his wife with my *amiga* taking up my tail. With our combined female force we zoomed under his fleshy arm and breathed a bit of balmy air before we once again became a human sandwich.

The booming noise from the Potato Head float had the sidewalk crowd springing forward ready to catch beads and spray cans. Everyone was holding their ground. They were not happy when my partner and I interrupted their game with a push.

What happened next I was totally unprepared for. It was like pressure building up in a keg and we were the exploding gas. The brunette and I were tossed out into the street. A blue-uniformed cop caught me. He gave me a strange look before he threw me back in.

Making it out into the street if only for a brief moment gave me an idea. This would be the way to catch up to Janine. And now that I was on the edge of the crowd, it would be easy enough to get back out into the street. Without the police to stop me, I did. I was now officially part of the dancers preceding the next float. No, not the same blue satin merengue dancers. These had plumed headdresses and skimpy Vegas-type showgirl costumes in a brilliant emerald. Right behind them came the float. I had to step it up. The float loomed above me. They were all egg-people—extra large brown and white Humpty Dumpty eggs.

I had no time to admire this unique culinary concept. Jim was close and that meant Janine was nearing the square. She must have thought that would be the best bet. Police were everywhere in the town center.

Las Palmaras was just ahead. It was known for its American style breakfasts. Unlike the other restaurants along the Raphael Melgar tonight, it was open, although, the staff seemed to be on break.

"Sugah, whatcha doin' here?" A big dude took my arm. "The ladies need another disco girl."

When I twisted out of his grasp, he laughed and swung me up in his arms. Like a prize trophy he brought me over to a bench where three women were gyrating to the music and set me down in the middle.

"This lil' gal looks like she wants to join ya'll."

The women tittered. Linking arms with me, they started to groove to the music. The big guy brought over a beer. "Looks like you need some, honeh. Open up."

Thinking I'd be able to make my escape if I go along with him, I let him pour a bit down my throat. It actually felt good. I was feeling the heat and my anxiety was coating my body with pearls of sweat.

"Lookee, over there. What's with that can, Sherry-Lee?" All the women stared at a tall brunette with a can in her hand. She waltzed straight over with a big grin on her face. Instead of answering, she pressed a button and a puff of pink foam shot out into the go-go dancers' faces. I saw it coming and leapt to the floor, landing hard on the tiles.

From above me, a woman asked, "You okay, honeh?"

"Mm-mm."

That was the wrong answer. The next second I felt the foam cover my neck and hair. The sticky mess was awful but on the plus side it distracted the rest of them. It was my chance to take off.

Rounding the corner, I entered the square. Cobblestones surrounded a landscaped treed area. On one, beer side stands and outdoor cafes had been set up. Luckily for me I saw Jim. With the place buzzing like a bee hive, even a big guy like him had trouble getting through.

Between Lorita's and the next restaurant there was a gap between the buildings. I saw Jim head into the alley and disappear out of sight. Speeding up, I followed, making my way between the tables. My pulse was racing as fast as my legs. I stopped to get my breath and wipe my forehead. But my mission was an urgent one. There was no time to indulge myself. Janine's life depended on me.

* * *

Dark shadows loomed ahead. My heels clicked on the stones as I made my way further into the alley. My eyes shot around nervously. I was wondering where they had gone. The humid night air had the rancid smell of old garbage. I covered my nose with my hand. My stomach was cramping and a wave of nausea hit me. I bent over a moment. And then gathering my resolve, I trekked into a junction where two alleys met. An empty can clattered as I accidentally knocked it with my foot.

It was brighter here. Moonlight flicked fragments of light through the shifting clouds on the cobblestones. I paused to look around and listen. With a whirl of wings, something swooped through the air, brushing my arm as it flew by. A black-winged creature. Shivers raced down my spine.

My Logical voice spoke up sternly: Get it together, girl. It's not a vampire. If it had wanted your blood it would have been glued to your neck sucking it up right now.

But I was spooked. Bats—bad omens. I was afraid. If Jim was on to me, I was walking into a trap. It would be best if I hung closer to the walls and surprised him. I was tempted to take off my shoes but was more afraid of stepping in broken glass. Creeping closer along the wall of the building, I paused, wondering which way to go.

Shouting voices came from the alleyway on my right. I hurried but was careful to make my approach silent. Then I saw him. His back was to me. I assumed Janine was in front of him but my view was blocked. This was it. I had to take him down.

Two strides and I was there. I kicked out to the back of his knee. It was too easy. He fell forward and slumped down on the cobblestones, almost knocking over Janine. But she reacted quickly enough, stepping back. It was then that I saw the gun in her hand.

Janine giggled. "You are amazing, girlfriend. Took him down, just like that. Of course Jimmy boy is on his last legs so to speak. The beer and ketamine combo is rather deadly. Don't you just love it when a plan goes so perfectly?"

I stared at her. Janine—it had been her all along. I felt so stupid. "Jim wasn't going to kill you, was he?"

"Smart girl. No, sweetie, although the dork might have tried later. Let's just say he was a loose canon—didn't care which side his bread was buttered on as long as he got it all. He knew I took out ol' Dean. At first he enjoyed it as much as I did—hated Dean as much as everyone else, but then the guilt set in. It wouldn't be long before he'd cave. He'd tell loverboy. If I was convicted, he'd take my share."

"You wanted the money so badly you killed Dean?"

"The money was a definite plus but it was something else. A video. The perv posted it on the net."

"How?"

Janine laughed. "He had cameras in all the bedrooms—blackmail. That's how he forced me to breakup with JJ and marry Jim. If I did that he said he'd delete the video."

"And so you came into his room and…"

"It wasn't quite that simple, babe. There was some prep time. I wasn't alone."

"Jim?"

"Sam. We smoked weed, the three of us—Sam, Dean, and I. Dean's margarita was spiked. Took ten minutes. That's all." She grinned like the cat who swallowed the canary and pointed to her chest proudly. "Brilliant, wouldn't you say?"

"Sam was in on it?"

"No, but she was my alibi. I sent her on an errand and waited for Dean to pass out. And pass out he did." Janine's eyes burned feverously. "It was so satisfying to cut his throat."

I shuddered. "All that blood. "

"Disgusting and inconvenient. But I was prepared. I wore a raincoat for the job." Janine tittered. "He bled like a stuck pig. You know, Adie, it was gratifying. I never knew how enjoyable murder could be until I cut his throat. But don't feel sorry for that piece of shit. He had it coming to him. You should know as much as anyone. Besides, how much pain could he feel drugged up like that?"

I'd never seen her like this. She was not the woman I'd come to know and love. Where was that whimsical loving friend? How could I have been so wrong to trust her? But with time running out, I had to get myself out of this fix. I tried to think but a strange overwhelming tiredness overcame me. I brought my hand out to the wall and steadied myself.

"I think the K is hitting you, Adie."

"How?"

"In the beer, babe." She swept the gun up. "Whoosh! Up into that tunnel, girlfriend. But don't worry. Once that stuff enters your system—but you know all about that already, don't you? Remember your K-trip at the resort? I'd bet lemonade never tasted so good."

"So you planted the pills in my tote. And it was Jim that lifted me as you changed my sheets?"

"You are quick. Such a shame that you and I..." She glanced over at Jim squirming on the ground. "Look at him." Janine pointed her gun at Jim. "He's down in the hole, I'd swear," she murmured. "First Jimmy and then you. A perfect plan, Adie."

"Listen to me. You can give yourself up. I'd help you—I promise. I'm your friend."

Janine grinned. "Yes, you are. And a loyal one, too. Such a sweetheart. I should thank you for coming to my rescue tonight. I was counting on that. I'd heard Wolf brag about you and your adventures, but going after Jim was your mistake—your last mistake." She chuckled. "Funny, isn't it? I owe you, girlfriend. If you hadn't come for the wedding, I'd have had to set up someone else. Please understand. None of this was personal. You're a good kid. I really like you. And Jim's an okay guy, too."

"Then don't do it, Janine. Don't kill Jim."

"Me? No, sweetie. You're killing him. And then I will have to kill you. No one would blame me for shooting a psycho chick who murdered two men." With one hand she tugged out a knife from her bag. "Just look at me." She giggled. "I feel like a regular *bandita*. A pistol in one hand and a knife in another. Maybe I should have been on the pirate float with Wolfie, eh?" She licked her lip thoughtfully. "I wonder if he'd go for me with you dead?"

My legs were tingling. I'd had only a sip of beer but the drug alcohol combination was affecting me. My eyes shot over to Jim. He'd had much more than I had—the whole can. On his back he stirred restlessly, muttering softly, his eyes staring at something we couldn't see.

"See how his lips move. I think he's hallucinating, don't you?" Janine dropped the knife on the stones. "Pick it up."

Janine blurred before my eyes, morphing into a cobra. I backed away.

"No, you don't. You're stayin' right here. You have a job to do, girl. Pick up that knife."

I wanted to say something but the words wouldn't come out. A wave of dizziness struck me.

Janine waved the gun at me. "Come on, Adie. No time to waste. A little thing like you will be droppin' over any second. Go on—pick it up."

She was right. Even a little bit could bring it on. I had to think how to get out of this.

"Now, Adie."

I stepped closer and stooped down to pick up the knife. My other hand held on to my umbrella.

"That's it. Now, slit his throat." She gargled out the words, her voice distorted like someone speaking through water.

I knelt down beside Jim.

"Come on, girlfriend. He won't feel a thing."

I glanced up. Janine's head had turned green and reptilian. I lifted the dagger high. I took another look at her. Omigod, she was a cobra. I snickered. Don't they cut the heads off cobras?

"Stop laughing, bitch. Do it! You hear?"

I squinted up at Janine, trying to focus before I let the knife fall. It clattered on the stones. The drug was hitting me like a brick. I didn't have much time.

"What the fuck?" She stepped to me and aimed the gun at the side of my head. "Pick it up," she shrieked, "now!"

I bent forward as if to pick up the knife and straightened up. With a quick sweep of my Burberry I struck her forearm, knocking the gun down before I ploughed the umbrella point straight into her chest. Hitting the cobblestones, the gun fired. The boom deafened my ears.

212

Janine stumbled before she fell. On the ground, she pushed back with her hands to stand up. I kicked at her temple. At this point I should have made sure she was out but as I stepped towards her, the alley became a kaleidoscope of spitting cobras swaying in front of me. My legs crumbled. Dean's face zoomed in and I spun into a deep black hole.

18

Like millions of tiny candles, the stars lit the endless expanse of midnight sky. An ocean swim in the dark was a surreal experience with the sea unusually warm and calm, the current only lightly tugging us back as we swam into shore. A cool breeze fanned my skin when I stepped out onto the powdery sand. It felt good to be alive.

The salt nipped my body as it dried—a reminder to mere mortals to respect the ocean's power. And I did. Tonight, I felt reborn. My fears conquered, I safely strolled down the beach, my hand secure in Wolf's larger one. The east coast was deserted. Away from the hubbub of tourists, this was the wild part of the island—unpredictable like life.

The moon backlit the house perched high on the hill. There weren't many homes on this coastline. This one was an old-style Spanish bungalow with a white stucco exterior and red tiled roof. Set back from the road, a cluster of palms gave it privacy. The few cars traveling by made me conscious of how isolated this tropical hideaway was. "That swim felt fantastic." I stared out at the shimmering waters of the Caribbean, magically lit by nature's beacon. "Isn't it beautiful?"

Wolf gazed at me. "You are beautiful, Adie Sturm."

I glowed from the warmth of his words. "You too, Wolf Du Lac."

"Thanks, babe, but guys aren't usually described that way. I think maybe something like—you're the greatest lover I've ever had."

I laughed. "Can't give you a swollen head. You already have one."

Wolf glanced down.

I poked my finger into his chest. "That's not what I meant." I shivered, my body suddenly chilled. I regretted not having brought a towel. Even a tropical place like Cozumel can be cool on a February night. "I think a shower would feel great right now—a steamy hot one."

"I like steamy." Wolf draped his arm around my shoulders.

"Hold on, babe. We're almost there."

The darkness and the shadows from the trees made it difficult to see the wooden stairs that wound up to the house. The outside light illuminated our way as we climbed up the steps to the back entrance.

Wolf held the door open. "First the shower and then—and, hey, this time I'm prepared."

I stepped into the hallway and turned to him. With his wild imagination I was scared to ask. "Prepared for what?"

Wolf shoved the door shut. "It's time to celebrate."

"Sounds like fun but, Wolf, but I'm a little puzzled. We just had Fat Tuesday and now it's the start of Lent. All the celebrating stopped with Ash Wednesday, didn't it?" I teased. "Aren't we supposed to be fasting?"

Wolf placed his finger on my cheek and slid it down slowly. I tingled all the way down to my thighs. In his husky voice he asked, "Supposed to? Am I speaking with Adie Sturm—the woman who breaks all the rules?"

I cocked my head and met his eyes. "Rules aren't so bad as long as they're mine."

Wolf flashed his even white teeth in a smile that would have melted a polar icecap. "I like your thinking as long as I get to make some myself."

"Fair is fair." I gazed up at my rugged sea god. "Take note, though. It'll still be my choice which ones I'll follow."

He shook his head and ran his fingers through his hair. "What have I gotten myself into? It would have been so much easier falling for some other female—a more traditional type."

What had he just said? I couldn't believe it. Could Wolf Du Lac have real feelings for me? Heat flushed my cheeks. "Um-mm," I said nervously, "what exactly are we celebrating anyway?"

"You." Wolf leaned down. His lips pressed on mine and with their heat he awakened my body. As if in answer to my silent request, he slid his hand over my damp top, his fingertips playing with the soft skin on the rise of my breast.

My lips parted for him to enter. When his tongue flamed the sensitive skin inside my mouth, I melted. He was magnetic—a sea god. I was more sure than ever that Wolf was not like the rest of them. But should I plunge into this? I was a love-survivor and with that came a protective wall. Still I needed to evolve from that sorry state I'd been in after Jack had exited my life. The karate motto I'd learned was "unity of body, mind, and spirit". My body and spirit were willing, eager even to trust in love again, yet a twinge of doubt remained in my mind. I glanced up. "You want to celebrate me? Why is that?"

Wolf laughed. "You must have had quite the K-trip. Don't you remember anything?"

I frowned. "Bits and pieces. I know Janine had me completely fooled. Eduardo told us before she was involved in some porn and I felt sorry for her. Someone had taken advantage of her innocence. Not 'til last night did I understand the whole thing. Dean was a control freak. He liked the power he had over her and Janine hated him for that. When I came along...." I bit my lip and looked up at Wolf, "do I have sucker written on my forehead? From the very beginning she'd set me up to be the patsy in Dean's murder." I gazed wistfully at him. "I believed her. I thought she was my friend. How could she have done this to me?"

"Don't kick yourself for that. We've all been fooled by so-called friends. You know that chick wasn't normal. She had a major personality disorder."

"Besides being a druggie."

"I think it was obvious she was flaky but no one would have thought she was capable of murder." Wolf took my hand and we started down the hallway. "How did you see Jim's part in all this?"

"He knew she'd murdered Dean but he needed money to keep his lover happy. Did you know he was gay?"

Wolf nodded. "He had those vibes."

I grinned. "The guy definitely found you more attractive than me."

"I think he had to hide the fact that he was gay from his family. He'd told me one time how conservative they were."

"So he went along with Dean and married Janine. A coverup with financial benefits."

Wolf took up my hands and gazed into my eyes. "Enlighten me on something. What happened in the alley before we came? Alvarez and I couldn't believe it when we saw all three of you lying there unconscious. How did you stop her from killing you?"

"When I left the float I took my Burberry with me for a weapon.

Janine had told me Jim was the killer. I figured with Jim being so tall it would be the edge I needed. Funny thing is, I was learning my sais at my dojo and just before I left, I'd asked my teacher what would be similar to a sword in real life." I grinned. "It was surprisingly easy to flip the gun out of her hand."

"And then?"

"I think I stabbed her with the umbrella."

"She was bleeding on her temple."

"I vaguely remember kicking her head before I passed out."

He grinned. "Your heel. Dangerous weapons those stilettos." He stroked my cheek. "You know, babe, with that drug in your system you were very lucky you didn't fall down into that K-hole first. What I don't understand is why you thought you could handle all this yourself, especially, if you thought Jim was the murderer. Kick-ass you might be, but seriously, Adie, that guy outweighed you by about eighty pounds. Why didn't you ask me to come with you?"

"You were dancing with your ex at the time. If I'd taken those precious minutes to drag you away from Sam, I would have lost Jim in the crowd and that was a risk I didn't want to take. I was sure he was out to kill Janine."

"You're a cat with nine lives and last night you lost one, princess."

"And Janine?"

"Jan's gone for good—hospitalized. You, on the other hand, are alive. So let's celebrate," his eyes locked with mine, "you being alive."

I smiled. "As long as we also celebrate my rescuers."

Wolf's mouth twitched. "I don't mind you paying tribute to me. There are numerous ways you can make me feel good," his eyes glimmered mysteriously, "but please, no talk of Eduardo or Alvarez. Every time I try to help my little Wonder Woman, that Joker arrives to cut in on my action."

"Diego cares what happens to me."

"I don't blame him for that." Wolf kissed my lips gently. "You are a special woman—above the rest."

I ran my hand along his bicep. "Tell me what happened."

"Alvarez got a call. I told the sheikh to contact the police and I'd go after you. Alvarez should have stayed on his float and let me deal with it. Playing the sheikh is the type of thing he does best. The guy is so self-centered, I'm surprised he sacrificed winning the grand prize to go after you."

"And what did Eduardo have to do with it?"

"He followed you and called Alvarez. There was no way he would be able to catch up with you."

"Why?"

"Did you forget what happened to him? Broken toes are not great to run on." Wolf smirked. "I'd say that's one thing that Alvarez arranged that got my vote. When the bastard phoned, I told the sheikh to call the police. In the mean time, I'd go after you. We were almost at the square anyway. That's as far as he could hobble. He was afraid of losing you in the crowd. But, no, Alvarez decided he was coming too." Wolf steered me down the hall. "I could have handled the situation just fine without the godfather."

"Did you forget you had a bullet wound, Superman?"

"I'm still in prime shape and you know it. I went off the float at Las Palmaras. I hardly expected Alvarez to tag along as my sidekick."

I lifted an eyebrow. "Your sidekick? Strange description. Are we speaking of the same Diego Alvarez? The man who is a master with a knife and numerous other weapons." My lips twitched after I'd said that. Diego did have several bodylicious weapons that bore further investigation. I was rather upset I'd missed their rescue attempt. Imagine two sizzling hotties arriving like knights in shining armor only to see the damsel in distress lying on the dirty cobblestones, passed out. "Well, he got the police there in record time. Janine was lucky Don has a powerful friend. With Diego's influence, she at least ended up in psychiatric care instead of prison."

"She wouldn't have survived long in jail. But my main concern was that you are free, no longer a suspect. And yeah, I'm glad Alvarez straightened out the police on that. Now we definitely have a reason to celebrate. So let's not ruin the night. Why don't we forget about him? There are other more interesting subjects."

I pulled his head to me and kissed his sensuous lips. "Sure thing. Subject's closed—promise."

As we passed the living room door, I stopped, attracted by the flickering light from the fireplace. "You made a fire, Wolf? How nice." Feeling chilled from the swim, I looked forward to cuddling up in front of the warm blaze. It would be romantic too. I was about to turn away when something on the table near the couch caught my attention. I started forward to see what it was but Wolf deliberately blocked my view.

"What are you hiding?" I tried to peek around him. "Goodies for a private party?"

Wolf's sapphire eyes glittered. "No way you're going to see anything now, woman!" With a sudden motion, he swept me up in his arms and strode down the hall. "Curiosity killed the cat, remember?"

"Hey!" I protested, but was definitely aroused by his he-man behavior.

"My spicy woman is way too curious for her own good."

"Your woman? You sure about that?" I gave him a wicked look. "Maybe you're not the only man in my life."

Wolf paused in midstride and swung around. Returning to the living room doorway, he looked from one corner of the room to another.

"What?" I tried to see what was on the table but a chair hid it from my view.

Wolf frowned. "Damn—forgot to check behind that couch."

"For what?"

"You mean for whom? Well, let's see now. There's those guys back in Canada, your so-called friends and there's always the karate guys you hang with, but I was thinking while we were swimming he might have landed his helicopter and sneaked in here."

"Who?"

"Alvarez."

I elbowed his chest.

He grimaced in the middle of a laugh but held onto to me even tighter. Wolf definitely liked having the upper hand.

Down the hallway and around the corner we entered a spacious bathroom—ivory marble tiles on both floor and ceiling. "Evil woman. A man has to be continually on the look out for the competition." He shook his head. "You make my job increasingly difficult." He set me down on the floor and turned on the faucet.

"And what job would that be?"

Steam filled the large tilted room. Wolf turned to me. His eyes glittered with an intense flame before he pulled me into the shower and shoved me against the wall. His lips flamed mine. Primal energy pushed his tongue into my mouth. I thrust back. We parried in lustful combat. His lips tugged on my lower lip. I nibbled back. Our tongues pushed in a wild rhythm—a naughty game where everyone won.

Water pounded against his powerful shoulders and rolled down his muscular chest. I leaned back against the tiles. Spray spritzed my face. His heavy-lidded eyes glinted with his need. Untying the straps of my bikini, he let them fall. Bending down, he gripped my shoulders and brought his mouth to my neck. My body tingled with the pressure of his lips.

Pinning my arms back with one hand, he grasped my top and forced it away. Stooping lower, he cupped my breasts and brought his head down to nuzzle the valley between. I grew weak as heat surged through my body. His teasing tongue licked his way over the crests of my mounds. When his mouth captured my nipple, a moan surfaced from somewhere inside of me.

Sliding his hands down my sides to my hips, he lingered to caress the fullness of my ass. I hardly knew when that other tiny scrap of bikini joined its partner on the shower floor. His hands and lips explored my body and with his every touch I was swept into paradise. My breathing erratic, I lost myself in the flicks of his tongue. Shuddering uncontrollably, I screamed out my pleasure.

When I opened my eyes, the sea god stood before me, magnificent in his natural splendor. The vapor rose around him like a magical haze. Water coated his body in a wet slick—broad shoulders, strong arms, and taut abs and yes, an enthusiastic display that would rev any red-blooded woman's motor.

His eyes burned as my hands glided over his muscular body. Every part got my attention. My fingertips caressed his package. He caught his breath and let out a groan. Throwing a pile of towels on the floor, he pulled me down with him. His passion unleashed in a fury. Like a wild panther he fiercely buried his head in my neck and made his mark. My legs lifted to his shoulders. Hard heat drove into me. I squeezed him tighter. Like two people possessed, we rocked furiously.

As we rolled over and twisted onto our sides, Wolf wrapped his arms around me and pulled me into him. His fingers stroked my wet body. Tantalizing licks and kisses assailed my neck. I brought my hands to his waist and slid them to his firm ass. His lips torched mine. Steam and sweat coated our bodies. We clung to each other as he pounded inside me. Dynamite blasted my core. Our bodies cried out in sync. Groans collaged with screams. I collapsed back against the towels.

Our eyes met, my bliss reflected in his. Breathlessly I asked, "Now will you tell me?"

"What?"

"Tell me what you think your job is?"

He smiled wickedly. "Simple, my curious little cheetah." He stroked my cheek. "To keep you purring. Loud and strong."

"I think you're on the right track."

Wolf raised an eyebrow. "You do, do you? But I sense some uncertainty. Not to worry, I have a plan. It'll take your full cooperation but it's guaranteed to make you very happy." He pulled me to my feet and into the spray. As he squeezed a bottle of shower gel, the delicious aroma of chocolate wafted in the air.

My part was to stand there passively and let Wolf smooth the lotion over every conceivable area of my body. A chore I didn't object to. "Your choice of shower gel shows you're a man of discerning taste. Mm-mm, I'm happy already." He lightly stroked my skin. I added, "Your hands are doing excellent work but…"

He shot me a look. "But what?"

My purring became stronger and throatier when I slipped my hands on his chest. It was time for him to be my toy. "I need some play time, too, tiger."

* * *

I drew my legs closer to my chest and let the fire warm me. Wolf lay on the bear skin rug, his head resting on my lap. My back leaned against an oversized leather couch. I looked up at the high vaulted ceiling. There'd been changes made since last I'd been here. Wolf had opened up the heavens for us with a sky light. The night sky was enchanting. The room seemed to have all the elements—fire, air, and the sounds of the ocean. Only the logic of the earth element was missing.

The terry cloth robes we were wearing kept us comfortably

warm. The chill I'd felt earlier was gone. Of course, that sizzling session in the shower had been a major contributor to my elevated body temperature.

When Wolf got up, I was curious. He was way too quiet. One glance at Wolf and I knew this was only the calm before the storm. He was a man with a mission.

"Time to start our celebration." He reached over to the end table to what looked like a coffee carafe. Filling two mugs, he topped them off with whipped cream. "Only the best for my mermaid." He handed me a steaming cup.

I took a careful sip and tasted pure nirvana. "This is exceptional, Wolf." I let the frothy mixture heat my insides. "I'm feeling this incredible rush in my system. This isn't just coffee. What is it?"

Wolf eyes glinted mysteriously. "Nothing ordinary for you, princess. With Ixchel as your guardian I sensed you needed the nectar of the gods."

"Mm, there's that for sure. Chocolate—decadent mocha." I drank more.

Wolf's eyes glittered over the brim of his cup. "And Kahlua. Together we will release those endorphins."

"The pleasure principal….good idea." Where his robe gaped open, I reached in and stroked his muscular chest. Dipping my finger in my drink, I ran it over his nipple. The tip of my tongue followed.

Wolf groaned. "Ah, baby, you must have taken Tease101 in college." Before I could do it again, he put his hand up to stop me. "I love your licks but I have something else for you to experience." He dipped his hand in a ceramic pot sitting on the hearth. "Close your eyes."

My nose picked up an incredible scent. His fingertip touched my lips. With my tongue I licked up chocolate. "Mm-mm." I opened my eyes.

Before I could say anything more his mouth sucked my lower lip. "Belgian chocolate." Rising up on his elbows, Wolf lifted himself up, and stared deep into my eyes. "Tonight is for you." He brought the mug to my lips next and I had a sip. It was more than a mere drink. Giving me the thing I craved, I knew, meant something to him.

"Finished?" Wolf took my cup and set it on the table beside

him. "The next part requires you to let go."

"You think I'm inhibited?"

Wolf pushed me down on the bear skin rug. "Not at all. You're a wildcat. But you tend to be a stickler for cleanliness." Undoing my robe, he pulled it open. "So let loose, princess. Tonight, you'll be my dessert."

"Oh?" I grinned, seeing his eager expression. "How so?"

Reaching back into the pot, his hand coated with chocolate slid over my neck before his mouth came to feast. Quivers raced down my spine as the tip of his tongue licked the thick molten cocoa until every bit disappeared. As he made his way to my breasts he paused and tantalized my lips once again with chocolate. I sucked it up. His journey became more playful with chocolate covering the ticklish area of my sides. Every lick tickled, yet at the same time aroused my senses.

I let myself relax as his hand brushed the decadent mixture between my breasts trailing to my nipples. With his tongue cleaning up bit by bit, I sighed, escaping into the sensuous experience. "It's the first time I've enjoyed a dessert I'm not eating," I said softly.

"Good," he murmured, his expression intense. Coating my belly thickly with rich brown syrup, he licked the chocolate off slowly, the tip of his tongue circling as it lingered at my belly button. His silky hair brushed my thigh as his exploration lit on the tender skin behind my knee.

I no longer thought of anything except where his tongue and mouth would go next. The scent of the chocolate wafted through the air and into my mind, releasing every reservation I ever had. I was his. That wall I had built around me crumbled. I would let him in.

*****

www.AnastasiaAmor.com
Anastasia.Amor@hotmail.com
https://www.facebook.com/Anastasia.Amor.author

http://anastasiaamor1.blogspot.ca

ABOUT THE AUTHOR

OKTOBERFEST Woman of the Year finalist,Epic and Global Award nominee, ANASTASIA AMOR is a university psychology and education graduate. She is the proud mother of two, a pet-mom and a teacher. She also speaks German and is learning Spanish. Art and writing are her passions but she loves to dance and is a known chocoholic. Twenty years in Mexico, and research of Mayan ruins and Cozumel cultural experiences inspired the popular Adie Sturm Mystery Series. As a martial artist she puts realism into the fight scenarios. For DEAD DELICIOUS she learned to scuba dive. Psychic experiences, Cuban journeys and karate training sparked the fantasy-paranormal suspense romance HAVANA HEAT. Her Canadian heroines are intelligent and fearless as well as sensual. Amor also writes erotic romance.

*HAVANA HEAT...a paranormal fantasy romance...**5 stars!***

"Havana Heat is a sensory experience. It's a sultry pleasure trip that rouses all the senses and won't let go. I think that the best attribute of this novel is its ability to surprise and engage. Every chapter, every scene, thrusts you in a different world, a varied experience that transports you utterly into magical realms and otherworldly adventures. The story has many threads woven into the plot but they are seamlessly pulled into the finish line and tied together. The paranormal aspect is highly original and captivating. Havana Heat makes you breathless. It will take you to Cuba with a one-way ticket and refuse to let you leave. I wanted to be there with Reese and Anise, Francisco and Sylvie. Your heartstrings will be pulled quite ruthlessly and in some poignant parts, you won't be able to stop a tear or two from falling.

***Fast paced and drop dead sexy...*"

—*Natalie G. Owens*, author of ***An Eternity of Roses***

"Twists and turns in this tropical romance make it a paranormal reading adventure that will keep you on your toes until the last word!"

——*Barbara Huffert*, author of ***Linked***

*EXPLORING IRRESISTIBLE...erotic romance...**5 stars!***

"Exploring Irresistible is as decadent as fine dark chocolate and tropical drinks. Amor's vivid descriptions put me right there. What I love best is that I can come back and enjoy this story over and over again. This book is sensuous romance at its best. Hot sultry Puerto Rico. When Aleese sees sinfully irresistible Arman—a man like chocolate...the tiger inside her is unleashed! A fight for control over her life surges into a burning adventure of passion and erotic fantasy...

***Irresistible in every way!*"**—*Michelle Stinson Ross*